WALK IN SILENCE

J. G. Sinclair was born in Glasgow, Scotland. He is the author of the novels *Seventy Times Seven* and *Blood Whispers*. As the actor John Gordon Sinclair, his first film won him a BAFTA nomination for Most Promising Newcomer to a Leading Film Role, and his first outing in London's West End won him an Olivier Award for Best Actor. He lives in Surrey with his wife and their two children.

by the same author

SEVENTY TIMES SEVEN

BLOOD WHISPERS

Walk in Silence

J. G. SINCLAIR

FABER & FABER

First published in 2017
by Faber & Faber Ltd
Bloomsbury House
74–77 Great Russell Street
London WC1B 3DA

Typeset by Faber & Faber Ltd
Printed and bound by CPI Group (UK) Ltd, Croydon CR0 4YY

Epigraph from Francis Thompson's 'The Mistress of Vision', in *New Poems* (Boston, 1897)

The right of John Gordon Sinclair to be identified as author of this work has been asserted in
accordance with Section 77 of the Copyright, Designs and Patents Act 1988

A CIP record for this book
is available from the British Library

ISBN 978-0-571-32663-1

FSC
www.fsc.org
MIX
Paper from
responsible sources
FSC® C020471

2 4 6 8 10 9 7 5 3 1

For Shauna, Eva and Anna.

To my dad –

'Yer some man for one man, big-man,
by the way, n'at, know.'

All things by immortal power,
Near or far,
Hiddenly
To each other linkèd are,
That thou canst not stir a flower
Without troubling of a star;

Francis Thompson

One

'The birds are singing again, draw back the curtains.'

'I think there's still someone in there.'

'They left over an hour ago.'

'I just heard a voice.'

'You didn't hear anything. They're gone. Draw back the curtains and let what's left of the day in.' Rozafa was in her late seventies. Her face – thin and dry – buckled inward along the line of a toothless mouth. Her hair – swept up in a loose bun – looked like a small stack of ashen hay sitting on top of her head. The old woman broke open the shotgun she was holding, pulled both cartridges from the barrels and placed them back in the box of shells resting on the arm of her chair. 'I saw two ravens leave the trees out back,' she continued, 'carrying the souls of the dead away.'

'There were six shots.'

'Sure, but only two souls got taken. Birds fell silent at the first pull of the trigger and didn't make a sound till all the shooting was done, did you notice that?'

Rozafa's daughter Lule stood near the window of the small cottage, head bowed, staring at the floor. 'I wasn't listening to the birds.'

'They know things.'

'Why're you putting the shotgun away?'

'The men are gone. Watched them climb into their car and

head off down the hill. Four of them – not in any hurry, either. Big white car – threw up a cloud of dust.'

'Watched from where?'

'Side of the house.'

'They might have seen you.'

'They weren't looking. You have the sickness in your mind where you think everyone's watching you. If they were coming for you they'd have been in here by now and the birds would have another two souls to take with them.'

Rozafa lifted a sheet of oiled linen draped over the back of the chair and carefully folded it over and around the shotgun. 'When I'm finished we can walk down to the village and call the Policia.'

'Stop talking crazy, we can't let anyone know we were here when this happened. No one.'

'We won't call from here, we'll phone from the village. Open the curtains.'

'It's already dark.'

Rozafa threw her a look and waited.

As Lule drew the drapes aside she noticed the remains of a spider's web stretched across the corner of the window frame, its thin strands dusted with specks of dry, sandy soil – thrown skyward by the wheels of the departing car. She stopped and stared, wondering how – having lost everything – the spider would find the strength to start again.

That was when she saw him, the young boy Ermir – from the house next door – staring at her through the dingy pane of glass, his face covered in blood.

Two

Keira Lynch pulled herself onto the edge of the swimming pool and drew a large bath towel over her shoulders. She'd lost count of how many lengths she'd swum, but she was out of breath so figured she'd either done more than usual or she wasn't as fit as she'd thought. The view from the Hotel Shkop's poolside deck stretched out across the deep blue Adriatic, revealing the curve of the earth. The early morning sun was showing just above the horizon, but she could already feel its warmth on her face.

Keira had arrived in Durrës late the night before. Her room – a superior double with a balcony overlooking the sea – was fresh, modern and a third of the price of anything in mainland Europe. Except for the occasional glow emanating from ships passing far out to sea it had been too dark to see much beyond the lights of the poolside area below. The light breeze had carried with it an aroma of fried fish, garlic and spices. She could hear the waves lapping along the distant shoreline and a gabble of voices drifting up from a promenade that separated the hotel from the beach. After emptying the minibar of four cold beers and smoking a couple of roll-ups on the balcony, she'd gone back inside, lain down on the bed and tried to sleep. *The New York Times* listed Albania as one of the top four holiday destinations in the world but Keira wasn't there on holiday.

'Lady, your visitor has arrived. You would like him out here or are you come in?'

An older guy wearing the Hotel Shkop's light cream and brown staff uniform was standing over her, checking out the scars on her wrist and the small circular areas of raised tissue on her shoulder and side.

The guy didn't seem too fussed that she'd caught him staring.

'They're bullet wounds,' said Keira.

'Yes,' he replied. 'Everyone in Albania has gun. We have lot of holes in us here. I have a cousin they call the Sieve.'

'Where are yours?'

'Not me. I'm not having any, but my son he was in the army, the stabilisation force in Bosnia. NATO. He got shot.'

'Did he survive?'

'Sure he's okay. Got hit in the leg and gives him small limp. He's in the Policia now. Was tired fighting everyone else's battles. You married?'

'No.'

'If you want to meet him you let me know. He's handsome boy.'

'As good-looking as his dad?'

The old guy smiled. 'When they made me they used up all the handsome. My son only got what was left. You are pretty, like a true Zana. I think you'd get on. How long are you stay, I'll bring you photograph.'

'I'm fine thanks. I'm only here for a few days. What's a Zana?'

'It is the Mountain Fairy. But you don't come across that many with bullet wounds. You don't look like the type of woman who gets herself shot, what is happened?'

'Does anyone look like the type to get themselves shot?'

'Sure. I know plenty that would be better off with a bullet in the head. One day you will tell me the story, yes? Maybe you're the crazy woman. Is that why people shoot you?'

'Maybe.'

'My name is Xhon. Is pronounced like your John but spelt with an X. Every time you say it, it comes with a kiss.'

He'd obviously used the line plenty times before, but Keira smiled like it was still fresh.

'What would you like I say to your guest, Zana?'

'I'll come inside.'

She pointed at her clothes on a nearby lounger. 'I'll dress and come inside, yes?'

John-with-a-kiss shook his head like he didn't understand, smiled and left.

*

Keira appeared at the far end of the hotel lobby wearing faded, skinny jeans cut just above the ankles, a loose crocheted, cream top and a pair of scuffed Gommino loafers in black patent. She felt good after her swim.

Daud Pasha was smaller than Keira had imagined. She'd only heard his voice over the phone, but had it in her head that he was a big guy. His tawny Mediterranean skin, shaded by a few days growth of dark stubble, did nothing to soften the angular features of his face and shallow, lazy eyes. When he stood to greet her he brought with him an unpleasant waft of stale tobacco and sweat. The suit draped over his bony shoulders looked like it didn't belong to him.

Keira extended her hand to greet him. 'Mister Pasha? *Unë quhem* Keira.'

'D'you speak Albanian?'

'Just a few guidebook phrases. "*My name is,*" and "*Can I have another beer?*" What else d'you need?'

'You are not . . . how in my head I see you. Much prettier . . . and in great shape.'

'You're not what I imagined either,' replied Keira, 'If you want to sue your tailor I know some people could help you out.'

'You don't like my suit?'

'I didn't say I didn't like it. I'm saying it could probably fit you better. Did you borrow it from your big brother especially for today's meeting?'

'Why are you mentioning my suit?'

'The same reason you're mentioning my appearance.'

Daud Pasha gave her a thin smile and changed the subject. 'You want breakfast?'

'I've already eaten,' replied Keira, 'But if you want something I'm happy to take a seat.'

'No, I'm thinking we go. It is a long drive.'

'I have a hire car. I thought I could follow you.'

'It is better we go together. The driving in Albania is a little crazy. Also we can talk on the way.'

'Okay.'

'We discuss on phone the money. You can bring this with you?'

'In my country you don't usually pay until the job is done.'

Daud Pasha's shoulders drooped and he clicked his teeth like some cheap villain in a cowboy movie. He looked around, slowly surveying the scene, then delivered his bit-part line. 'We ain't in your country.'

Keira had sat in too many interview rooms with guys far

tougher than Daud Pasha to react with anything other than complacency. 'You've adopted other countries' customs like saying "ain't" instead of "are not". You sure you don't want to give the "I'll pay you when the job's done" custom a try too?'

'Lady, I'm not go anywhere without first I have some money. Is like a deposit. If you are not happy, at the end then I give you it back. I explain already, this is the finder's fee.'

'What if you've found the wrong boy?'

'Is not the wrong boy. You will see this.'

'I can give you half of it now and the rest when we get back. Is that okay?'

Daud Pasha stared at the floor, shrugged and said, 'Maybe... I think this is okay,' in a way that suggested it wasn't. 'When we confirm it's the boy you will give me the rest, yes?'

'If we're certain it's the right boy.'

'I'm not ask you to come all this way if there is mistake.'

Pasha stayed where he was, waiting for her to hand over half the money before he'd lift his skinny frame up out of the chair.

Keira took a folded envelope full of euros from her pocket and passed it to him. She'd been expecting to pay something today, but not just moments after they'd met. Pasha took the folded bills from the envelope and started to count. When he'd finished he made another clicking noise with his tongue – like it would have to do – then placed the cash in an inside jacket pocket.

As she followed him through the hotel's deserted lobby towards the exit, Keira had already made her mind up she didn't like him.

Across the street from the hotel sat a Mercedes 420se W126

in black with an overweight guy in the driver seat, window down, drawing on a cigarette. As Daud and Keira climbed into the back he pinched the lit end between his stubby fingers before pocketing what was left and starting the engine.

'This is Fat-Joe Jesus. His name is Fatjo. In Albanian, this means "our fortune", like, "our good luck", but he has no luck at all so we say, *Fatjo i cili nuk është me fat.*'

Hearing his name, Fatjo caught Keira in the rear-view mirror and nodded before pushing the gearshift into drive and pulling away from the kerb.

'It means "Fatjo who is not lucky". So we call him just Fat-Joe Jesus.'

'Must have taken a while to think that up. The Fat-Joe bit I get, but why "Jesus"?'

Daud Pasha didn't answer. He was staring out the window, not paying attention. 'You have flown over from England?'

'Scotland. I travelled from Glasgow.'

'This is where you live?'

'Yes.'

Fat-Joe Jesus glanced over his shoulder and spoke for the first time. 'Mogwai.'

Keira nodded. 'Yes, home of Mogwai.'

'You like?'

'I love.'

'Favourite album?'

'*Young Team.*'

'Track?'

'"Mogwai Fear Satan".'

'You have watched live in concert?'

'A few times.'

'Loud, huh?' A small smile spread wide over Fat-Joe Jesus's face, 'You can still hear what I'm saying?'

'Sorry, I didn't catch that,' replied Keira.

Fat-Joe Jesus's shoulders started shaking up and down. '"I didn't catch that", she says. Ha ha, you hear, Mister Pasha? She makes the joke,' he said, shaking his head in approval. 'You're okay, lady.'

Keira stared out of the window at the small-town bustle. The centre of Durrës was much more built up than she had imagined. Modern concrete apartment blocks rising seven or eight storeys high, sat at odds with some of the older colonial buildings, all of them covered in satellite dishes. Wide avenues full of cars gave way to smaller streets laced with telephone cables. The pavements were lined with market stalls selling everything from fruit and vegetables to rugs and electrical goods.

The traffic ahead was being held up by an old man leading an ox tethered to a wooden cart along the centre lane of the busy road. An elderly woman wearing a rich blue headscarf sat slumped like a sack of black cloth near the edge of the pavement, weaving a basket of wicker as though she'd been sitting there since the Middle Ages.

Everywhere Keira looked was a mess of colour and noise.

Nearing the outskirts of the town, Fat-Joe cut a junction, narrowly avoiding a collision. Daud caught Keira's reaction and said, 'We have only had cars in Albania since nineteen ninety-two. Most people still think they are on a horse and cart.'

'You've only had cars for twenty-odd years?'

'Yes – cars, but not yet the roads. In most countries you get stopped by the police if you are swerving all over the road. Here the roads are so bad they pull you over if you are driving in a

9

straight line. Only drunks drive in a straight line in Albania.'

Daud Pasha left it for a few moments, then started again.

'So what is it that is so special about the boy?'

'There's nothing special about the boy. It's his circumstances that mark him out.'

Daud waited for Keira to continue, but that was all she was giving him.

'Okay, so why this kid?'

'I owe his mother.'

'But she's dead, right?'

'Right.'

'What happened to her?'

'It's a long story.'

'We going to be in the car for a while. I'm a good listener.'

'I'm not a good talker,' replied Keira. 'If I'm not staring out the windscreen with my hands on the steering wheel I get travel sick. Best I just concentrate on keeping my breakfast down.'

Fat-Joe Jesus suddenly swerved to the left and brought the car skidding to a halt in front of the oncoming traffic. Keira had to brace herself to avoid falling on top of Daud, who had smacked his head against the side window.

He leant forward, giving Fat-Joe a hard time, Fat-Joe waving his arms around and giving some of it back to Pasha.

The street around them filled with the sound of horns blowing as cars tried to navigate their way round the stalled Mercedes.

One car drew alongside; the driver, window down, was shouting at Fat-Joe.

Keira saw Fat-Joe Jesus pull something from inside his jacket and point it out of the window.

Just as quickly as the other driver had drawn to a halt, he screeched off down the road again.

After two more failed attempts Fat-Joe managed to start the engine and swing the car back on to the right side of the road.

Daud was glaring at him from the back seat. Eventually he turned to Keira with a forced smile. 'Fat-Joe says we have swerved because the manhole cover was missing in the road. Says we're lucky we are not driving in the goddamn sewer now. I tell the son of a bitch he's falling asleep at the wheel.'

Keira wasn't listening. Her view had been partially obscured, but she was sure Fat-Joe Jesus had just pulled a gun on the other driver.

Three

Forty kilometres south of Durrës the black Mercedes took a slip road off the busy motorway and swung left onto Rruga Beklehem: a route that followed the course of the river Shkumbin towards the market town of Peqin. Fat-Joe steered the car left and started to climb a steep dirt track just wide enough to take the Merc.

A screed bank fell away to the right, but as they climbed, the barren slopes soon gave way to thick vegetation.

Eventually they came to a halt outside a solitary worker's cottage nestled in the lee of the surrounding hillside. The cottage had a collection of grey, broken timbers leaning against the far gable: the remnants of a garage or outbuilding that had collapsed from old age.

Fat-Joe jumped out of the car with a smile on his large, round face and held the door for Keira.

The sweet smell of pine and eucalyptus hung in the warm spring air.

Daud Pasha led Keira over a small area of rough ground that marked the front garden, rapped on door of the cottage and entered without waiting for a response.

Quarter-length pelmets of embroidered lace hung from poles, blocking the windows on either side of a small open fireplace. The mantel was draped with a floral-patterned cotton cover on top of which sat a mix of faded black-and-white images in small wooden frames: a curly-haired child, a rural village scene, a handsome man in suit and tie, his hair swept up in a fifties-style DA.

Set hard against the skirting on either side of the fireplace, resting on wooden pallets, sat two mattresses that doubled up as settees – covered in red woollen throws with an array of dull cushions and pillows lining the wall. Behind one of the settees, hooked onto a picture rail that ran the length of the wall, was a pair of worn workman's trousers, a large framed sketch of two cherubs holding hands and a guitar with only three strings. A long, narrow tapestry showing a street scene of Tirana in sepia tones covered the wall opposite.

There was no television, no books and – save for the photographs on the mantelpiece – no other ornaments.

The small kitchen-diner also housed four chairs and a table at the far end, seated at which was a middle-aged couple whom Daud Pasha introduced as Korab and Leonora. Korab was easily recognisable as the guy in the photograph. His hair – still slicked back – was grey and thinning now; his once smooth face was scored with deep grooves. Leonora looked nervous as she surveyed the photographs Keira had laid out on the table in front of her. She was shaking her head from side to side. '*Po. Ajo është e saj.*'

Keira looked to Daud. 'What's she saying? It isn't Kaltrina?'

'The opposite! She is saying she recognises her niece.'

'Why is she shaking her head?'

'I am telling you before, we have different customs. In Albania, when we shake our head from side to side it means yes. If we nod it means no.'

'Can you ask them when they last saw Kaltrina?'

Daud spoke to the couple in Albanian. Leonora shrugged and made a face.

'Do they know what happened to Kaltrina's parents?' continued Keira.

Daud answered for them. 'I already asked them this last week. Leonora is Valbona Dervishi's sister. The boy, Ermir, was found at Valbona's home in Dushk when the neighbours heard shooting and are calling the Policia. The Policia phoned Korab and Leonora to pick the boy up. They bring him here to look after him, but they have no money and don't know what to do with boy. They know who is responsible for what has happened at the house and worry that they will come here. They don't want any trouble.'

'What did you tell them?'

'I say what you told me. That you have money for the boy from his mother, but they think you are here maybe to try and buy the boy and take him away.'

'I'm trying to make things right. Can you tell them I'm only here to help. Is the boy here?' asked Keira, picking the photographs off of the table.

Leonora seemed to understand and pointed to the back of the house. '*Ai është duke luajtur jashtë.*'

'He's outside,' said Daud.

'Can I see him?'

Daud spoke to Leonora again. When she answered this time her eyes filled with tears. '*Ai nuk flet. Sytë e tij nuk janë këtu. Ata ia ngul sytë në asgjë.*'

'She is saying that he does not speak. His eyes are not here; they stare at nothing. He has only the shadows for friends now.'

'Would it be okay for me to see the boy?' said Keira directly to Leonora. 'I don't want to upset you, or the child, but I have to be sure it's him. Is that okay?'

The woman shook her head and replied, '*Po.*'

Daud and Keira followed Leonora through a small pantry area to the back door and out into the garden.

At first the cleared patch of ground at the rear of the building appeared to be empty, then Keira caught a movement over by a large oak in the far corner: a young boy sitting on the ground with his back to her rocking gently back and forth.

'Ermir!' called Leonara. The boy didn't respond. She tried again. 'Ermir!'

This time the boy turned and glanced over at them. He was no more than five years old, but his soft, round face and hard stare gave the impression of someone much older.

'Would you mind if I showed him the photographs?' Keira held them in front of her and gestured to Leonora. 'It's okay?'

The woman looked uncertain, but again shook her head.

As Keira approached the boy he flinched and turned away, as though he was expecting her to strike him.

She moved round and squatted directly in front of him.

'Ermir.' She spoke in a soft, low tone. 'Ermir, my name is Keira. *Unë quhem* Keira.'

The boy kept his focus on the ground. Keira placed three photographs face up on the dirt in front of him and waited. She was in no hurry, prepared to give the boy as much time as he needed, but out of the corner of her eye Keira could see Daud Pasha shifting around impatiently and wished that this encounter was taking place in private.

The sound of the river far below and the rustle of branches caught in the current of warm air from the valley floor faded until there was nothing left but the stillness between them. Eventually, the boy lifted his head and stared at Keira, holding her gaze until she started to feel uncomfortable. After a while he glanced briefly at the photographs and spoke: '*Pastë e butë*'.

The tone of the boy's voice was as flat and emotionless as the expression on his face.

'"*Pastë e butë*"? What is "*Pastë e butë*", Ermir?' asked Keira, but the boy turned away and she knew instinctively that it was over.

The encounter – as brief as it was – had been difficult, but Keira had seen enough. Picking the photographs up from the ground she slowly rose to her feet and left Ermir staring vacantly at the patch of dry earth in front of his crossed legs.

Back in the kitchen Daud was eager to conclude the deal.

'You will pay now the rest of my fee?'

'The money's back at the hotel.'

Ermir's aunt spoke in Albanian, gesticulating with her hands before falling into a chair and burying her head in her arms as they rested on the table.

Keira had to wait for Daud to translate. 'They have no money and Ermir is a burden on them. They know they have no option but to look after him. Leonora says she has prayed for someone to help them and you are the answer. She loves the boy like her own, but they need help. He is troubled and cries if they leave him. It is very difficult to work when they cannot leave him on his own.'

Leonora lifted her head and stared up at Keira.

'If it is money that has been left to the boy,' continued Daud, translating as she spoke, 'she will give thanks for this miracle and blesses you for saving him. She misses her sister Valbona and young Kaltrina and wishes they would come back. Every time someone comes to the door she expects it is them. She says she would rather be poor and have them alive than rich like Sahit Muja and be in this situation.'

Keira knelt down and put her arm round the woman's shoulder in an effort to comfort her. 'Please tell her not to be upset. I have to go back to the hotel now and think of the best way to handle this, but I will make everything all right.'

Daud produced an official-looking form from his jacket and smoothed it out on the table. 'Do you want her to sign this just now?'

'No, but she will have to at some point. Does she have any documents saying that she is the legal guardian?'

'Yes, I have copy I can give you.'

'Can you ask her if she knows what *Pastë e butë* means. The boy said it when I showed him the photographs.'

'I don't have to ask,' replied Daud Pasha. 'It means "Mummy".'

Four

By the time Keira arrived back at the Hotel Shkop the sun was dimming the last of its rays. The final few kilometres of Fat-Joe's route took them along the coast road with views out across the Adriatic as far as Brindisi in southern Italy. Colourful rows of parasols and sunbeds littered the beach in front of the various hotels that lined the edge of the large bay.

As attendants folded loungers and collapsed umbrellas the first of the early-bird holiday-makers were starting to appear on the streets looking for somewhere to eat.

The lobby hummed with the sound of couples at low glass tables murmuring across their cocktails. The doors leading to the pool area lay wide open, allowing a cool sea breeze to flow through the lounge as waiters and waitresses glided between tables with trays of drinks and bar snacks.

Keira spotted the old guy who'd given her the message by the pool earlier that morning, John-with-a-kiss, serving a table, the same placid look on his face, but wearing a different uniform now.

The receptionist waved her over – 'Miss Lynch?' – then handed her an envelope. 'Message for you.'

'Thanks,' replied Keira folding it and putting it in her trouser pocket unread.

Daud Pasha was at her elbow. 'You want to find a table here or go somewhere more private so that we can talk.'

'Maybe see if there's one outside; I could do with a smoke,' replied Keira. 'You find a table. I need to go to my room for a second.'

'You getting the rest of the money?'

'Yeah, that. And I need to pee.'

'D'you want a drink?'

'The coldest Korça they have, please.'

Keira was heading for the stairs when a thought struck her. 'Mister Pasha.'

Already on his way out, Daud Pasha turned back, 'Yeah!'

'Don't order anything hot. My guess is you'll be leaving before they've had a chance to light the hob.'

*

The envelope the receptionist had handed Keira lay torn on top of the bed, a sheet of A4 bearing the hotel's logo sitting alongside with a typed message on it.

Keira stood out on the balcony and tugged on the tight single-skinner she'd rolled until the end glowed a fiery orange and she was able to draw down some smoke.

On the patio area below Daud Pasha sat at a table with his back to her. As she leant out over the balustrade to get a better view he turned – somehow aware that he was being watched. He looked up and caught her peering over at him. Keira cursed under her breath as she ducked back out of view.

After taking another slug from the bottle of beer she'd lifted from her mini bar and drawing hard on her cigarette to finish it off, Keira left the room and headed downstairs. As she approached the table Daud made that clicking sound with his tongue again and threw her a look. 'Your beer was cold when they brought it; now, I'm not so sure. What happened – you need to shit as well?'

Keira slipped into her seat without answering and eyed the packet of cigarettes sitting on the table in front of him. Without asking she reached forward, picked it up and tapped one out. 'You have a light?'

Daud stared at her for a few moments like he was going to take her on, but then thought about the money she owed him and decided to play it cool until she'd handed the rest of it over. Flexing his hip, he reached into his trouser pocket and pulled out his Zippo. He held the lighter up without thumbing the spark wheel.

Keira didn't budge, just sat, waiting to see how far he was willing to push it. After a moment she decided to nudge the tension a little further. 'Is this another one of your customs?'

Daud looked back with a puzzled expression on his face: playing it like he didn't understand.

'In my country that's considered impolite, not to light a lady's cigarette.'

'In my country it's considered impolite to keep someone waiting. I figure you've already had a smoke out on your balcony, so maybe you've got a nicotine buzz goin' on s'making you act a little crazy.'

'You're not going to give me a light?'

'It's not your cigarette.'

'I paid for it.'

'How'd you figure that?'

'I gave you all that money this morning.'

Daud screwed his face up. 'Only half! You didn't give me *all*.

This is what I'm saying: you got that lady logic thing going on there. The money is mine.'

'I thought it was a deposit.'

'Sure, but I made a mistake earlier; it's non-refundable. You employed me to find the boy and that's what I did. Then, the whole journey home you don't say a word. Just staring out the window, pretending you've got the car-sick thing.'

'I wasn't pretending. You and Fat-Joe really need to have a conversation about personal hygiene. Usually a return journey from an unfamiliar place seems quicker, but that took twice as long.'

'You're doing it again. Being disrespectful. I see you up there hanging out on your balcony, keeping me waiting without asking. Then you come down here and take my smokes without asking and I don't see you carrying the rest of my money unless you got it hidden somewhere on your body. You want me to go hunting for it?'

'Now you're being unpleasant. I'm only asking you to light my cigarette.'

'It's not your cigarette. See, now I'm thinking twice about even giving you this,' said Daud, making to put the Zippo back in his pocket. 'If I give you my lighter, you gonna want to keep that too?'

'Maybe.'

'Okay, your cigarette, my cigarettes ... either way, lady, you're starting to piss me off. What's say you take them all.' He threw the packet over to her, then continued. 'Just give me the rest of the money and I leave you to have pleasant evening in your hotel. All I want is for you to pay me what you owe then I can go back to the office and finish off the paperwork.'

'Where is your office?'

'Why, you want to come visit?'

'Yes! I was thinking I could come by tomorrow and drop off the rest.'

Daud Pasha shook his head. 'Lady, if this is your way of telling me you're sitting there empty-handed, I got to tell you this is not a good situation.'

'This is my way of telling you that the address at the bottom of your emails doesn't exist. The reason I didn't come down from the room straight away: I was reading a message from my secretary back home saying your office is nonexistent.'

'You can come with me now if you like and I'll show it to you.' Daud tilted his head to the side and smiled.

John-with-a-kiss appeared over Keira's shoulder and held out a lighter.

'You want a light, Zana?'

Keira lifted the cigarette to her mouth and, taking Xhon's hand, lit her cigarette. Before letting go she gave his wrist two quick squeezes.

'Daud, this is my friend John-with-a-kiss, he works in the hotel. John, this is Mister Pasha.'

John looked over at Daud Pasha and nodded, but got nothing in return. 'John's son and I are going out on a date tomorrow night,' continued Keira.

John-with-a-kiss was straight on it. 'This is right. He looks forward to it. And, he will be picking you up here if that's okay.'

'What is it he does for a living again?'

'Policia: but he is promising to leave his gun at home. You got enough holes in you.'

'Thanks for the light, Xhon.'

'Is no problem. You need another beer?'

'Sure. This one got warm while I was on my balcony trying to figure out the best way to repel an annoying little mosquito before I got bitten.'

'You want a nice fresh one?'

'Actually, I'll wait until Mister Pasha has left, so that I can enjoy it without getting a nasty taste in my mouth.'

John-with-a-kiss left the table without asking Daud Pasha if he wanted anything.

'You think you are getting me worried with your little act there. You think I care your "boyfriend" is Policia. You don't know anything.'

'I know that the best client a lawyer can have is the boss of a criminal organisation,' said Keira, tilting her head the same way Daud Pasha had and returning his stare.

'Yeah?'

'Yeah. I've never met one yet that isn't polite, courteous, does what they're told. Because at their heart they are just business-men and they know I'm going to do my best for them because my business is the law.'

'You're a lawyer? You're way too pretty to be a lawyer.'

'And you're just ugly enough to be a cheap little hustler. You and your muscle man Fat-Joe Jesus are at the lower end of whatever organisation it is you work for. I can tell by the way you conduct yourself that you're not the boss, you've got no class: just an employee near the foot-soldier end of the line. You're one of those guys, oversleeps in the morning, leaves for work late and wonders why their life's spent stuck in a traffic jam. Are there bears in Albania?'

'Lady, you are so random. What the fuck do bears have to do with anything?'

'Do you hunt?'

'Bears?'

'Anything.'

'No, I don't hunt.'

'Don't ever take it up.'

'Yeah? Why's that?'

'A bear has a brain one third the size of most humans, but they can pick up the scent of shit from miles away. They'd smell you coming before you'd even left your house.'

For a moment it looked as though Daud was going to throw a punch, but he managed to hold it together: only one thing on his mind now, 'Just give me the money.'

'You're not getting any more money, Mister Daud. In fact I'd like you to return the cash I've already paid. Or I'm going to have to have a word with my date tomorrow night and maybe ask him to come and get the money from you.'

Daud leant towards her and spoke under his breath. 'You're making a big mistake, crazy lady. I'm going to give you one last chance to pay up and we stay friends or I'm going to get up and leave, but what happens after that is out of my hands. You asked me to find the boy and I find him.'

'I asked you to find *the* boy. All you found was *a* boy.'

'I did find the little fucker,' said Pasha, his act starting to melt, 'so you are owing me the money.'

'The photographs I showed the boy you claim is Ermir . . .'

'He recognise straight away,' interrupted Daud, 'he knew straight away that it was his mother.'

'Then I must be Ermir's sister.'

'Now you're confusing me.' Daud Pasha turned away as if he was looking for someone to back him up. 'You start talking about bears and now you're Ermir's sister? Where the fuck did that come from?'

Keira took a last draw on the cigarette, stubbed it out in the ashtray in the middle of the table then took a swig of her warm beer. 'The photographs I showed the boy were of my mother, not his.'

Daud stared at her like he was unfazed, but Keira knew he was already trying to think of an exit line.

After a few moments he stood and said, 'I need to go pee.'

Keira shouted after him as he headed back towards the lobby: 'Is that the best you can do?'

Keira ordered a cold beer from one of the other waiters and picked another cigarette from the packet Daud Pasha had left behind. Over the sound of the mood music playing in the background she could hear the waves folding against the shore somewhere in the darkness beyond the dim lights of the patio. When the waiter returned with her beer Keira asked, 'Where's the old guy, Xhon?'

'He's on his break,' replied the waiter.

'Where does he take his break?'

'Usually out the back of the kitchen. He does not have long. Is everything all right?'

'Is it possible to ask him if he wants to take his break with me?'

The guy looked uncertain. 'I'm not sure if he's allowed to sit with the guests.'

'Am I allowed to sit with him ... out the back of the kitchen?'

The waiter shrugged. 'I think it is up to you. You're the guest, you can do whatever you like.'

Keira handed the guy a 500-lek note and told him to keep the change.

'Can you show me?'

*

Stepping out into a dim yellow pool cast by the bulkhead light at the kitchen door, Keira saw Xhon sitting on a stack of up-turned beer crates over by the bins, smoking a cigarette and holding a small coffee cup in his other hand. 'I still don't get this shaking-your-head-for-yes thing.'

Xhon immediately stood, gesturing for her to take a seat beside him, which she refused. 'Thanks, but I've been sitting all day. I need to be up and moving around.'

'I forgot to bring you your beer. Sorry!'

'It's fine . . . Is this your coffee break?'

'Dinner break, but I'm not hungry. A coffee and smoke to get me through. You want a cigarette?'

'I've just finished three, thanks,' replied Keira. 'What time d'you finish?'

Xhon shot her a glance. 'I'm married. Don't get any ideas. I finish in few hours, but my wife can put hole in you just with her stare. Does the mosquito know you're here?'

'He went to the toilet and never came back. Turns out he was a con man, but I didn't find that out until after he had made off with half my money.'

'If you want a loan, I'm thinking maybe you are come to the wrong guy. I earn enough to pay my travel to work and from work with a little over for the food.'

'I don't need money, I need help.'

'Got plenty of that. Had some delivered this morning, nice and fresh. Best help in the whole of Albania. How much d'you need?'

'Could be a little, could be a lot . . . I don't know yet.'

'Well, let's get started and see.'

'I wondered if I could talk to your son. I'm trying to find someone . . .'

'You need address?'

'I have a rough idea where they were last seen.'

'A missing person?'

'Not really . . . I don't know. I don't know if they're missing so much as I don't know where to start looking. I thought maybe your son might have an idea. I have a name . . .'

Xhon looked sceptical.

'. . . and a crime,' continued Keira.

'If there is also a crime, then maybe is the chance. Depends what sort of crime and how long ago. Also, will depend on who did this crime. In Albania there are some people for who the keeping of records is not with the diligence, you understand? One of our main industries is corruption. If you shake an official's hand, clasp both of them, otherwise his free hand will be stealing from your pocket, you know what I'm saying?'

'I do.'

'When did this crime happen?'

'Not that long ago. This year.'

'I can see in your eyes it was a bad thing. Can you tell me what it was?'

'A murder . . . Two murders, in fact.'

'And your bullet wounds . . . they have something to do with this?'

Keira wanted to be straight with Xhon, but only up to a point. She hesitated before answering, 'In a roundabout way.'

'Don't worry, I will not ask for you to explain more. How long are you here for?'

'I'm supposed to fly home on Thursday, so only one more day.'

Xhon took a moment to think.

'Is that a problem?' asked Keira.

'Is maybe problem. Tomorrow I am not here at work, my family has the funeral. My son will be there also.'

'If it's easier I could talk to him on the phone tonight or first thing in the morning.'

Xhon thought some more, then said. 'You should meet. I think it's better. You okay with funerals?'

'Not on a first date.'

'You can be ready early in the morning?'

'How early is early?'

'Nine a.m.?'

'Meet before he goes to the funeral?'

'At the funeral, but it is a few hours' drive.'

'I don't want to intrude. A funeral might not be the best place.'

'It will be fun day. I will send a car.'

'I have a hire car. All I've done so far is drive from the airport to the hotel. It could do with a run.'

'You will never find us: I'll send a car. You can meet lots of real Albanians. We are like the Scottish: friendly and warm when you get to know us. But we are better-looking.'

'Like the Irish, then.'

Five

At 8.35 a.m. on Wednesday morning Keira was sitting by the pool drinking coffee. The intensity of the thick, chalky liquid was like nothing she'd ever tasted.

She liked it.

A basket of freshly baked pastries sat alongside a saucer on the small glass table in front of her. Aside from a waiter busying himself nearby in preparation for the other breakfast-goers, the pool area was empty. As she lifted the tiny cup to her lips Keira noticed two police officers standing at the concierge's desk. The concierge nodded in the direction of the patio, then pointed at her. Keira finished the coffee, placed the cup back on the saucer and watched as the officers in their light blue cotton shirts headed through the lobby and out towards her.

'You are Miss Lynch?' asked the taller of the two as he approached the table.

'Yes.'

'You would like to come with us.'

'I'm not sure. Would I like to come with you?' replied Keira.

'You can finish your coffee and we will wait for you outside.'

'I'm finished already. Can I ask what it's about?'

'The funeral.'

'Are you my car service?'

'Yes, we are here to drive you.'

'One of you is Xhon's son?'

'Xhon's son is our colleague. He is at the burn already so asked if we would take you for the lift. Special escort. It is quite far so we must leave soon.'

'Okay, I'm ready.'

Keira offered them a pastry, which they both refused, then, grabbing one for herself, followed the officers through the lobby and out into the cool of the shaded street.

All three climbed into a dark blue Volkswagen Golf with a decal reading POLICIA that was parked on the pavement right outside the front entrance to the hotel.

'Where are we headed?' asked Keira from the back seat.

'Gjirokaster,' answered the officer who was driving. 'It is known as "The City of the South". It is very nice place. It has a castle, a bazaar that is very old, lots of coffee shops and tavernas. It is a good place to live and a good place to rest when you are dead.'

'What's the burn?'

'Sorry, not understand.'

'You said Xhon's son was already at the burn.'

'It is the place where they are putting the dead body in the fire.'

'The crematorium?'

'Yes, this is the place. *Krematorium*. Same in Albanian.'

The lights changed to red as the Volkswagen approached. The officer flipped a switch on the dashboard to sound the siren then accelerated towards the crossing. Keira's knuckles whitened as she clutched the door handle and pushed herself deeper into the seat. She braced her knees against the back of the driver's seat as the police car cut through the stream of traffic in front.

The officer sitting in the passenger seat turned and shouted over the wail of the siren. 'Gezim is very good driver. The best in Albanian Policia.'

The driver then cocked his head over his shoulder and – keeping one eye on the road – added, 'Gezim is off sick today, but I'm pretty good too.'

*

Just over two hours later the police car came to a halt outside a squat, umber-coloured, municipal building in the centre of the hillside town of Gjirokaster. John-with-a-kiss left a small group of people gathered in the shaded courtyard area outside the entrance and hurried over to open the car door.

'Come, I'll introduce you to everyone.'

Keira followed Xhon through the small gathering to a line of family members standing just inside the entrance waiting to receive the mourners.

'You must leave your shoes,' whispered Xhon as they approached.

Keira slipped her shoes off, placed them alongside rows of others laid neatly to the left of the door, then stepped into the dark corridor.

'*Zoti ju lasht shnosh*, is what you say at funerals. It means, "Let God leave the others untouched."'

With Xhon walking along behind making introductions in Albanian, Keira made her way along the line of people, shaking each of their hands in turn, saying, '*Zoti ju lasht shnosh*,' and adding, 'Sorry for your loss,' under her breath to each of the family members. As she extended her hand to the last in line

31

– a man of a roughly similar age to her – he replied, 'Don't be sorry . . . he was a shit.'

Keira turned as she walked away and saw that he was smiling after her. She noticed straight away that he was a younger version of Xhon. Same eyes, same shape face; only difference was a narrower frame and slightly darker hair.

Following those in front, Keira made her way through into a large reception hall where drinks were being served from a bar comprising two trestle tables laid end to end. A large plastic bin filled with ice was being used as the wine cooler and beer fridge. Two long rows of tables covered in white embroidered linen ran the length of the hall, with simple place settings for over a hundred people arranged neatly along either side. Apart from a huge Albanian flag – a two-headed eagle silhouetted against a deep red background – hanging on the far wall, there were no decorations.

Xhon was at her shoulder with a bottle of beer. 'Thought you might need this.'

'Thanks,' replied Keira, accepting it from him and taking a drink.

'It's a beautiful town. Is this where you live?'

'Two doors down from here.'

'A long walk home, then?'

'Less then thirty metres, but my wife will be so drunk I will still have to call for a taxi.'

'What about you?'

'I am working at the hotel later, so I take it easy.'

'Shouldn't you be in the line-up? Are you not family?'

'I have done my duty at the crematorium. They are now just greeting the stragglers and those that missed the burn.'

'Should I have been here earlier?'

'No . . . not necessary! You are only come for the fun part.'

'I take it the guy on the end is your son?'

'Yes. Is okay, you will sit with him at the meal. Then you can talk: ask him about murder and the missing person you're not really sure is missing.'

*

'What brings you to Albania? And more, what brings you to the funeral of a stranger?' Xhon's son had just pulled up his chair alongside Keira and introduced himself as Pavli Variboba the cop.

'I'm happy to wait for another time,' replied Keira. 'I did say to your father that we could talk on the phone.'

'We're not here to celebrate the life of my grandfather, we're here to celebrate his death; most of the people you see in this room – the older ones in particular – have come only to make certain he's dead. If you look over at my grandmother you will see no grief on her face, only relief. My grandfather served under Enver Hoxha as a member of the Sigurimi. They were the intelligence service, the secret police. Now they are called National Informative Service or SHIK, which is same dog, different bark. They were not liked – did lot of terrible things. Only my father would have anything good to say about the old man. But my father has only good things to say about everyone. He still believes that people are good.'

'You don't?'

'I'm with Zola. Inside every human there is a beast: *La Bête humaine.* I have seen too many bad things to think it is any other way. So don't feel awkward that we find ourselves in this setting. We can talk here just as we can talk in any other place. My father mentioned that you are trying to find someone. This is correct?'

'Yes, a boy.'

'But, is not straightforward?'

'No.'

'There was murder connected to this, yes?'

'Two murders . . . his grandparents.'

'You have their names?'

'I have the family name, and a good idea of where they lived, but I have no idea where the boy is now, or even if he survived. I could be wasting your time.'

'Can I ask what is your interest in the boy?'

Keira found herself pressing the scars on her wrists firmly together under the table. She took a moment before answering. 'I let his mother down. I want to try and make amends. She left behind some money. I thought if I could track the boy down, maybe I could give it to him or whoever is looking after him and somehow make his life a little better.'

'You are his guardian angel?'

'Just trying to do the right thing.'

'Where is the mother of the boy?'

'She's dead.'

'What is happened to her?'

'She was also murdered.'

'At same time?'

'No, she was murdered in Scotland, but I believe it was the same killer in both cases.'

Pavli looked puzzled. 'The grandparents are killed in Albania, the mother of the boy is killed in Scotland, by same person?'

'The perpetrator is already in custody awaiting trial.'

'Here?'

'In Glasgow – Scotland. He definitely killed the mother.'

'You are sounding very sure about this.'

'I was there when it happened. Unfortunately, I'm the prime witness in the trial. And I'm fairly certain he killed the grandparents too, but that's irrelevant at the moment. I'm only interested in finding the boy.'

'And you have flown all the way to Albania to do this? To find this boy.'

'To try.'

Pavli reached across and lifted a bowl of tabbouleh from the table and offered to spoon some on to Keira's plate.

'Thank you.'

'Some bread to go with?' he said, pulling a large platter covered in circles of wheat bread across the table and tearing a piece into strips. 'We're lucky that it is my grandfather's funeral we are meeting at. Normally the men and the women would have to sit in separate rooms, but my grandmother deliberately mixed it up to upset his rotten, dead soul. It is her act of defiance. She wants to show him disrespect and let the people here know that she is on their side, not the side of the Sigurimi. He would be furious with this arrangement. This also why she had him cremated. There will be no gravestone.'

Keira watched Pavli pinch some tabbouleh with a stub of bread between his fingers and pop it in his mouth. 'Bread, salt and heart,' he said as a toast. Following his lead, she did the same.

The table was covered in a selection of large platters each containing a different entrée.

'What's in the stew?'

'It called paçe. You don't want to know what's in it. All you need to know is, it tastes good. You want to try some?'

'Sure.'

Pavli spooned some on to her plate then lifted Keira's glass and hovered a hand over two bottles placed nearby. He leant in to be heard above the din of voices echoing around the large bare room. 'Wine or rakia? The wine is sweet; the rakia is strong.'

'I'll try the wine.'

Pavli poured out two large glassfuls then handed one to Keira.

'You like the wine? Before you answer, I have to tell you my grandmother makes it.'

The clear, yellow liquid had a fruity taste, more like a dessert wine.

'It's sweet. I'm a cold beer kinda girl.'

'It has the taste of friendship in it, I think. The first year she made it she let the plums overripen. Everyone in my grand-mother's village preferred hers to the rest of the villagers' efforts so she makes it that way ever since. Okay, if I can, I am try and help you,' continued Pavli. 'First, I need to know more about what has happened. Where did the grandparents live?'

'A place called Dushk.'

'Yes, it is a small village, north of Fier.'

'I don't have a street name.'

'It won't have one. You don't want to be postman in Albania . . . there are still a lot of roads with no name.' Pavli sipped some wine before continuing. 'And you have any idea why all these people they are murdered?'

'The grandparents were murdered to put pressure on my client.'

'Who was your client?'

'The boy's mother, Kaltrina Dervishi.'

'The girl was your client?' Pavli sounded surprised. 'What is your job?'

'I'm a lawyer. Kaltrina was due to give evidence in a trial against a drug dealer and as a result she was marked down for execution – is the short version. The guy ran a prostitution ring, trafficked girls, smuggled drugs ... multi-talented.'

'The girl was Albanian?'

'And the hit man. And the drug dealer.'

'So you have a good impression of my country, eh? Hopefully today you will see another side, albeit at the funeral of someone who used to be in secret police. Okay! I'm starting to get the picture in my head. This is a little more complicated than first I thought. You are leaving tomorrow, yes ... you can't stay any longer?'

'No, I have to get back.'

'I will take some notes before you leave here and do some checking, but I won't be able to do this now until tomorrow.'

'That's fine. I appreciate you giving up your time.'

'If I find anything I will call you or email you. You can come back?'

'Yes. Not straight away – the trial is about to start, but if you find anything I'll see what I can do.'

'So, you know the killer's name?'

'Engjell E Zeze. He was contracted by a guy called Fisnik Abazi.'

Keira studied Pavli's expression for any change, assuming he might have heard of them, but if he did recognise the names his face gave no hint of it. Instead he said, 'My grandfather wanted to be buried, but my grandmother would not grant this wish. She has destroyed all photographs and burned his clothes. It is her belief that – for all the suffering he brought to this world – his time on the earth should have no reminders.' Pavli turned to Keira and asked. 'Do you think she is right to do this?'

'It's sad to lead a life that no one wants to commemorate, but I can understand her logic.'

'This thing you are trying to do for the boy – it is a good thing. You will be remembered for this.'

'I'm not doing it for the boy; I'm doing it for me,' replied Keira.

Six

The idea was to finish packing, head down for a quick swim then take a walk into the market area of Durrës in search of something to eat, but Keira felt tired. She lay on the bed and closed her eyes, then almost immediately sat bolt upright again. One of the french doors leading to the balcony had slammed against its frame with a loud crack and was now knocking against the metal railings.

The setting sun had given way to a grey blanket of cloud and the room was now in darkness. Feeling the sudden drop in temperature, she hoisted herself up from the bed and secured the door, bolting it top and bottom. Outside, small droplets of rain stained the terracotta floor of the balcony dark grey. Before long there was rainwater cascading from the overhang; the gulleys and downpipes quickly overwhelmed by the sudden rainstorm. Her watch read 21:47: she'd been asleep for nearly four hours. Through the torrents of water that streamed across the glass panels of the french doors she could see the heavy droplets bouncing off the deserted boardwalk.

Keira made her way over to sit on the edge of the bed. She lifted the receiver from the bedside table and – since it was too late to head out now – dialled room service.

'Hi, is the kitchen still open?'

'Yes! You would like some food?'

'Do you have paçe?'

The guy at the other end of the line laughed. 'Zana?'

'Is that you, Xhon? I thought I recognised your voice, but I wasn't sure.'

'We didn't feed you well enough today?'

'You did, but I've been asleep since I got back and somehow managed to work up an appetite.'

'I told Pavli he shouldn't have driven us back. He had too much of the wine. But he's a cop, who's going to arrest him? No father should have to endure listening to their own flesh and blood being so awkward in the presence of a female. He brings shame on the family.'

'I think your presence made him a little awkward.'

'You think if I hadn't been there he would be up in your room with you now?'

'I'm here to find a boy, Xhon, that's all. Pavli's a nice guy, but that's it.'

'I hear what you are saying. We don't do paçe in this hotel. Only sandwiches available now: with the ham or cheese. You would like this with some chips?'

'That's fine; anything, really. How long will it be?'

'Ten–fifteen minutes. I'll make them fresh. Is okay?'

'Could I get a large whisky sour as well?'

'Of course! I will bring this up as quick as possible.'

'Xhon, I need to be at the airport for about six a.m. tomorrow. What time should I leave?'

'You will not get much sleep tonight. The traffic will not be bad, but you will still have to be on the road maybe 5 a.m. You want I should give you lift?'

'Thanks, but I have the rental car. I need to take it back.'

'Okay. I will now go to kitchen.'

Keira slipped the phone back into its cradle and headed into the bathroom. She'd slept for too long. A quick bath and a night in seemed like the only option now.

Keira twisted the mixer tap, held her fingers under the stream of water until it was warm, then left the bath to fill while she picked through the small bottles by the sink in search of some bubble bath. The shampoo, conditioner and shower gel all smelled the same so she emptied each of the bottles into the flow from the tap and watched as folds of bubbles started to appear.

Keira undid the top two buttons on her blouse then pulled it up and over her head. She took off her bra, then unzipped her jeans, hooked her thumbs in the waistband and pulled them down over her hips, dragging her panties along with them.

Standing naked in front of the mirror, she slowly raised her arms to the side so that her body made the shape of a crucifix, then closed her eyes and let her head fall forward until she could feel the muscles in her neck stretch and tighten.

A draught of cold air swept into the bathroom, then a noise from the bedroom made her turn.

She listened for a moment, before calling, 'Xhon!'

The bedroom was shielded from view by the bathroom door. A step sideways and she was peering through into the darkness.

'Xhon, is that you?'

There was no answer.

Keira figured the sound must have come from the room next door and was about resume her meditation when she heard it again. There was no mistaking this time. The noise had come from somewhere in the bedroom.

With the bath still running, Keira stepped out into the

darkness, heading for the main light switch by the bedroom door. The french door opened a fraction then slammed shut, letting cold air blow in through the gap. 'Shit,' said Keira to herself, 'I thought I'd closed you already.' She bent down and pressed the bolt at the bottom of the door firmly into place, then stood to fasten the top bolt. As she reached to the top of the door frame Keira caught a movement: something darker than the shadows approaching from the side.

She turned too late to avoid the blow. A gloved fist slammed into the side of her face, the force of the impact causing her to stumble sideways and crash against the wall. Before she had time to react to the first punch, there came a second, then a third in rapid succession. Keira tried to raise her arms to protect her face but the damage was done. A roundhouse to the stomach and she was down.

Keira dropped heavily onto her knees, gulping at the air as she struggled to fill her lungs again. The figure loomed out of the darkness with both fists clenched together and struck Keira full in the face, spraying blood up the wall as she fell unconscious to the floor.

Half an hour later reception got a call from the room below, the guy screaming down the phone, 'There's water pouring from the light fitting. It is all over my bed and my clothes!'

Xhon was the first to arrive.

*

Keira lay on her back, strapped to a trolley in the back of an ambulance on the way to hospital. The area around her right eye was dark and swollen. Two lines of dried blood extended from her nostrils out along her top lip and down the side of her cheek. There was blood seeping from a row of puncture wounds where her front teeth had penetrated her bottom lip due to the force of the blow. The paramedic had just given her a shot of morphine, which was already starting to take effect. Keira could sense a warm familiar feeling starting in her toes and spreading up along her legs, over her thighs and across her chest till it finally reached her head and the sharp, stabbing pain eased a little.

She was aware of a slight pressure on her right hand and, glancing down, realised that Xhon was sitting beside the stretcher with her hand clasped between his rough palms. She squeezed lightly and saw his big friendly face staring back at her.

'I came up with the tray, but I didn't want to disturb you . . . I'm sorry. I heard the bath running and when you didn't come to the door I pushed a note under. I'm very sorry.'

'You got to see me naked before Pavli,' replied Keira.

Xhon smiled back at her, but couldn't think of a comeback.

Eventually Keira mumbled, 'Where's my whisky sour?'

Seven

The guy in the white lab coat pushing Keira's wheelchair along the fluorescent-bright corridor of the American Medical Center in Durrës was talking to her in Albanian. A couple of times Keira tried to cut in, but he wasn't listening.

She spotted Pavli Variboba limping along the corridor toward them: he looked very different in his uniform. 'You decided to stay a little longer?'

Lifting the cold compress away from her eye, she tried to smile, but the bruising down the left side of her face and swelling around her mouth and cheek meant that nothing moved.

'Can you tell this guy I don't know what he's saying. I can't understand him.'

'He's not talking to you,' said Pavli as he reached her. 'He's making notes on his phone.'

Keira tried turning to get a better view, but the movement in her neck and shoulders was limited. 'When he's done, can you ask him if I'm in good enough shape to fly?'

'You can ask me yourself,' replied the doctor in a New England accent as he steered the wheelchair into a private room off the corridor. 'I'm making notes for my secretary. He's Albanian.'

The room was cold and uninviting, lit with the same fluorescents as the corridor and filled with a nondescript modern desk, two chairs and a metal filing cabinet. 'My advice would be to take it easy for the next day or so,' continued the doctor, taking his place behind the desk. 'You have a concussion. It appears to be a mild one, but you need to rest. Keep using the ice compress and I'll give you some meds to take with you.'

'I'm supposed to be flying back to Glasgow in a few hours.'

Keira caught the look between Pavli and the doctor.

'It's almost midday,' interrupted Pavli. 'Your flight left five hours ago.'

The doctor leant forward and placed his elbows on the desk, his face serious. 'I would advise you not to fly for at least forty-eight hours.'

'I need to get home. I have to be in court on Monday.'

'Ideally I'd keep you in for observation, but you're probably okay to go back to the hotel and hang there if you'd rather.'

'Can I drive?'

'If you feel up to it, but if anything happens your insurance would be invalid, so you have to weigh up if it's worth the risk.' The doctor slid a printed sheet of A4 across the desktop. 'This is just to say you're leaving of your own volition. We can't keep you here if you don't want to stay: just to cover ourselves.'

'I'll give you a lift back to the hotel,' said Pavli, taking hold of the wheelchair. 'You want to stop in for a coffee somewhere and we can talk some? You feel up to it?'

'Only if the espresso comes with a straw,' replied Keira.

*

The glass-fronted Pelikan café opened onto a narrow pavement at the corner of Rruga Pavaresia and Rruga Bajram Curri. A two-metre-high fibreglass ice-cream cone marked the entrance, which led to rows of enclosed glass display cabinets containing pastries, cakes and a variety of colourfully wrapped sweet treats.

Keira and Pavli sat in the shade of a palm tree at one of the tables outside, talking above the noise of traffic. The previous night's storm had rinsed the air clean.

'The view's not as satisfying as the coffee,' said Keira, lifting the straw away from her swollen lips and placing it and the double-shot cup back on the table.

'Their pastries are very good too and not expensive. I stop in here in the morning on the way to work . . . the people who work here are friendly.'

'You don't have to convince me Albania's a good place . . . I know I've just been unlucky.'

'So far you've been ripped off and beaten up, robbed . . . you've only been here a few days. Just as well you're not staying for a few weeks.'

'I'm a lawyer. I see the consequences of crime all the time. Violence is not part of my everyday experience, but dealing with its aftermath is. It's not pleasant, but I can rationalise it. I'm not going to write off an entire country because of a few unfortunate incidents. Only civilised people can make coffee this good . . . Relax.'

'That's nice of you to say, but none of the news I have is good.' Pavli glanced down at his notebook. 'The security cameras at the hotel were not working so we have no way of knowing who attacked you. It is most likely to be this Daud Pasha – or someone working for him – but we can't be sure. His name doesn't check out; unless he's the same Daud Pasha that was the grand vizier to the sultan.'

'You still have a sultan?'

'Not since the fifteenth century. Pasha – or whoever he is – probably gave himself the name from a book. If you are not so ill, I thought you could come down to the station and maybe check out some ID shots. See if anything comes up and maybe give us more of a description.'

'That bit of shell you get in your last mouthful of boiled egg. He was like that.'

'Might need a bit more than that to go on,' replied Pavli. 'I can show you what we have. Not today: tomorrow morning maybe, if you feel up to it.'

'Do I have to?'

'No. I probably have enough. If all that was in the safe in your room was the money – then chances are you were just unlucky.'

'My passport too.'

'Your passport was also in the safe?'

'Yes. I told one of the cops at the hospital.'

Pavli frowned. 'This I didn't see on the report. It may cause you more of a delay getting home, but I will talk to some people and see if we can rush through a new one. You will need to talk to your embassy as soon as possible.' Pavli took a sip of coffee and continued. 'Every so often there is a spate of robberies from the hotels. I'll check around and see if any others happened at the same time. It's just as likely to be this. We checked out Pasha's phone too – the mobile number you gave us. It's just as temporary as his name and no one is picking up now . . . so, I'm sorry, but my news, it's not so good.'

'What about the boy? The Dervishi family? The unnamed road in Dushk?'

Pavli shook his head. 'I checked the records: everything over the past few years. The girl's family the Dervishis are definitely registered there, but there is no record of the boy. There is also nothing about any murders. If we drove up there just now we'd probably find the grandparents sitting out in the garden enjoying the sun. Your client, the girl Kaltrina, maybe she was lying?'

Keira shook her head. 'No. They sent a video of the mother and father telling her to stop. Under duress . . . to scare her: trying to make her think twice about giving evidence.'

'Could have been a fake?'

'I watched it. They knew they were going to die.'

'That look you get when you realise it's not the dying, but the length of time it takes to get over it?'

'Yeah, "eternity fear". If you've ever woken up in the middle of the night and felt the dread you know what I'm talking about. It wasn't a fake.'

'There's only two other scenarios I can think of. One is best option but unlikely, the other is more likely, but worst option.'

Keira lifted her coffee, took another sip from the straw and waited for Pavli to continue.

'There's the possibility the murder did happen, but not in their home. So far I've only looked in the location of Dushk. I can check the national database – widen the search. But my feeling is this would be a waste of time.'

'The worst-case scenario?'

'Not every crime that's committed in Albania is reported. There are a lot of very dangerous people with a lot of influence whose best interests are not served by reporting or recording crimes. Judges, politicians, police officers are paid to look the other way. These organisations are run like the Mafia. They are families, with strong ties and little humanity. If they are the ones that murdered the girl's parents then no one will speak out against them. Even if the police have been to visit the scene of the crime they may not have filed a report or even opened an investigation. If the Clan is involved in these murders I would advise you to rest as much as you can in the next few days, then travel to the airport and get the first plane out of here. Forget the boy, forget trying to be his guardian angel, forget your guilty conscience. Get on the plane and go home. My grandfather's funeral was fun . . . Yours wouldn't be.'

Eight

Keira had been assigned a different bedroom in the hotel. The new balcony extended the length of its outside wall and was wide enough to accommodate a double lounger, and a small glass table. She perched on the edge of the lounger holding a glass of cola in one hand, a roll-up in the other, and checked her watch. Two hours had passed since she'd taken the last lot of painkillers and her head was starting to hurt again. The label read *Two to be taken every four hours*, but Keira had already decided she couldn't wait that long. Cupping her hand, she tipped out another couple of pills from the bottle, opened her mouth as far as the swelling would allow and swallowed them down.

The view of the sea was restricted by the quoined corners of the hotel's exterior, but she could still see a section of the crowded beach and a short strip of boardwalk.

In the last hour, Keira had phoned the airline to rebook her return flight, contacted the British Embassy in Tirana, called her secretary, Katy, and extended the rental on the car. The flights out were mostly full, but she'd managed to secure a seat for early Sunday morning. It was twice what she'd paid for the original round-trip ticket, but Keira didn't care; she needed to get back.

The hotel management were convinced her attacker must have climbed onto the balcony and entered her room from there, but whoever it was would have been easily spotted. To climb up from the patio area or drop down from the room above would have left them too exposed. The only safe way in was along the hotel corridor and in through the door and the only way they could have done that, thought Keira, was with a key.

As she drew down some smoke from the roll-up Keira noticed a figure standing on the boardwalk with a phone clamped to his ear. He was looking up at the hotel, his face turned to the side, making it difficult to pick out any features, but there was no hiding the broad shoulders and thick neck squeezed into the Puerto Rican peg-pant suit.

Fat-Joe Jesus.

Keira followed his line of sight and realised he was staring up at her old room, as if waiting for her to appear on the balcony.

Keira stood too quickly and thought for a moment she was going to faint. When the dizzy spell had passed she headed out into the corridor and down the fire escape until she reached the ground floor. A quick left at the bottom of the stairs, past the reception desk and she was out at the pool area. On the first morning, before her swim, she'd noticed a gate at the bottom of a set of wooden steps that provided access for the hotel guests to the beach. As she made her way between the tables set for lunch she scooped a steak knife from a place setting in front of a couple who had just taken their seats, mumbling, 'I'll bring you a fresh one.'

With the handle of the knife held loosely in her right hand and the blade concealed by the sleeve of her shirt, Keira disappeared out onto the crowded boardwalk.

A steady stream of holidaymakers filed past as she tried to

orientate herself. The steps leading down from the pool were directly in line with her previous room. Fat-Joe Jesus should be standing a few metres to her right, but the spot he'd occupied a few minutes earlier was empty.

She looked up to her new room and tried to work out the angles. There was no doubt in her mind this was the right spot, but where had Fat-Joe gone?

Keira stepped down from the wooden boardwalk on to the sand and started towards the shoreline, glancing over her shoulder at the flow of people moving in both directions along the walkway.

The adrenaline rush was over: she was starting to feel nauseous.

She stopped and closed her eyes, taking a moment to bring her breathing under control and prevent another dizzy spell. When she opened them again, there he was standing on the corner. From there he could keep an eye on the front entrance to the hotel and the balcony at the same time.

With a properly weighted throwing knife Keira's 'sticking distance' was around three metres. Over that span of flight the blade would make one full rotation and stick point first into the target. As she crossed the beach towards Fat-Joe she let the steak knife slip into the palm of her hand and flipped it so that the blade rested comfortably between her thumb and forefinger. Keira knew she could hit him anywhere on his body: the head being the easiest target to ensure a 'stick', but all the weight was in the handle. The trajectory of the knife would be unpredictable. If the butt struck first the knife would bounce off. Keira decided it would be better to get as close as possible and stab the knife into him, wound the son of a bitch enough to slow him down, then call the cops.

Keira circled round so that she could approach him from behind. She would drive the knife as deep as possible then continue moving past. Hopefully the element of surprise should give her enough time to get back to the safety of the hotel before he realised what had happened. Keira continued until she was past his right flank, then cut in towards the boardwalk.

She fell in behind a group of holidaymakers and started towards him.

The knuckles on her hand tightened around the handle, but just as she drew her arm back ready to strike, Fat-Joe turned to face her.

Keira stopped dead in her tracks. She was less than a metre from him, her eyes screwed shut, fighting against the intense, throbbing pain inside her head. Another wave of nausea had Keira reaching out, but there was nothing there, nothing to brace herself against. The knife slipped between her fingers and dropped to the ground, sticking point first into the boardwalk.

She was falling.

The last thing Keira saw was a large pair of hands reaching out towards her. The last thing she heard was Fat-Joe Jesus's voice, 'Mogwai lady. I've been looking for you.'

*

She became aware of a presence: someone nearby. Keira heard a shuffling sound, then felt her wrist being lifted and gently squeezed. When she opened her eyes there was a man she'd never seen before squatting beside her studying his watch while he took her pulse.

'I'm hoping you're a doctor.'

'So am I,' replied the man in heavily accented English.

Keira lifted her head and looked around. She was back on her balcony. For a brief instant she wondered if she'd imagined seeing Fat-Joe down on the boardwalk, then she spotted the steak knife resting on the glass table next to her. Sitting beside the knife was a tattered envelope: the one she'd handed over to Daud Pasha.

'How did I get up here?'

'Fat-Joe. You took sick down at the beach. He brought you here and called me.'

'You're a friend of his?'

'Not friend! I help him out sometimes if he needs doctor.'

'Is he inside?' said Keira, tipping her head in the direction of the french doors.

'He didn't stick around.'

'Ever heard of a guy called Daud Pasha?'

The medic nodded slowly. Keira waited for him to say something, but that was it; just the nod.

'Are you doing that nod thing that means no?'

The guy shook his head. 'There was a grand vizier called Daud Pasha. D'you mean that guy?'

'No. This guy's one of Fat-Joe's acquaintances.'

'I never heard of a Daud Pasha.'

The man started packing his stethoscope and notepad into a leather briefcase. 'You're good. If I was you, I'd take it easy for a bit. And try to eat something. You shouldn't be taking these on an empty stomach.' He held up the bottle of painkillers the hospital had given her.

'How do you know I took them on an empty stomach?'

'Experience.'

'D'you know where I can get a hold of Fat-Joe?'

'His number's on the back of the envelope: said to give him a call.'

*

Keira placed the small tray of sandwiches, the whisky sour and the bowl of fries room service had just delivered on the balcony table and lifted the envelope that Fat-Joe had left. There was no doubt that it was the same one she'd handed to Daud Pasha two days earlier – the only difference being it was now splattered with what looked like tiny droplets of dried blood. Keira peeled it open and raised her eyebrows: it was still full of euros.

She freed the bundle of notes from the envelope and counted them. All there! Not including the money that had been taken from the safe, but the exact amount she had handed over to Daud Pasha.

Keira swapped the cash for her sour sitting on the table and – using the straw – drained it in one.

She picked up the envelope again and, moving back inside, headed for the telephone by the bedside, flipped the envelope on to the bed and dialled the number written on the back. It was answered almost immediately.

'*Kush është ky?*' The voice was female, shouting to be heard over the music in the background.

'I'm looking for Fat-Joe?'

The female spoke in English now, 'Who is this?'

'Is this Fat-Joe's phone?'

The female turned away from the phone and shouted to someone in Albanian. It sounded like she was in a busy bar or nightclub. There was a muffled response in the background, then she was back.

'You are Mogwai lady, yes?'

'Yes. I wanted to speak with Fat-Joe, can I do that?'

'You can come to Bar Fiktiv tomorrow night. Rruga Taulantia.'

'I don't want to meet him in a bar. I'd just like to speak to him on the phone, can you put him on?'

'Fiktiv. Nine o'clock,' repeated the girl, before hanging up.

Nine

The bar could have been anywhere in the world. The music was loud, the lighting too low and the air filled with the sweet scent of overpriced, cheap-smelling perfume. Below the NO SMOKING signs sat ashtrays full of cigarette butts. Keira spotted Fat-Joe's table in the far corner and squeezed past the crush at the bar. A heavily made-up woman in her mid-thirties sat on a blue velvet bench seat next to Fat-Joe giving Keira the once-over as she approached. Keira figured it must have been her who had answered the telephone the night before.

Fat-Joe stood as Keira approached and edged his way round to pull a chair out for her. He was wearing the same clothes as he'd had on the day before. His tie had dark streaks of grease and the shirt was stained with salsa and other marks that were harder to identify. The jacket hung open, exposing a brown leather holster out of which protruded the solid, steel butt of his handgun.

'This is Ardiana,' he said, pushing Keira's chair in for her as she sat.

Ardiana stayed seated, but extended her hand. Keira took up the offer and felt Ardiana grip her fingers tight, like she was squeezing a lemon. Up close Keira could see that the woman was at least ten years older than she'd thought – a slab of make-up doing a good job of hiding her true age from a distance.

'You're doing well from fall?' asked Fat-Joe.

'I'm doing well . . . Better, yes. Thank you.'

'I'm speaking better English than Fatjo,' said Ardiana.

She pronounced his name with a silent 't' so that it sounded more like Fahyo. 'He understands it more than he can speak it. I am his interpreter for the evening. You would like a drink?' A smile at the end warmed what had so far been a wary, disinterested expression.

Ardiana and Fat-Joe were both on coffee, but it didn't stop Keira ordering a beer.

Fat-Joe made a few hand gestures to someone behind the bar, then slumped against the padded-velvet seatback and smiled across at Keira.

'Do your miming skills stretch as far as being able to ask for a straw?' asked Keira.

Fat-Joe and Ardiana didn't get it. They stared back at her with blank expressions.

'You brought your gun?' said Keira, moving on.

Fat-Joe didn't have to look down: he knew where it was. 'Always I have the gun, but is never pointed at you, so no worries.'

He spoke the next few sentences in Albanian, then paused as he waited for Ardiana to do her bit.

'Fatjo wants to know what happened to your face?'

'I was kind of hoping he would tell me.'

'He's asking if you got the little package.'

'If he's talking about the envelope full of cash, then yes I did,' replied Keira, 'but I'm a little confused as to why.'

'Fatjo wants to help you find the boy. He is giving you the money back and hopes that you and he can start again. When he has found for you what you are looking for then you can pay him the money.'

'Why only half? Why not give all of it back?'

58

A frown appeared on Fat-Joe's face. He spoke to Ardiana out of the side of his mouth, all the while keeping his eyes on Keira.

'He gave you everything there was,' continued Ardiana. 'He's confused why you say it is only half.'

'What about the money that was taken from my room the other night? The money in the safe – and my passport.'

A quizzical look spread across Fat-Joe's face as he replied and Ardiana translated.

'He doesn't know what you are talking about.'

Keira had been watching Fat-Joe's responses closely. Even though he was speaking in a language she couldn't understand it was clear that he was telling the truth.

'Okay, so you didn't come to my room and take the rest of the money and my passport?'

'Is correct,' replied Fat-Joe.

'So this envelope you're giving me contains the money I gave to Pasha?'

'Is correct, also yes.'

'Where is he?'

At the mention of Pasha's name Fat-Joe launched into a drawn-out speech, animated with more sweeping hand gestures.

'You no longer have to worry about Mister Pasha,' said Ardiana after he had finished. 'He has left town. He lied about being paid any of the money at all. He told Fatjo you had not given him any money then tried to cut Fatjo out of the deal. So he paid for his deception. Fatjo would like to help you now and hopes that his giving the money back will help you to trust him. He is giving his *besa* to you.'

'I don't know what that is.'

'S'like his word of honour.'

59

'So neither Fat-Joe nor Daud Pasha broke into my hotel room the other night and did this to my face?'

Fat-Joe had caught the drift of what Keira was saying and shrugged his shoulders, pointing at himself with both hands. 'Me! I hurt that you think it was me.'

'What about Pasha?'

'When did this happen?'

'Wednesday evening.'

Fat-Joe was talking Albanian again, with Ardiana translating simultaneously.

'Fatjo says that it could not have been Daud Pasha, because he had already left town by that point.'

'Left town?'

'Sure . . .'

Keira waited for more. When it didn't come she asked, 'Okay, where did he go?'

'It was far away.'

'I'd like to speak with him. D'you have a contact number?'

Fat-Joe leant across the table like he wanted to whisper something, then waited for Keira to do the same.

'I can give you his number . . .' he said, his voice just audible above the din. 'But in hell there are no telephones.'

Keira's beer arrived at the table along with another round of coffees and a bowl of salty snacks. The waiter placed the items on the table along with a small saucer on which sat the bill. Fat-Joe threw some notes on top of it and waved the guy away.

Keira caught the waiter's arm. 'Could you bring me a straw?'

The waiter shook his head and headed back to the bar, returning seconds later with it.

Keira waited until she'd poured her beer and taken a sip, before she said, 'I came here to help a young boy in the hope that something good would come out of the tragedy surrounding his mother's death. As much as I appreciate your offer of assistance – I already have someone helping me. What I wasn't prepared for and what I don't want to do is get involved in anything that might compromise that . . . and, more importantly, compromise me. As I see it, not only am I now in possession of a piece of material evidence, namely an envelope splattered with blood, but I'm also party to some information regarding the possible disappearance and murder of someone I've been in contact with in the last few days. I'm booked on a flight first thing Sunday morning. I'd go sooner if I could, but a mild concussion and lack of travel documents mean that's not going to happen, so I'm stuck here – in the shit – for the moment. I don't need any more shit to happen during the remainder of my stay, so what I'm going to propose is this. I'd written off the money in the envelope. I'd be happy to give it and the piece of evidence – the envelope – back to you for your troubles. In return, all I ask is that we forget this conversation ever took place. You're not my client. I'm not your lawyer. There's no way of passing this off as lawyer–client privilege. If you're telling me what I think you're telling me then I should really head to the nearest police station and report everything I've just heard . . . but . . . I don't think that's in anyone's best interest.' Keira took the envelope from her shoulder bag and placed it on the table in front of Fat-Joe. 'Did you get what I just said? I don't want any more shit.'

Fat-Joe stared down at it for a moment then turned to Ardiana, as though it was down to her to make the next move.

After a few moments Ardiana reached across, picked up the envelope and emptied it of the bills. She tucked the money into the front pocket of her jeans then slid the empty envelope across to Keira, saying, 'We'll keep the cash, you keep the evidence as security. When we find the boy you can pay us the rest of the money . . . the other half, then you can return the envelope to us.'

'Maybe I didn't make myself clear,' replied Keira. 'I don't want your help.'

'You do, but you just don't know it yet. Pick up the envelope and put it in your purse. If anything goes wrong you have something you can use against us. This way we can trust each other, I think.'

Keira stared back at Ardiana for a moment, then fished a throwaway lighter and soft pack of Marlboro from her bag. She tapped out a cigarette before offering them around, but both Ardiana and Fat-Joe refused. Keira sparked the wheel and lifted the small blue flame to the tip of her cigarette. The swelling around her mouth made it difficult to keep the tip clamped between her lips: the only place where they met was still raw and painful.

With the throwaway still alight, Keira lifted the envelope and held the corner of it over the naked flame until it caught.

As the pale blue flames rose towards the top corner Keira placed what was left in the ashtray and watched the envelope burn to black. 'I have all the help I need, thank you.' She took a long drag on the cigarette then stubbed the rest out in the ashtray, crumbling what was left of the envelope into ash.

Keira started to pack her things back into her purse. 'You can keep the money.'

'I have a friend who lives in Dushk,' said Ardiana.

Keira stopped what she was doing. 'So.'

'She was there when the men came to kill the girl's parents.'

'In the house?'

'No, she lives in the village. She heard the shots and saw

the police cars.'

'The police were there?'

'Of course.'

'You sure about that?'

'Is what she told me.'

'Does she know the family?'

'She knew the mother. She knows of the boy.'

'Knows where he is?'

Ardiana shrugged. 'I'm not sure.'

'Can I meet her?'

'She says the police came, but there was no mention of the killings on the news or in the papers. There was a rumour that the Clan were involved and this has made everyone afraid to speak of it.'

'So, can I meet her?' repeated Keira.

'She will talk to you, but I have to come with you. She does not want to get involved and you must promise not to bring the police or tell them that you have met her. She will also want to be paid. It doesn't have to be much, but something, at least. I will give you my address. If you want to go see her, you will come to my apartment at nine o'clock tomorrow morning and I will take you there. You have car?'

'Yes.'

'It is okay I can drive?'

'I guess so.'

'Did you understand everything what I just said?'

'I did.'

'You still don't want any more shit?'

'If you're up to your waist wading through it, you might as well be up to your neck swimming in it.'

Ten

Keira drove in a low gear through the multi-storey valley of concrete apartments looking for Ardiana's building. A watchful cur padded in front of the car before disappearing behind an overflowing set of wheelie bins nestling in the shade of a tall palm tree. When she spotted – on a brick gatepost – the dark-blue ceramic with the figure eight painted in white, Keira pulled over to the kerb and cut the engine.

Ardiana's apartment was situated on the top floor of the shabby pink-painted block in front of her.

The stray followed Keira with a fixed stare until she'd entered the building before returning its attentions to the scraps of food that had tumbled onto the pavement next to the bins.

The apartment was small and cramped. There was one bedroom off the hall, a kitchenette and a lounge with an L-shaped sofa and double bed squeezed into the tight floor space. The lounge looked like a scrapyard for clothes and shoes.

Ardiana stood framed in the kitchen doorway hand on hip, cigarette hanging from her bottom lip. Either Ardiana didn't feel the need to tidy up or she hadn't expected Keira to come to the door. She was still in her underwear: a few threads of lace and embroidery designed for show rather than anything practical.

Clearing a space on the red cotton sofa, she offered Keira a coffee. 'I don't have any milk. D'you take sugar?'

'No thanks,' replied Keira.

'Good; got no sugar either.'

'Do you have coffee?'

Ardiana shot Keira a look, like it was too early in the morning for wisecracks.

'Am I early?' asked Keira, taking in her surroundings.

'You're not early; I'm late.'

'D'you mind if I use the bathroom?'

'Go ahead. The cistern doesn't flush properly, you have to hold the handle down and wait for the water to come through. Sometimes it's better to do that before you've finished: it can take a while.' Ardiana pointed to a door near the front entrance. 'Toilet's there!'

'When's Fat-Joe Jesus coming?' said Keira over her shoulder as she headed into the hall.

'He's not! My friend she doesn't want Fatjo to know where she lives and Saturday's his day off anyway. Just you and me, but don't worry, we don't have to talk.'

When Keira returned from the bathroom, Ardiana was standing by the front door dressed and ready to go. She'd finished her make-up and pulled a crop-top denim jacket over her white, embroidered linen blouse. Ardiana handed Keira an espresso cup, full of coffee. 'Where did you park? You have to park in a bay.'

'I didn't see any bays. I just parked on the street at the front of the block.'

'Drink up. If the police see you're not in a bay they'll give you a ticket. They take your plates off. You get an even bigger fine if they catch you driving around with no plates. So you've got no choice – you have to go to the station and pay the 'fine'. Trick is, to pretend you've got no money, sometimes they let you away with it, but if you're a tourist they'll rip you off for double.'

Keira downed the coffee and handed the cup back to Ardiana. 'D'you live here on your own?'

'Is my place, yeah.'

Ardiana gulped back her coffee then placed both cups on the side table in the hall. She fished around in her bag for a set of keys and pulled the front door closed as they stepped out into the communal hallway.

*

While Keira scanned the deserted street Ardiana checked under the front of the car before climbing into the driver's side. 'We've still got plates.'

'Where are the bays?' asked Keira.

'There are no bays. That's how the assholes get you.'

Keira strapped herself into the passenger seat and handed Ardiana the car keys. 'If we crash, I'll pretend to be you. You can pretend to be me. You're not insured.'

'We crash, nobody's going to pay up anyway, except you,' replied Ardiana.

Before turning the ignition she pulled a bright pink headscarf from her bag then leant over to place the bag in the footwell in front of Keira. 'When we get closer I need you to put this on,' she said handing her the scarf, 'like it's a blindfold.'

*

Because it was the weekend, the traffic was light and it wasn't long before they'd cleared the outskirts of Durrës and were motoring along the SH84 expressway, heading south towards Dushk.

Keira stared out of the window, her mind picking over the events of the last few days. She was puzzled why Pavli had told her there was no record of Kaltrina's parents being murdered in Dushk. She was on her way to talk to someone with a different side of the story to tell.

Keira became aware of a voice. Ardiana was saying something.

'What?'

'You're so far away in your head you can't hear what I am saying.'

'What were you saying?'

'I have cigarettes in my bag.'

'It's a no-smoking rental car.'

'Who gives a shit. Pass me my bag up.'

Keira pulled a Marlboro soft pack out of her pocket. 'If you keep your eyes on the road you can have one of mine.'

She pressed in the cigarette lighter, waited for it to pop, then lit both cigarettes simultaneously before handing one to Ardiana.

'They're actually Daud Pasha's cigarettes, we can blame him.'

'Your face looks better today. The swelling is not so bad,' said Ardiana through a cloud of grey smoke.

'It doesn't feel so tight.'

'You worked out who did it to you yet?'

'No.'

'Could just be a coincidence.'

'In my experience coincidence is what happens when common sense is taking a nap.'

'What does this mean?'

'It means I don't believe in coincidence. Everything happens for a reason.'

'What is the reason they would beat you up?'

'Who knows, but it wasn't a coincidence.'

Both women sat in silence for a few moments enjoying their cigarettes.

'Is it your day off too?' asked Keira eventually.

'Sure. Why you ask?'

'No reason. What d'you do, when you're not hanging out with gangsters?'

'Fatjo is a good guy. Everyone says he's not even smart enough to know how dumb he is. But even a mountain goat knows where the sweetest grass is. He has a brain in his head; he just doesn't show it. Plays things cool. Knows how to treat you right, though. Has six sisters, so he's not a jerk when he's hangin' out with the girls. Once he's on your side he won't take any shit from anyone as far as you're concerned.'

'I get the "Fat-Joe" bit, but where's the Jesus thing come from?'

'He keeps company with taxmen and harlots, like Jesus did.'

'Taxmen?'

'His brother works for the tax office: keeps Fatjo's dark affairs in order, so he doesn't get into any trouble.'

'And harlots?'

'Yeah. Fatjo runs a few girls.'

'What do you work at?'

'Sales and rentals.'

'Like, real estate?'

'No. I sell my ass and rent space in my vagina. I'm one of those girls. My working name's Eliza.'

'Why Eliza?'

'"Eliza Doolittle, but I do lots." Fatjo made it up. He laughed so hard he nearly choked to death. After that it just kind of stuck.'

'You want me to call you Eliza?'

'No.'

'You hook for Fat-Joe?'

Ardiana blew a jet of smoke out the side of her mouth. 'Who else d'you know has a double bed in their lounge?'

*

It wasn't long before the hire car was trundling along a rutted dirt track that ran between two uneven fences. The faded, upright pickets of each fence – standing just over a metre high – were bound together near the top with woven strands of willow. A dust cloud rose into the air behind the car as it climbed the shallow incline towards a group of houses at the foot of the tree-covered hill.

'We're almost there. You are okay to put the blindfold on till we get inside? It's dumb, but my friend is nervous to have the house identified.'

'Sure.'

At the far end of the track a mature olive tree stood in front of a two-storey detached house with a red terracotta roof. Moments later the car pulled up in front and Ardiana stepped out into the warmth of the midday sun. Keira pulled the headscarf a little tighter around her eyes and waited for Ardiana to guide her out.

The friend – a woman who, by the sound of her voice, Keira

guessed was roughly the same age as Ardiana – opened the garden gate and beckoned them through. Keira heard them kiss each other on both cheeks, then felt Ardiana take hold of her arm and lead her up a set of shallow stairs into the dim shade of the house.

'Kafe turke?' asked the friend.

Ardiana tapped Keira. 'You want a real coffee?'

'As opposed to what?'

'Instant.'

'I'll go real.'

Ardiana led Keira into the kitchen, manoeuvred her to a seat by a large solid table and held on to her as she sat. The air was filled with the aroma of freshly ground coffee. Keira listened as the young woman filled a pot with water then spooned in some of the coffee and brought it to the boil. 'You can take the blindfold off now.'

The kitchen had a rustic look. The table took up most of the floor space. A simple range cooker with pots hanging overhead sat below a small wooden window that let in little light.

'*I ëmbël?*' asked the woman as she turned from the stove.

'Is better sweet. Otherwise it tastes like shit,' said Ardiana. 'My friend is asking if we want it with sugar.'

'However it comes,' replied Keira.

Ardiana shook her head and the woman tipped four heaped spoonfuls of sugar into the pot.

Her voice had been misleading. She was younger than Ardiana, wearing a simple blue cotton dress covered by a ragged, work-stained apron. When the brew was ready the young woman poured out three small cups of the dark brown liquid and placed them on the kitchen table.

'This is my friend Helena. Helena, this is Keira.'

The woman held out her hand and gave a polite shake.

'I am sorry for the blindfold, but it is better this way,' said Helena.

'It's okay,' replied Keira. 'I understand.'

'You want to tell her the story?' said Ardiana.

Helena was apprehensive. 'I don't want to bring trouble.'

'It's okay. You can trust her,' said Ardiana.

'I just want to find the boy,' said Keira, cutting in. 'I promise I won't mention your name or discuss with anyone ever having met you. I knew the boy Ermir's mother, Kaltrina, and I want to help him, so anything you can tell me would be great. You knew Kaltrina's family, is that right?'

'I know Kaltrina also. Edon is the father. He used to work at garage here in Dushk and her mother, Valbona, worked as cleaner in Fier. You know what has happened with Kaltrina? No one has heard from her. Everything is strange. We thought she would have come home to bury her parents, but no one has heard from her. You have come to get the boy and take him to her?'

'No ... I'm not here to take the boy anywhere ... I'm here to fulfil a promise I made to Kaltrina.'

'But you know where she is?'

'I do know where she is,' replied Keira, struggling to find the words, 'but I'm afraid ... it's not good: the news is not good.'

'She is in trouble? Ardiana told me you are lawyer. Kaltrina is in trouble with the law?'

'She's not in trouble ... It's a long story which doesn't have a good ending. You'll forgive me if I don't go into too much detail.'

'I will not ask more. Her parents, Valbona and Edon, were very proud of her. They missed Kaltrina when she left. I think I hear what you are saying. She is not coming back?'

'No. She is not coming back.'

'I understand. Hopefully they are all together once again. I will think this when I remember them.'

'Do you believe that the parents were murdered?' asked Keira. 'I've seen a video where they were threatened, but the police here have no record of any crime being committed. They say the video could have been made to scare Kaltrina, but it's probably a fake.'

'The house is near the top of the hill. Is just over three kilometres, but even from here I could hear the gunshots. I hear the sirens and can see the lights flashing blue in the sky. If you go you will see, but no one enters into the house. People they are afraid. What has happened to the bodies, there has been no funeral? No one will live there ever again, it is haunted by their ghosts.'

'Did you know Kaltrina well?'

'Kaltrina left Dushk just over two years ago for travelling. I don't hear from her since. But there was a girl living in next house; she was Kaltrina's best friend. I think if you are looking for boy, this is where to go first.'

'Does she live there now?'

'Rozafa, the mother, is there, but she won't talk to you.'

'What happened to Kaltrina's friend?'

'She left. The day after the shooting she disappeared. Rozafa says she has no idea where to, but I think maybe this is not true.'

'You've spoken to her, the friend?'

'No. I saw her one day in Fier. Her name is Tallulah, but

everyone calls her Lule. She had changed very much, her personality. She liked to have fun, but I think she got involved with the Clan. I hadn't seen her around for a long time and when I did she was different... She was all the time nervous and scared. Her mother was concerned because she didn't leave the house. Not often.'

'Did Lule have the boy with her?'

'When?'

'When you saw her in Fier.'

'I can't remember. She had her hood up and lots of make-up to cover her looks. I shouted after her, but she turned and walked in the other direction.'

'It was definitely her?'

'Sure. Her mother is not well, sometimes my *mama* takes her food. Sometimes she takes Rozafa medicine. This is how I know these things.'

'D'you think Lule may have taken the boy with her?'

'I think yes. When the men came Lule thought they were there for her. This is what Rozafa told my mother. I think that is why Lule has gone.'

'What men?'

Helena picked up her cup and stared nervously back at Keira, like she'd already said too much and was reluctant to go any further.

'Do you know who killed Kaltrina's parents?' asked Keira.

'I don't want any trouble. It's just the rumour, but if it is true, then it is very bad.'

'What is the rumour?'

'If I speak his name you must not say it was me.'

'Promise.'

73

Helena looked nervously to Ardiana then back to Keira. Eventually in a quiet whisper she said, 'He has lots of names. The Black Angel, the Watcher . . . he is a demon. Everyone in Dushk believes that it was this man. His real name is Engjell E Zeze.'

There was a long silence in the room.

'You are quiet I think maybe because you have heard of this man?' asked Helena.

'I've heard of him, yes. A few months ago he tried to kill me,' replied Keira. 'He shot me three times.'

'I've never met anyone that's come into contact with E Zeze and lived,' said Ardiana. 'What happened?'

'I shot him back.'

Eleven

'Smells like an ashtray in here.'

'Better than some of those air fresheners you get, Cotton Candy and Sea Breeze Fizz: got all these fancy names, but give you a goddamn headache.'

'Are we taking the scenic route? Feels like we keep turning left.'

'Just following Helena's directions. Only a few more minutes and you can take the blindfold off.'

'If you're trying to disorientate me, I wouldn't waste your time. I could see how frightened your friend was. I'm not going to say anything to anyone about our meeting.'

'Everyone is paranoid. The Clan are very dangerous. People don't like to talk openly about them around here. Engjell E Zeze may be far away in Scotland facing the rest of his days in jail, but that doesn't mean he's out of commission.'

The car slowed to a halt. 'See: that's us here.'

Keira pulled the pink headscarf from her face and waited for her eyes to adjust to the sunshine streaming through the windscreen.

The car had stopped near the crest of a hill, outside the cottage belonging to Kaltrina Dervishi's mother and father.

'You sure you want to go in? You see all those little purple flowers everywhere.' Ardiana indicated with a nod of her head the overgrown garden in front of the house. It was covered in a blanket of black hellebore. 'They're planted to ward off evil. I've got a feeling it didn't work too good.'

'Just for a quick look round. When I get on that plane tomorrow I want to feel I've tried everything. I don't know when I'll get another chance.'

'Why don't you just wire the kid the money via Western Union? That's what everyone else does around here.'

'I have to find him first.'

'What about old Rozafa? Let's go knock on her door, see what she has to say.'

'After this we'll go next door.'

'We?'

'You don't have to come.'

'Yeah, I might sit this one out. Witches used to throw handfuls of those flowers up in the air to make themselves invisible. Might be some of them standing in the garden right now and you wouldn't know.'

Keira shot Ardiana a look.

'I don't want to get any closer to this situation than I already am, you know. I'm just doing Fatjo a favour, I don't want to be seen as one of the players.'

'That's fine,' said Keira as she climbed out of the car.

It was warm and – except for the occasional click and hiss from the cooling engine – everything was quiet: no birdsong, hum of insects or rumble of distant traffic to break the silence. Keira stood for a moment taking in the view. The dirt road leading to the cottages quickly disappeared out of sight, cutting in a long arc down towards a plain of fields and farm buildings in the distance.

Keira turned towards the house. Tall grass and other weeds

hid the wheels and upright stanchions of a collection of disused farm equipment, rusted by the wind and rain, which lay scattered around the garden. The path leading to the front door was covered in long weeds, with clumps of grass growing through the gaps in the broken flagstones. Keira stepped through a tumble of boulders that marked the perimeter wall and made her way to the front door.

The door handle was difficult to turn. Keira applied more pressure, but the stem had rusted to the dark metal rose on which it was mounted and didn't move. A faint buzzing made Keira turn her head to help locate the source, but the sound was so slight it was difficult to tell which direction it was coming from.

A loud clunk made her spin on her heels. Ardiana had slammed the car door closed and was now leaning, back against the bonnet, facing out across the valley – a cloud of cigarette smoke rising into the air around her.

Keira turned her attention back to the door. She tried peering through the panel of glass – no more than thirty centimetres square – in the middle of the door near the top, but there was nothing to see. The glass was obscured by a piece of black cloth that made it opaque except for a small chink of light in the bottom right-hand corner.

Keira made her way around to the rear of the cottage, checking for any other entry points. All the windows were shuttered or had curtains blocking the view inside and all of them were locked.

Keira walked back round and launched a kick at the front door. Then, leaning in with her shoulder she grabbed hold of the handle again and tried twisting. That was when she noticed that the glass panel was now clear. The cloth covering had fallen to the floor, shaken loose by the impact of her kick. She pushed her face against the glass and tried to peer inside, then instantly recoiled. The buzzing sound was there again. Just as suddenly as it had cleared, the panel turned opaque again. Keira's view inside was almost instantly obscured by thousands of insects regrouping on the inside of the glass.

Keira took a step back and stamped the flat of her foot hard against the door again. This time it screeched open twenty centimetres before jamming up against something inside.

A cloud of insects swarmed towards Keira, who lurched backwards, arms flailing as she tried to shield her face. The air around her was filled with the sound of buzzing as hundreds of flies collided with her face and became entangled in her hair.

The flies brought with them the stench of putrefying flesh. The odour gripped Keira's throat like a vice and had her reaching to cover her mouth and nose to avoid inhaling the rancid air, but it was too late. Keira staggered along the path towards the car – and vomited into the long grass.

Ardiana was already over the boulders and heading her way.

'What the fuck is it? Are you okay?'

Keira shook her head in response and retched again.

Ardiana caught a hint of the foul-smelling air. 'We must leave this place.'

Keira stumbled past, making for the car.

'Get in the car and let's get out of here,' continued Ardiana, the panic rising in her voice.

'Do you have any perfume in your bag?' spluttered Keira.

'Any what?'

'Perfume . . . with you?'

Keira hauled open the passenger door, stretched inside and pulled out the pink headscarf, at the same time lifting Ardiana's bag from the footwell and handing it to her.

'Please, let's just go.'

'Perfume,' repeated Keira.

Ardiana rummaged around in her bag and pulled out a half-empty bottle of Gucci Rush.

Taking the bottle from her, Keira held the scarf in one hand, depressed the atomiser and covered it in a thick, sweet-smelling mist. Scrunching the piece of pink cloth in her fist, she pressed it to her face, making sure to cover her nose and mouth, then set off back along the path.

'What the hell are you doing? You're not going in there,' said Ardiana, calling after her. 'Please! This is bad ... very bad. We should leave,' but Keira was already gone.

*

Flies continued to buzz around her as she squeezed into the tight opening between door and jamb. Keira tried to widen the gap, but whatever was on the floor was stuck fast. The perfume helped block out the rancid smell, but it wasn't enough; Keira started to gag.

Leading with her right arm and shoulder, she tried to squeeze her hips and torso through into the hallway, but twisting sideways and craning her neck for the final push was too painful. Each nudge wedged her more firmly into the gap. Her head movement was restricted. She tried edging back out towards the garden, but that didn't help. She was stuck, lodged between the door frame and the edge of the door.

Keira took a deep breath, sucked in her stomach and managed to tug her belt buckle free from the door handle, then with one final effort she pushed through into the darkened lobby.

What little light there was spilling in through the open door cast shadows in the gloom. It was just possible to make out the outline of a kitchen table and beyond that the arm of a sofa in the far corner. A solid, misshapen mass lay heaped on the near side of the table, shimmering in the darkness. With one eye on the shadowy mound Keira dropped to a squat and ran her hand along the bottom of the front door. Her fingers came to rest on something soft, jammed underneath. Applying a little pressure to the door, she yanked the object out and held it to the light. A child's soft toy, an animal of some kind, too stained to be recognisable beyond that.

Keira was now able to open the door fully, allowing the lobby and kitchen to fill with light and cleaner air.

The misshapen mound in the kitchen was now clearly visible.

The remains of two bodies collapsed against each other, sitting where they had died, their clothing stained dark with blood. Ermir's grandparents.

Valbona Dervishi sat nearest, arm across her chest, a withered, skeletal hand clutched to her throat. Her husband Edon's body was slumped in the chair next to her, head flopped back, the hole in his ribcage visible through what remained of his shirt. The little flesh they had left was being slowly devoured by a plague of maggots and cockroaches. The insects crawled and writhed across their faces and exposed limbs in a seething mass, giving the impression that the cadavers were somehow alive. In the gloomy silence it was possible to pick out the buzz and click of thousands of tiny jaws consuming the rotten meat.

Behind them on the mantel sat a collection of memorabilia: trophies, ornaments and a number of framed photographs. In one, the fresh face of a young girl, barely in her teens, stared thoughtfully into the room. An unguarded moment of innocence at odds with the scene it overlooked. Her face was swollen with childhood and softer than the Kaltrina Dervishi that Keira had known, but she recognised the young girl immediately. In the frame next to Kaltrina's a young boy of four or five with the same expression as his mother: the same eyes and soft, high cheeks, his head tilted to one side, nuzzling something between his chin and his shoulder.

This was Keira's first glimpse of Kaltrina's son: she was in no doubt that the boy staring back at her was Ermir.

Filling her lungs, she drew the headscarf from her mouth and used her hand to steady herself against the near wall. As she stretched across the dead bodies towards the mantel her leg brushed against the chair, causing Valbona Dervishi's hand to fall from her chest and knock against Keira's thigh.

She jumped back.

'Shit.'

The car horn sounded outside.

Keira took a step closer, taking care to avoid any further contact. Balancing on the tips of her toes, she braced herself against the wall again and this time managed to hook her fingers round the back of the nearest frame and drag it along the mantel until she could grip it properly. Using the frame to extend her reach Keira tipped the photograph of Kaltrina so that it clattered face down onto the mantel where it lay – blind now to the horror in front of it.

Moments later Keira was back on the garden path, retching until there was nothing left in her stomach.

*

'You okay?' frowned Ardiana as Keira approached the car.

'Thanks for your help.'

'You're lucky I'm still here. I was all set to steal the car and get to hell away from this scary shit. We all done?'

'Nearly.'

'Don't even think of telling me what's in there. Whatever it is, I don't want the picture in my head.' Ardiana craned her neck to look at the photograph Keira was carrying. 'This is the boy?'

'I'm pretty sure, yeah.'

Ardiana nodded in the direction of the cottage. 'Please, it's not him in there that smells so bad.'

'It's not him.'

'The grandparents, like you said?'

'I thought you didn't want to know.'

'I don't want to know what they look like. I am just checking you were right.'

'I was right.'

'This is what they do to keep people afraid.'

'Who?'

'The Clan; they don't let anyone near the place to get the bodies for a funeral. It's to show everyone they are in charge of everything round here: whether you live or die, whether they will let you go to the afterlife. Even when you are dead, still, they are in charge of you. They are cursing the family. It is not good what you have done. They will know. We must leave here straight away.'

'I need to talk to Lule's mother.'

'You think old Rozafa there will have anything to say to you?' Ardiana wagged her index finger in the air. 'The people in that tomb were her neighbours. She will know what's in this house – what has happened – and her mouth it will be stitched tight. You will get from her, nothing. We must leave here.'

'I think she knows where the boy is.'

Twelve

Lule was on her way to drop off some shopping at her mother's house in Dushk when she got the call. Rozafa was talking in whispers.

'They been at the front door three times now.'

'They?'

'She . . . a woman.'

'On her own?'

'Just a woman on her own and another one sitting in the car.'

'There are two of them?'

'Been peering in through the windows 'n' looking over the fence into the back yard.'

'Where is she now?'

'In her car.'

'Both of them are in the car?'

'Parked right outside the gate: I can see her plain as day.'

'Which one?'

'The one who was at the door. Looks like they're gonna wait there. They're both in the car now, talking to each other.'

These days most of Rozafa's experience of the world came via the television, which was nearly as old as she was and sat babbling away in the corner of her living room. Her politics came courtesy of TV Klan's long running political show *Opinion*, but her favourite was the American show *Gruaja a Mirë: The Good Wife*. The only time she left the house was to tend the vegetable patch behind the house and feed the chickens picking over what was left of her dusty lawn. Lule had told her this day would come. She'd warned her that people would come looking for her, but Rozafa had dismissed her daughter's concerns as paranoia. Lule had not been the same since returning from her travels. Her youthful confidence was gone: whatever happened while she was abroad had hollowed the girl out; made her nervous and withdrawn.

'D'you think this is it?' continued Rozafa. 'Is this the thing you said was going to happen one day . . . is this it happening?'

'I don't know, Mom. You think maybe they're Policia?' asked Lule.

'More like someone from a bank – the one that's come to the door, anyway. Plain, not showy; an accountant maybe.'

'Why would someone from a bank come visit you?'

'I'm just saying what she's dressed like.'

'What sort of age?'

'Hard to tell what she looks like: her face is all beat up, like she's been in a fight. Doesn't have any smile lines round her eyes; definitely not Albanian. The other one is. She looks familiar. I've seen her before.'

'You got close enough to see the lines around her eyes?'

'The beat-up one came right up to the front of the house. Was peering in the windows. I was standing on the other side of the nets looking straight at her.'

'Have they gone next door?'

'The car parked up about an hour ago. Figure they went in to have a look. Got a rental sticker on the windshield; could be she's from out of town. You want me to go get the shotgun; ask her what the hell she's doing? I could end this right now.'

'No,' said Lule. 'Don't do anything. Do they know you're in the house?'

'Don't think so. Where are you?'

'I'm nearby. I've been to the market. I have a couple of bags for you.'

'You have the boy there too?'

'He's asleep in the back.'

'Turn around and go back to your apartment. Don't come here, Lule. I'll take care of it.'

'I'm at the bottom of the hill.'

'Take him away from here, Lule. You can bring the shopping tomorrow.'

'I don't have the car tomorrow.'

'Wait, I hear something.'

'Don't go out there, Mom.'

'I'll call you back.'

'Don't go out there,' hissed Lule, but the phone was dead.

Just past the turn-off to her mother's house, Lule eased her foot on to the brake and steered the light green W115 Mercedes onto the verge. The soft tyres bulged and bounced along the potholed surface until the car eventually came to a stop. In the rear, the boy's head rested at an awkward angle against the car window. A small teardrop of saliva escaped his mouth, ran down over his soft chin and dripped onto his shoulder, turning a patch of light-blue cotton T-shirt a darker shade. Lule cut the engine and sat for a moment taking in the silence. She wound down the window and let the car fill with warm air from outside. Where her arm rested on the top of the door panel she could feel the sun's heat on her bare skin.

When she'd dressed for work earlier that morning it had

crossed her mind that today could be the day. It wasn't intuition; she'd had the same thought every morning for the past few months. Ever since the boy had walked through the garden and into her mother's house – covered in blood, his eyes wet with tears, his stomach cramped with hunger – she'd wondered when they would come. From the moment she'd decided to take the boy and look after him she'd barely slept. The least noise: the creak of a door or crack of a floorboard would have her sitting up in bed fighting to catch her breath. Ermir would wake too and start asking for Hathi, whoever or whatever that was. The rest of the night would then be spent trying to comfort the boy back to sleep. Money was tight: she worked part time in a grocery store in Tirana and shared a flat with her friend Nikki Shyri, but that wouldn't last. Nikki was already making noises about Lule finding somewhere else to live and now this: two women outside her mother's house.

Ermir would be awake soon and it would be impossible to deliver the shopping to her mother without him becoming distressed. Ermir was afraid he was being taken back to the house where his grandparents had been murdered. He would become agitated, start crying – wail until he made himself sick. The only options were to leave him with a neighbour or drive to her mother's house when he was asleep and drop the shopping off without even getting out of the car. Leaving him with a neighbour caused the boy to become even more anxious. He couldn't bear to be separated from her. It was the same for Lule: she couldn't bear to be separated from the boy. He'd barely spoken since the day his grandparents were murdered: just one word that he repeated over and over again. 'Hathi'.

When Lule asked him what it meant he would stare back

at her with tears in his eyes and say it again, 'Hathi,' like she should already know.

Lule looked over at his small round face – his dark eyes closed as he slept in the back of the car. She stared at him and hoped his dreams were somewhere to escape to and not somewhere to fear.

Lule leant across and opened the glovebox. She pulled a flat-black Beretta from inside and placed it beside her empty handbag on the passenger seat.

The phone started to buzz. Lule snatched it up and pressed it to her ear.

'The beat-up one's going back to the car,' her mother hissed. 'I think they're leaving.'

'Did you go out to them?'

'No.'

'Okay, I'll be up in a minute, but come to the gate. The boy is going to wake up soon.'

*

Ardiana revved the engine and leant across to open the passenger door as Keira approached the car and climbed in. 'Told you it's a waste of time. Even if the old woman's in there, she's not going to tell you anything.'

'Can you write a message for me in Albanian?'

'Then we can leave?'

'Then we can leave.'

'What does the message say?'

'"I want to help Ermir."'

'That is all?'

88

'I'll put the number of the hotel and my office number back in Glasgow.'

'Why not your mobile, too?'

'I don't use a mobile.'

This time Ardiana shot Keira a glance. 'You don't use a mobile? Albania's still playing catch-up with the rest of the world on a lot of things, but everyone has a goddamn cellphone. How d'you stay in touch?'

'Your question assumes that I want to stay in touch.'

'Now you are talking like a lawyer. What is there to write on?'

Keira lifted the car rental agreement from the glovebox and discarded the paperwork. 'Use this envelope.'

'D'you have a pen?'

'Got some eyeliner.'

Ardiana wrote the note and handed it back to Keira, who then signed her name and added the telephone numbers. 'Be back in a minute.'

Keira scanned the front door for somewhere to post the note but there was no letterbox. It was tight, but eventually she managed to work the envelope under the storm sill at the bottom of the door.

Instinct made Keira turn and look over her shoulder as she headed back towards the front gate. A twitch at the curtain told her what she already knew: someone was watching from inside the house. It was frustrating, but all she could do now was wait and hope that whoever it was would pick up the note and give her a call.

*

'You got plans for your last night in Albania?' asked Ardiana as they pulled away. 'I'm meeting up with Fatjo. Why don't you come have a drink with us?'

'I have to pick up new travel documents. I'm going to drop in at the police station.'

'You have to have passport photograph done with your face all bruised?'

'A temporary travel permit: I'll apply for a new passport when I get home.'

'So you want to come for a drink? I'm supposed to be working, but we can maybe go for one quick one.'

'By the time I've picked up the papers and got back to the hotel, I doubt I'll have time. It's an early flight tomorrow.'

'Don't even think to tell anyone what you have seen today.'

'Two dead bodies in a house: it's not something you come across every day. We should let someone know.'

'You don't understand. The police, they already know. The whole of Dushk knows. You and me are the last to find out, that's all, but everyone else knows. If the Clan leaves two bodies as a warning, you have to listen to the message. Don't get involved. You go into the police station, you're going to be talking to a Clan member wearing a uniform. He'll say, "Why you don't listen to the message?" and arrest you for being deaf.'

Ardiana slowed the car as it approached the bottom of the hill and flicked the indicator stalk to turn right.

At the junction Keira looked up to the left, checking for oncoming traffic. Twenty metres from the corner, pulled over to the side of the narrow road, sat an old Mercedes with a young woman staring out from behind the steering wheel. Her body was stiff, her eyes alert, like a wary deer in the field watching for predators. A figure lay slumped in the back, asleep, the features indistinct.

The young woman held Keira's gaze until the rental car had turned right and was heading off down the road.

Keira twisted round to check through the rear window. A puff of oily exhaust rose into the air behind the Mercedes.

'What you looking at?'

'Slow down for a second.'

'You left something behind? I'm not going back.'

'There's a girl in the Merc. Back there . . .'

Ardiana checked the rear-view mirror. 'Yes?'

'Slow down, I want to see if she turns into the lane.'

'Car's parked up.'

'She's just started the engine.'

Ardiana slowed to a crawl. The next junction opened onto a busier tarmacked stretch of open road that in turn led to the motorway back to Durrës.

'Take a left, then double back as soon as you can,' said Keira.

'Shit. Do we have to?'

'There's no other turn-off until you get to here. If she's coming down the road towards us then I've no idea who she is. If the car's gone, the only place it could go is up the hill . . . and my guess is that whoever's driving has gone to visit her mother.'

Ardiana pulled left out of the junction, passed a few low-rise houses, then turned in a tight arc until the car was heading back in the opposite direction.

The spot the old Mercedes had occupied was vacant.

Keira signalled for Ardiana to slow down as they rounded the bend near the top of the lane. The girl standing outside the Dervishis' next-door neighbour's house reacted immediately when she saw their car approaching. Keira watched her run back to the car, pull open the passenger door and reach inside.

'Stop and let me out.'

'What's she doing?' asked Ardiana.

'Stop here! I don't want to scare her.'

Ardiana stamped on the brakes and Keira swung the door open, ready to jump out.

The girl was just fifty metres away, screaming as she marched towards them, arms extended.

'She's not scared, she's pissed off. Stay in the car. Bitch's carrying a goddamn nine in her hand,' said Ardiana, raising her voice.

Before Keira could pull the door closed there was a bright muzzle flash followed by a loud crack and the hire car's windscreen shattered. Through the fractures Keira saw another flash and the whole screen exploded in on top of the two women.

Cowering down behind the dashboard, Ardiana managed to pull the gearshift into reverse then started the car backwards down the slope. There was another loud crack as the wing mirror was hit. Ardiana steered the rental car blind, swerving from side to side, with the accelerator pedal pressed hard to the floor. Near the bottom of the road the car missed the turn and came to a halt with a sudden jolt as its rear bumper slammed hard into a drystone wall.

Keira tried her door. It was jammed shut. She put her shoulder to it, but it wouldn't budge.

As she wound down the window and started to climb out Ardiana hissed at her, 'Where are you going? You got to stay in the car.'

The door was lodged against a shallow bank of earth. With

her arms resting on the roof Keira managed to pull herself free and clamber out.

The sound of an engine revving into life and the crashing of gears filled the valley.

Keira jumped down from the embankment and started along the lane towards the oncoming car, Ardiana shouting something behind her.

Moments later the Mercedes appeared from the belly of a dust cloud, hurtling around the bend as it sped towards her. Keira stopped dead and planted her feet firmly in the middle of the track.

The car continued to accelerate. Just as Keira was preparing to dive out of the way she heard the sound of brakes squealing against rusty discs. The old Mercedes swerved into a skid then slid to a halt with the chrome bumper touching the crease of denim at Keira's knees.

The dust cloud drifted over quickly. When it cleared, Keira saw the girl's china-blue eyes staring back at her through the windscreen, a handgun pointing at her out of the driver's window. Keira raised her arms above her head.

There was some movement behind the girl. A child. It was difficult to make out the features properly, but Keira knew who it was.

Both women held each other's gaze, but said nothing. Eventually, Keira stepped clear of the bumper – her movement tracked by the barrel of the Beretta pointed straight at her chest – and broke the silence.

'I'm here to help. I want to help the boy ... Ermir ... and you, Lule.'

It was a few seconds before the girl spat back at her, 'If I ever see you again, I will be the last thing you ever see.'

The car lurched forward and sped off down the hill.

*

Ardiana was sitting on the bonnet of what was left of the rental car smoking what was left of her cigarette. She held it out in front of her and shouted up the lane to Keira. 'You want some, you better be quick! It's the last one.'

'You go ahead . . . You think there's any point chasing after her?'

'Don't have to. I know where she's heading.'

'Where?'

'Tirana.'

'What makes you think that?'

'The plate on her car; starts with 'TR'. Means the car is registered there.'

'Did you get the whole number on the plate?'

'I did.'

'Did you write it down?'

Ardiana held out the flat of her hand, showing a scribble of letters and numbers. 'Used your eyeliner.' She took a long drag and flicked the cigarette into the dirt. 'Why didn't she shoot?'

'I think she was just trying to scare us off.'

'What did you say? What did she say?'

'I told her I wanted to help. She answered me in English,' replied Keira, starting back down the hill.

'So? Lots of Albanians are speaking English these days.'

'With a Scottish accent?' replied Keira.

Thirteen

In front of the two patrol cars sat a light blue Opel with a rental sticker on the rear window and a gaping hole where the windscreen used to be.

On the bank – a safe distance from the motorway traffic – stood one of his officers alongside Keira and another female.

Pavli took his time walking around the rental car, then stood for a while studying the front end, making a show of it for Keira. He pulled the passenger door open, checked the interior then made his way round to the boot. He popped the lid open and spent a few minutes examining something inside.

When he was finished Pavli scrambled up the bank to join them.

He nodded to the traffic officer and had a muttered conversation with him in Albanian.

Keira had no idea what was being said, but figured Pavli had told him he would take over because a few seconds later the officer descended the slope, climbed back into his patrol car and drove off.

Pavli turned to Keira. 'You should stand under a birds' nest and hope that one of them shits on you.'

'After a thorough examination of the wreckage, that's the best you can come up with?'

'It's good luck for a bird to drop shit on you from the sky. I'm thinking you could do with some.'

'I'd need a flock of them to fly over.'

Pavli looked across to Ardiana. 'What is your name?'

Ardiana hesitated before answering. If she gave her hooker name the cop might ask more questions, but if she gave her real name she'd be easier to trace. She opted for hooker. 'My name's Eliza.'

'Second name?'

Ardiana couldn't think quick enough so gave her real second name.

'Kastrati.' She was trying to play it cool, but Keira could see that she was nervous.

'From the north?' continued Pavli.

'Way back in time, yes, my family were from the north, but we are lowlanders now.'

'Where do you live?'

'Durrës.'

'What is your job?'

'Sales and rentals.'

Keira shot her a glance.

'You two know each other?'

'Eliza was showing me round,' interjected Keira.

Pavli addressed the next question to both of them. 'You are going to tell me what really happened or are you sticking with the "we hit a donkey" story? There is a reason I ask. My colleague followed your car for some distance before he stopped you and he said there was no sign of a donkey on the side of the road. Also, I have examined the car and there is no impact to the front of the vehicle, but there is to the rear. Only the door mirror is missing and, of course, the windscreen. I think for insurance a better story would be that you have come back to the vehicle and found it this way. I would say also that you have no idea how it happened. What do you think?'

'Of what?' asked Keira.

'Of what is the best story?'

'"We came back to the vehicle and found it this way. We have no idea what happened,"' repeated Keira.

'Okay. That is what I write on the ticket. I give you this to show the insurance company and the rental company also.' Pavli pulled a notebook from his pocket and started jotting down some notes. 'Then, you tell me what really happened and why there is a hole from a nine mil in the padding of the rear seat and matching nine mil slug in the trunk of the car, but this can wait. Let me first write down the "official" version. Once that is done I drop you back at hotel and arrange to have car towed to a garage. You can not drive it any more.'

'What do I tell the rental company when I get to the airport in the morning?'

'Tell them you returned from a sightseeing trip in Gosë to find the car damaged and the car has being taken by the police.'

'What about the bullet hole?'

'What bullet hole?'

Pavli finished off his notes then gestured with his hand, 'Come, let us go get beer.'

As the three of them started back to the police car Keira asked Pavli a question that earned her a look from Ardiana. 'Is Tirana far from here?'

'Is quite far. An hour and a half, maybe quicker if I put on the lights. You want to go to Tirana for a beer?'

'If I gave you a number plate would you be able to get an address?'

'What is number plate?'

'Of a car . . . the registration number. Is that what you call it?'

'Is the licence I think, yes?'

'Yes, the licence plate.'

'Who is belonging to the plate?'

'That's why I'm asking. I don't know.'

They'd reached the police car. Pavli held the door for Keira to sit in the passenger seat and looked mildly disappointed when she stepped aside to let Ardiana through instead. Keira got into the back and slid along till she was sitting in the middle with her head poking through between them.

'I don't want to go to Tirana,' said Ardiana. 'If it's okay I will get out near Durrës and catch a furgon. I have to work this evening.'

'You are working on a Saturday night?' asked Pavli.

'Sure . . . so are you.'

'I'm just about to finish.'

'Lucky you,' was all she could think to say.

'What is the licence plate number? You have it here?'

Ardiana lifted the palm of her left hand. Her hands were sweating so much that some of the letters had been wiped off. She tried to read the black smudge of eyeliner.

'It is T R one, two, eight something . . . I can't make out the last number or the letter. It is maybe six, but the letter has gone completely.' She held it up for Keira to look at, but it was difficult to tell.

'What is the make of the car?' asked Pavli.

'A Mercedes,' replied Keira. 'A light green Mercedes. Old.'

Pavli pressed the call button on his radio and there was a

brief exchange in Albanian followed by a short silence.

A few seconds later the radio hissed and crackled out a response. Pavli gave them the translation. 'Tirana. First block of flats on the corner of Rruga Sami Frashëri and Bulevard Gjergj Fishta: apartment's on the third floor. The car is registered to a female, surname is Shyri. Do we need any more?'

'No.'

Pavli thanked the controller, replaced the handset and started the engine. 'You want to have a coffee with Miss Shyri or ask her to join us for a beer?'

'If you have the time, I'd like to talk to her.'

'Okay, we go.'

'Wait!' exclaimed Keira, opening the car door.

Pavli and Ardiana watched through the windscreen as Keira ran back to the hire car and ducked inside. She emerged a few moments later clutching a photo frame and a small furry toy. Seconds later she was climbing back in.

'Who's in the photograph?'

'I think it's the boy,' replied Keira, handing it over for him to look at.

'The toy you have in your hand is the toy he is holding in the photograph?'

It was caked in dried blood and almost unrecognisable as the one Ermir held squashed between his cheek and his shoulder, but it was the same.

'Yes, I think so.'

'Where you find this?' asked Pavli handing the frame back to Keira.

Ardiana shifted a little in her seat.

'Is it okay if I tell you later?' replied Keira. 'I'm running out of time and if it's possible to talk to the girl this evening, I'd really like to do that.'

'Okay. Now we go.' Pavli slipped the car into first, switched on the blue lights and pulled onto the motorway.

'I will call for back-up to meet us there, yes?' asked Pavli. 'I am thinking maybe Miss Shyri is the one put the nine mil through the windscreen.'

*

Ardiana was relieved to get out of the car. The cop dropped her off on the outskirts of Durrës at a layby that passed for an informal bus stop. A small crowd – a mixture of noisy tourists and stony-faced locals – had gathered waiting for the next bus into town. There was no way of knowing how long it would be, but she was in no hurry.

Ardiana checked her phone – three more messages from Fatjo asking what was going on.

She moved away from the crowd and thumbed in a number. It rang three times, then she hung up and dialled again. This time it was answered.

'Let me speak to the *krye*.'

'The boss is not here. What d'you want?'

'Don't dick me around. He asked me to call if I found out anything.'

'Who is this?'

'Ardiana Kastrati. Put him on.'

'Hold on.'

Ardiana heard a brief, muffled exchange then another voice came on the line. She recognised it straight away as belonging to Verbër Vedon, the boss. 'Where the fuck have you been?'

'Sitting in the front of a cop car is where I've been,' protested Ardiana. 'I couldn't call you.'

'You got busted?'

'No. We went to the house.'

'Did you go in? I told you not to go in.'

'I didn't go in. Let me finish. We went to the house and the lawyer lady forced the door open then went inside. She went in, I stayed in the car. There were bugs everywhere and the smell made me want to puke.'

'Where were you?'

'In the car, but I got out for a smoke. Even from there you could smell it – like sick and shit. It smelled like a bad death. I don't even want to talk about it. The lawyer went in and saw bodies. When she was done she went next door to neighbour's house. Tried to talk to the old lady, lives there, but she didn't even come to the door. She was in there – no doubt – but she ignored us.'

'You went to the old lady's door?'

'No, I stayed near the car, but this is what I want to tell you. When we left, a girl was parked at the bottom of the hill. The lawyer lady saw her. We turned round, and went back up, but then the girl pulls out a goddamn pistola and starts shooting at us.'

'Is this why the cops are involved?'

'No. She drove away . . .'

'Who?'

'The girl! But she's shot our car to shit . . . She drives away and we try to get back to Durrës and get pulled by the cops on the motorway, we've got no windscreen or anything.'

'So you didn't follow her?'

'Our car was fucked.'

'Did she have the kid?'

'Yes, I think so. There was a child strapped in the back.'

'He the one the lawyer's looking for?'

'Yes.'

'So where is he now?'

'This is what I'm calling to tell you. We got her plate.'

'You got her plate?'

'So, when we get into the cop car, the lawyer lady asks the cop to run the number – I think maybe they know each other – so he runs it for her.'

'Babe, are you calling me to tell me you have the girl's address?'

'Tirana. First block of flats on the corner of Rruga Sami Frashëri and Bulevard Gjergj Fishta: apartment's on the third floor. The car – a light green Mercedes – is registered to a female. Surname is Shyri. You need any more?'

'Ardiana?'

'Yeah?'

'This is very good.'

Ardiana found herself smiling.

'How long ago did they leave you?'

'I just got out of the car, so like, thirty seconds maybe. I called as soon as I could.'

'Where are you?'

'Waiting for a furgon just outside Durrës. Shkallnur.'

'Are they taking the fifty-six?'

'I think so, yes.'

'So they'll take about forty minutes to get to Tirana . . . how long since the girl with the kid left?'

'Maybe an hour.'

'Go home: don't do any work tonight, no clients. I'm going to give you a bonus, so no work. Go home, take a break, open a bottle of wine and keep your legs closed.'

Ardiana didn't find Vedon's comment funny, but she laughed anyway.

'What should I tell Fatjo? He's left me a hundred messages.'

'Don't worry about that fat dumb-fuck, I'll talk to him.'

'Should I call him at least? I feel bad, like I've gone behind his back.'

'Call him and tell him I said you're to have the night off. If he starts bitchin' about it, tell him to give me a call.'

'Okay.'

'Ardiana?'

'Yeah?'

'You think the cop would recognise you again?'

'Not without my make-up! I've got my eyes on and enough foundation to build a house. You think I should go back to being a brunette just in case?'

'Redhead . . . I always like the redhead look.'

'Sure.'

'Ardiana?'

'Yeah?'

'You done good.'

Fourteen

It was after six when Pavli's police car turned off of Bulevard Gjergj Fishta into the car park of the ten-storey apartment block. An ambulance blocked the main entrance to the building, but Keira's eyes were on the two police cars, skewed alongside. 'These your back-up?'

Pavli looked puzzled. 'This has nothing to do with me.'

It was clear that the ambulance had only just arrived. Its doors flew open and a team of medics clambered out, heading off at speed into the building.

A shock of adrenaline hit Keira the moment she spotted the blue flashing lights. She scanned the rest of the parked cars for the light green Mercedes, hoping that it wasn't there, but spotted it two cars behind where they had just parked.

'Wait in the car till I find out what is going on,' said Pavli, clipping his sidearm to his utility belt and climbing out. He approached another officer who was standing at the rear of the ambulance and started talking. She waited until they both had their backs to her then slipped out of the police car and ducked between the parked vehicles until she reached the Mercedes.

Keira laid the palm of her hand on the bonnet. It was hot.

She tried the door handle and was surprised to find that the door opened.

Sliding into the driving seat, she looked around. The passenger footwell was a mess of sweet wrappers and cigarette butts.

A child seat, covered in stains and stale crumbs, was strapped into place in the back. The faint odour of cigarette smoke and sour perfume filled the air. The scent was familiar, but Keira couldn't remember its name.

She had no idea what she was hoping to find, but there was nothing of any interest here.

Keira climbed out and stood for a moment taking in her surroundings.

The perimeter of the parking area was marked by a low wall on top of which sat a line of head-height metal railings. Beyond the railings, traffic rumbled up and down the busy road to the sound of car horns and the distant wail of sirens. On the far side of the stream of traffic crowds of pedestrians and holiday-makers made their way along the packed pavement past cafés, bars and restaurants.

Just as she was about to head back to the police car Keira noticed a figure standing stock still amongst the crowd: a young woman with a child next to her, holding her hand. At first she thought they were waiting for a break in the traffic then Keira realised that the young woman was staring across at her.

The distance made it difficult to make out her features.

Keira couldn't be sure, but the little boy standing beside her was enough to convince her that it was Lule.

A hand clamped Keira's shoulder.

'I told you to wait in the car. This is a crime scene now,' said Pavli. 'You must not go wandering off or you end up being the suspect. There's a body in the apartment.'

'A body?'

'Yes.'

'A girl?'

'A young woman.'

'Is she still alive?'

'No.'

Keira stared back at Pavli. 'Shit.'

'Someone got here before us.'

Keira glanced across the street, but the two figures had disappeared. Maybe it wasn't them. Maybe it was just a woman and her son crossing the street. A thought struck Keira, but Pavli got there before she could ask the question. 'There's no sign of the boy.'

'It must have just happened,' said Keira. 'This is the car. Feel the bonnet: the engine is still hot – not even cooled a little. She can't have been here for very long, so it must have happened recently.'

'Go sit in the police car,' said Pavli as he turned and started back towards the entrance of the apartment block.

The car park was a sudden flurry of activity. As Keira made her way back to the police car she saw uniformed officers running into the building, weapons drawn. Minutes later the whole area was swarming with cops as two support units drew up, sirens blaring, and blocked the entrance to the car park; the road outside too. More armed men poured into the building and started to search each apartment floor by floor. A steady stream of figures began to appear until eventually the car park was transformed into a sea of displaced residents.

Keira heard the rear passenger door open and felt the suspension spring a little as someone climbed into the back.

'Don't turn. You turn and I will blow your fucking head all over the windscreen.'

Keira felt a circle of cold steel press hard into the back of her neck. She lifted her gaze to the rear-view mirror and saw Lule staring back at her.

'Poison.'

'What are you saying?'

'Poison. I smelled it in your car earlier. It's the name of the perfume you're wearing.'

'Why is there ambulance?'

'There's a body inside. They think it's you.'

The girl cursed in Albanian then asked, 'Who are you, lady? What is you want from me? You see out there the chaos? You have brought this to me. Why you have done this?'

Keira made to answer, but the girl cut her off by pressing the barrel more firmly into her neck.

'I have a grave already is dug for you. You understand. If I see you again is where I put you. This is the last time I say this.'

'Where is the boy?'

'There is no boy.'

'I want to help Ermir.'

'Who is Ermir?'

Keira knew Lule was throwing her a line and pressed on. 'I know what happened. I know you are looking after him, I want to help.'

'Leave us alone, lady, okay? We don't want help. All we want is to be left alone.'

'I knew Kaltrina. I know what happened to her family. I'm here to try and make things better for Ermir . . . and for you.'

'Stop using that name, he is not that name any more. This is what helps him. He must not be known by that name. Is not safe for him. You are dangerous to him, lady. You think you are helping, but you have brought only trouble with you. Tell Kaltrina I am sorry for what happened to her parents. If I'd known what they would do I would not have run away.'

'Run away from where, Lule? I don't understand.'

'Tell Kaltrina I am keep the boy safe until she returns. This is my *besa*.'

'Lule, please, Kaltrina's . . .'

Suddenly Pavli knocked on the window. As she wound it down he picked up straight away on the expression on Keira's face. 'Sorry, I didn't mean to make you jump. The building is searched from top to bottom. Is safe, but you are right. This has only just happened. Medics are going back in to recover the body. You think you maybe recognise the girl, if she is the one that shot at you?'

'You want me to come look?'

'You don't have to, but it would help. They have made bad mess of her, so say no if you don't want to see. There is some confusion. The neighbours are saying Shyri is the name of the girl who is owning the flat, but there is another girl – with a son – who is sharing. The body, her face is so bad they don't know which one it is.'

'Do I have to come in? Can I wait until they bring her down and look then?'

'Sure, but only if you are up to it. I understand if you don't want to be involved.'

'I'm already involved, but I have to get on that plane tomorrow. If I take a look, I can't be written up as a witness. Nothing formal.'

'Nothing formal,' agreed Pavli. 'You can just look, then

someone will take you straight back to hotel. There are new travel documents for you to sign also, but I will meet you at the airport with them tomorrow and make sure with my own hand that you get on the flight. My friend at the embassy has made things happen quickly, but you will need to be there early.'

'We can't sort it out tonight?'

'I have now to stay here. It's okay for you to identify the girl?'

'I'll come over when they bring her out.'

'Okay. This will help us, thank you. I was hoping tonight we could share a bottle of rakia, but I'm cursed like you, I think.'

Keira stared after Pavli as he walked back to the building and disappeared inside.

Lule's voice came from the floor behind. 'Why are you hanging with the cops?'

'He's trying to help.'

'Cops in Albania are either corrupt or stupid, and if they are not corrupt it's because they are *too* stupid. You should be careful. If you want to help, tell them it's me on the gurney. If they think I am dead this will buy more time for me to get away from Tirana.'

'I don't want you to get away from Tirana. I want to help you and Ermir.'

Keira glanced over her shoulder as she heard the rear passenger door click open. 'Wait Lule, go to Hotel Shkop, room 415. I'm leaving tomorrow – flying back to Glasgow. We need to talk. Kaltrina's dead . . .'

The area behind the passenger seat was already empty, a lingering hint of Poison the only evidence that the girl had been there at all.

Keira jumped out, her eyes searching between the rows of

parked cars. She scanned the crowd of residents jostling impatiently in the car park, but the girl was gone.

*

Pavli was beckoning to Keira from the tailgate of the ambulance, where two porters were waiting to load the gurney.

As she approached one of the medics pulled the sheet from the corpse, revealing the badly beaten face of a young woman. Blood seeped from the fresh wounds and her eyes stared lifelessly into the growing darkness.

Keira muttered 'I'm sorry,' under her breath to the girl lying on the gurney then nodded to Pavli. 'It's difficult to be certain, but I'm pretty sure it's the girl who shot at us. Her name is Lule.'

Fifteen

Xhon Variboba was working the concierge station when Keira exited the lift into the lobby of the hotel. Half an hour under the shower and a change of clothes later she was ready for a beer and something to fill the empty feeling in her stomach. It was a relief to see Xhon's friendly face.

'Were you on the desk when I got back? I didn't see you.'

'Just started my shift. I'll finish in time to wave you off to the airport.'

'You on all night?'

'Yes, is so,' replied John with no hint that he was bothered by the prospect. 'You're back early.'

'Didn't realise I was on a clock.'

'My son has never been good at closing the deal. He's chickened out of asking you to go for a drink. He's not supposed to be working tonight: took the night off. I told him he's never going to find a woman until he eases back on the cop thing. I thought you two would be out till late. You were with him, yes?'

'Yes.'

'And he didn't mention the drink thing?'

'He dumped me for girl in Tirana.'

'She a looker too?'

'Maybe once. Right now she's staring at the roof of an ambulance headed for the morgue.'

'What'd she do?'

'Nothing to deserve what happened to her. They broke her nose and beat her till she stopped breathing. Pavli was the first senior officer on the scene. I don't think he had much choice whether to stay or go.'

'So, if it wasn't for this other woman you'd be interested?'

'In going for a drink maybe: but that's all.'

'Did you see the body?'

'I saw what was left of her face; that was enough.'

'You still hungry after seeing that? You want me to arrange some food and a cold beer?'

'Yes please, and bring ten straws just in case. One for each beer.'

Xhon liked that. 'Go join your friend outside and I'll see to it. I didn't realise you were in the hotel or I'd have called up to your room. I told her you wouldn't be back for a while.'

'What friend?'

'The young woman.'

'Ardiana?'

'Didn't give a name, but she said she'd wait. Tried to order some food on your room. I told her no, but got her a beer and some bar snacks 'cause she was looking kinda anxious. Told her it was up to her if she wanted to stick around, but if a resident needed the table she'd have to move . . . Beer's on my tab.'

'Where's she sitting?'

'First she was at a table by the pool, then she moved to hotel loungers down on the beach.'

*

The patio area seemed surprisingly busy, then Keira remembered it was Saturday night. Tea lights in the centre of each table lit the faces of the diners with a warm glow and strings of fairy lights hung overhead helped soften the mood. Most of the tables were occupied by couples. Keira scanned their faces as she snaked between them, then headed down the steps and out through the metal gates towards the beach. A roped-off rectangle, lit by hanging lanterns, marked out the perimeter of the Hotel Shkop's residents-only beach. Beyond this area where the sand sloped down to meet the water's edge sat three neat rows of loungers. The steady hum of conversation and low-volume muzak was replaced by the crash of waves rolling in along the shoreline as Keira made her way towards them.

A small orange glow briefly illuminated a woman's face.

Alerted by the sound of her approach the figure rose. 'The guy at the desk said you wouldn't be back till late.'

'I got stood up for a corpse.'

'Do the cops think it's me?'

'Yes, for the moment.'

'They've killed my friend Nikki. That's fucked up.'

'Yes.'

'You dating the cop?'

'In his mind maybe, not in mine.'

'You go for coffee three times with a guy in Albania, you're as good as married.'

'You said you needed time to get out of Tirana.'

'I'm out of Tirana.'

'I thought you meant somewhere slightly further afield.'

'I did.'

'You picked here?'

'It's the last place your cop friend's going to think of looking, but it's not my final destination.'

'The guy working the front desk is my cop friend's father; it may not have been the best choice.'

'It was your fucking suggestion and, like I say, it's not my final destination.'

Keira crossed to the lounger opposite Lule and perched on the edge.

'I'm not sure the police are the ones you should be running from.'

'I'm thinking this is maybe your first time in Albania. You don't think it's weird that we've never met before today, and yet this evening they showed up at my flat?'

'We took your licence plate.'

'And who passed it on to the two assholes I saw going into my apartment block? I knew soon as I saw them they were Clan. Was it you?'

'I don't know anyone in the Clan.'

'That's what you think. If it wasn't you passed on my address it was your cop friend or that bitch sitting beside you in the car this afternoon. Either way, you know someone in the Clan.'

'How come the killers didn't see you?'

'I'd crossed to the shops to buy some cigarettes soon as I got out of the car. Smoking's supposed to be bad for your health. In this case it saved my life.'

'Everything that's happened since I arrived in Albania has been weird, but I'm not convinced the cops are the enemy here.'

'Every cop in Albania has a brother or a cousin works with the Clan. You want anything done, someone taken care of –

you don't go to the Policia, you tell the Clan first. If they can't get one of their own to fix the problem then they get their cop cousin to sort it out. Make it look like an accident. You understand what I am saying? A butterfly flaps its wings in Albania, it's because the Clan controls the weather.'

'Why do you think they would be after you?'

'Is none of your business,' replied Lule as she swigged back some more beer.

'A few hours ago, outside your mum's house, you tried to shoot me. Earlier this evening, outside your apartment, you stuck a gun in my neck. It has become my business.'

Lule looked up, giving her the stare now. 'Okay, let's put it this way: I'm not in the fucking mood to talk about it.'

'D'you still have the gun?'

'In my bag. Why?'

'I miss it: feels like the edge has gone from our relationship.'

'I can get it out and point it at you if you want.'

'You ready for another beer?'

'Sure. Is there a bell you ring or something?'

'No.'

'How d'you order?'

'There's someone on his way already.'

'You want to go back inside?' asked Lule.

'Here's fine,' replied Keira. 'I'm not good with crowds.'

Keira arched forward and slid her hand inside the pocket of her jeans, hunting for roll-ups. That was when she noticed a slight movement over to her right. What had looked like a small bundle of clothes heaped on one of the nearby loungers shifted its position. In the twilight it was difficult to make out what she was looking at, but gradually her eyes were able to pick out the outline of a small boy tucked into a foetal ball, lying asleep under a thin cotton jacket that doubled as a blanket. Keira pulled a pouch of tobacco from her pocket and started to roll two smokes.

'Is that Ermir?'

'No.'

'Who is it?'

'I don't like using that name.'

'What d'you want me to call him?'

'Anything you like, he's asleep.'

'And when he's awake?'

'It doesn't really matter. He acts like he doesn't hear. I found him wandering around outside my mother's house covered from head to toe in blood. At first I thought they'd shot him too, but it was the blood of his grandparents. I think the boy thought they were just sleeping, tried to wake them. That's where all the blood came from.'

'How old is he now?'

'Five, nearly six.'

'Is he able to tell you what happened?'

'Not really. He said a few things at first, like he was hungry. That his grandma and grandpa wouldn't talk to him. After that he said nothing else. I am sure he has seen the killing. He was there and saw everything I think. He doesn't say this, but I know it. He doesn't say anything now, only one word, "Hathi".'

'What's that?'

'I don't know.'

'It's not an Albanian word?'

'No.'

'The name of one of the killers, maybe?'

'I don't know, but he repeats it, over and over. Doesn't say if he's happy or sad, or hungry now, just one word: "Hathi". I would do anything for his mamma, Kaltrina is like my sister, but this now I am finding hard. Not the thing where he doesn't speak, but looking after him. Kaltrina's mother and father were all the family she had. There are no aunts or uncles, so what can I do? The boy has no one else. He has been damaged and I am the same. I know the colour of his pain ... it is blacker than black. I want to help him, but it is maybe too hard. You ever wish you could take out the part of the brain where the memories are and bleach it clean? I do. I'd rather erase all of them than have even one. I think the boy would wish the same. I thought if two broken things are sent for repair at the same time it would be quicker, but I've learned that this is not so. It just takes twice as long.'

A voice came from out of the darkness. 'Miss Lynch! That you down there?'

'Yes.'

A few moments later Xhon emerged from the gloom with a tray full of food and drink. 'I hope you're hungry. I am bringing a selection. Only four beers, it's all I could fit on the tray and if you get too many up at the one time they get warm. You want I'll bring some more in a minute.'

'That would be great, Xhon. What's in the tall glasses?'

'The sour I owe you from the other night. Brought one for your friend, too. I hope you are liking meat. There is some lamb with the cumin, meatballs with tomato sauce, and some dolma. I forgot the bukë gruri: the bread, but I will bring some. You need anything else?'

'Does the hotel have any vacancies? My friend might need somewhere to stay.'

'For how long?'

'Tonight.'

'Is very busy,' replied Xhon, 'but I check and let you know when I bring the next delivery.'

Xhon placed the drinks tray on the edge of Keira's lounger then trudged off through the sand, back towards the hotel.

Keira shouted after him. 'Xhon!'

'Yes.'

'Sour's good.'

'You want another one?'

Keira handed Lule one of the tall glasses and watched as she drained it.

'Another two.'

Keira picked up a cube of lamb. The meat was tender and sweet in her mouth with a long finish of cumin.

Lule stared at the dishes, but didn't make a move.

'When did you last eat?'

'I'm fine.'

'I didn't ask you how you were feeling, I asked when you last ate.'

Lule ignored the question and, raising the highball glass, asked one of her own. 'What d'you call this?'

'A whisky sour.'

'Is a cocktail?'

'My favourite.'

'My first.'

'Whisky sour?'

'Cocktail.'

'D'you like it?'

'How much does it cost?'

'Will knowing how much it costs make you like it more or less?'

'We'll see.'

'I don't know.'

'You don't know how much it costs?'

'No.'

'Must be nice to sit on a beach in front of your nice hotel and order shit and not care how much it costs.'

'Are you trying to work out if I'm an asshole or not?'

'Everyone's an asshole. With you I'm trying to figure out how big an asshole.'

'If you think I'm an asshole now just wait till you get to know me.'

Keira finished her sour and ate another piece of lamb. 'You hungry?'

Lule didn't reply, just stared back at her. So far Lule had snapped back most of her responses: openly hostile. But Keira had been involved with plenty just like her. Clients who knew they were in trouble and needed her help, but still wanted to play the big shot.

Keira would give her a little more space to play before she bit back.

'Your cells can only divide a finite amount of times before they reach their limit and give up. At some point everything has to die. If you want to slow that process as much as possible you'd better eat something. Also . . . it's really tasty.'

Lule reached across and picked up one of the dolmas. 'You're starting to sound like an asshole.'

'That's because you're getting to know me.'

Keira fished a plastic throwaway lighter from her pocket.

She lit two roll-ups and handed one across to Lule. 'D'you want to wake the boy and give him something?'

'No. He usually doesn't sleep for long. It's best to leave him. He won't eat any of this. If there was a packet of Cocoa Crunch – that's all he eats.'

'Will I ask?'

'I doubt they'll have it,' said Lule, placing her empty glass back on the tray and starting on a beer. 'It's a kids' cereal.'

'Do you have a passport?'

'Sure.'

'What about the boy?'

Lule took a long draught of the ice-cold Korça before replying, 'No. He doesn't have one and it's impossible to get.'

'You've already tried?'

'I'm not his legal guardian so there's no point. Why are you asking for me a room?'

'I figured if you had somewhere else to go you wouldn't be sitting on a lounger outside the Hotel Shkop. You chose here over your mum's.'

'They would find me there.'

'Who?'

'Like I already said, I'm not in the fucking mood. Anyway, the boy is very afraid. He screams if we go anywhere near Dushk. He thinks maybe we are going back to the killing.'

'No other family?'

'The boy or me?'

'Both.'

'Unluckily for him, I'm all he's got. Unluckily for me, I have a brother, but he knows what happened to me and thinks it's my fault.'

'Thinks what's your fault?'

Lule ignored the question and kept talking. 'I stayed with him when I first came back. He has friends in the Clan. They told him stories about me. They said I fucked anything with a dick. They told him everybody knew I had AIDS and I screwed without a condom. It's not true, but dumb people believe dumb lies. My brother said I had shamed the family and if the Clan found out he was hiding me they would probably come after him too, so he threw me out.'

'Is there no one you could stay with? I'm leaving to go back home tomorrow. I can't put it off. I need to know you and the boy will be safe. What about friends?'

'I was staying at a friend's . . . but you saw for yourself . . . that didn't turn out too good.'

'I'm sorry about that.'

'You ever wonder why people with money think they are the ones with all the answers. You come here and think you can buy me with a room and a few drinks that you don't even know how much they cost. What makes you think I'm for sale?'

'I said I wanted to help, Lule, not pick a fight. As far as I'm concerned you're the sideshow. I came here to help the boy if I can; that's it. I'm offering to help you too, but I'm not going to take any shit from you. If you want to go your own way I won't raise a finger to stop you, but I can't let you take the boy. You are old enough to make your own decisions, but he has no say on the matter. If you fuck up your own life that's one thing, but you're going to have to get your gun out if you think I'll let you fuck up his any more than it already has been.'

Lule stared back at Keira like she was considering whether or not to take her on.

She took her time finishing her cigarette, then sat quietly looking out to sea. Eventually she said, 'Now it's your turn. You said you know Kaltrina? You have seen her recently?'

'I was her lawyer.'

'So you know what is her job?'

'Yes, although I wouldn't describe it as a job; forced labour, maybe.'

'She needs a lawyer because she is in trouble?'

'Not any more.'

'You say *was* her lawyer. You are not her lawyer now?'

'No.'

'Why not? It is something bad, yes?'

'It is something bad, yes. I tried to tell you earlier, as you were leaving the car, but I guess you didn't hear me. She was murdered, probably by the same people that killed her parents.'

The alcohol had hit home, making it difficult to think clearly. Lule took a moment to let the implications of what Keira had just said sink in.

A tear ran down her cheek. 'This is so fucked up. I knew Kaltrina was in bad situation, but still I am hoping she would contact me. I wonder she might be dead, but I don't want to think this is possible . . . She is not coming for her boy?'

'She is not coming for her boy. I'm sorry, Lule . . . That's why I'm here. I have money for Ermir. I want to help him if I can. I want to help you too.'

'What is money when you have no mother?'

Xhon appeared from the shadows, shuffling towards them.

'Brought another two sours and an ice bucket for the beers. Also some bread.'

Keira stood to take the tray from him, then placed it

alongside the other on the lounger.

'You have been telling everyone there's a party on the beach tonight?'

'What d'you mean?' asked Keira.

'Your other friend . . . she's not here?'

'What friend?'

'The one you made the face for earlier when you thought it was her. Ardiana . . . she was asking for you, just five minutes ago. I told her she wait in the bar and I will check where you are. The face you were making made me think I'd better be sure is okay to tell her you are here, but when I look up again she's gone. I think maybe she has come looking for you.'

'We haven't seen her.'

'I ask about room for your friend. None here, but I know the guy who runs the desk next door. Says he can do a double at out-of-season rates. Not as nice as the Shkop, but it's clean. When you're done, walk along the beach and go in through the back. He's keeping it off the books so cash only, if is okay. Tell him you're a friend of John-with-a-kiss, you'll be okay. There's no rush 'cause he's on all night, like me, so take your time and enjoy the evening.'

'Thanks, Xhon. Can I ask one more favour? If you speak to Pavli, I'd appreciate it if you didn't mention any of this.'

'Zana, I'm offended! My son, he is an idiot. I love him, but he should be sitting here now drinking beer, when instead he is being the big policeman. What do you want me to say if I see this Ardiana again?'

'I could just stand here and wait to hear what you're going to say, but I might not like it,' said Ardiana as she appeared over Xhon's shoulder. 'You're not a very good liar, old man. I could tell from your eyes that Keira was in the hotel.'

'Not lying – protecting privacy of our guests,' said Xhon as he headed away.

'Is okay I join you girls for a drink?' asked Ardiana, noticing that Lule had reached inside her bag.

'Sure, pull up a lounger,' said Keira. 'Ardiana this is Lule; Lule – Ardiana.'

Lule eyed Ardiana and gave her little more than a nod in acknowledgement.

'I thought you were meeting Fat-Joe Jesus,' continued Keira.

'He's not free till later and I've got the night off. I was walking right past the hotel and thought I would come in and say goodbye properly. I am too nervous with the cop around . . . couldn't wait to get out of the car. I won't stay long.'

'Stay as long as you like.'

'Is that the boy everyone's looking for?' asked Ardiana as her eyes fell on the sleeping bundle.

'Not everyone, just me,' replied Keira.

'Yeah sure, that's what I meant.'

Ardiana was behaving strangely. She was distracted, her eye movements slow and dopey. Keira figured she'd either smoked some weed or she'd stuck a needle in her arm. Either way, there was a chill in the atmosphere.

Ardiana picked up one of the sours from the tray and took a slug. 'What you holding in your bag there, Lule?'

'An insurance policy.'

'If I sit down on this lounger, you going to try and shoot me again or are we all best friends now?'

'Why don't you try it and see?'

'I'll stay standing. Don't want you pulling a nasty burner

outta that bag. Your aim's so shit you might just hit something and I don't want it to be me. Got to go pee, anyway.' Ardiana turned her attentions to Keira. 'Thought you were having an early night?'

'You checking up on me too?'

'You're an adult; you can do what you like. You will have one drink with me? I just go to toilet, then we can have a quick cocktail, then I'll go . . . Sound okay?'

'Sure.'

Ardiana headed back towards the hotel, leaving Keira and Lule in silence.

When Keira was sure Ardiana was out of earshot she said to Lule, 'Maybe you should go now. I'll make up an excuse.'

'You think she overheard Xhon saying I have a room next door?'

'No. Why don't you slip away before she gets back? Take Ermir and we can meet up in the morning. I'll have a quick drink with Ardiana and ask if she's been handing out your address to anyone. Then I'll go get hold of some cash for you: leave it at reception desk next door. D'you have a bank account?'

'What for?'

'When I get back I'll send some more money. I'll make sure there's enough for you to rent somewhere until we can figure out what's the best thing to do.'

Lule rose to her feet and started towards the hotel.

'Where are you going?' asked Keira.

'I need to piss, too.'

'What if the boy wakes up?'

'Ask him what the hell Hathi is? Be right back.'

Sixteen

Lule moved quickly between the tables on the patio area, through into the bright lights of the lobby: ahead of her was Ardiana, unaware that she was being followed.

Lule hung back, waiting until Ardiana had disappeared down the steps to the right of the reception desk, then made her way to the top of the landing.

Soon she was standing in a gloomy corridor outside the women's restroom.

Before putting her shoulder to the swing door Lule felt inside her bag and pulled her handgun free. With the Beretta hanging loosely by her side, she quietly opened the door.

The area over by the sinks was empty and all the cubicle doors – except for one – were open. Lule edged closer to the door that was closed and leant in until her ear was almost touching. On the other side she could hear Ardiana's whispered voice.

'I'll put my phone on vibrate. How close are you . . . ? Okay, well I can't stay in here all night. I think they are ready to leave, but they are waiting to have one more drink with me . . . The boy is with them, yes. He is asleep. Text me when you are outside so that I can get out of the way.'

Lule quickly slipped into the cubicle next to Ardiana as a young woman walked in and made her way over to the sinks. She checked her teeth in the mirror, fixed her make-up and left.

Lule waited, breathing heavily, her heartbeat pounding in her ears.

In the next cubicle she heard the sound of a bag being unzipped, and a small package being unwrapped. She knew what was coming next: the chopping and click of plastic on the cistern lid as the occupant cut herself a line.

When she'd finished, Ardiana slid the thin ink chamber back inside the barrel of the ballpoint pen she'd used as a straw, checked for signs of powder around her nose using her compact, put everything back in her handbag then pulled back the snib on the cubicle door.

A flash of movement to her right made her raise her arm instinctively in self-defence, but it was too late to parry the blow. The butt of Lule's Beretta caught the bridge of Ardiana's nose with a crack and sent her sprawling back into the cubicle. The heel of her left foot caught on her ankle and she stumbled, landing heavily on the floor, her neck snapping forward as the back of her head smacked off the rim of the toilet seat.

Ardiana looked up, eyes dazed, blood and white powder streaming from her nostrils. She touched her fingers to the back of her head and felt blood flowing freely from the gash that had opened at the base of her skull. Another blow landed, this time glancing off the side of her cheek: a punch to the head.

Lule was standing over her, framed in the doorway. Ardiana stared back with a puzzled expression on her face. As Lule drew her arm back and swung again, Ardiana pulled her legs to her stomach and kicked out. The soles of her shoes caught Lule on the shins and tipped her far enough off balance to make her miss.

The cocktail of cocaine and adrenaline was working to Ardiana's advantage. There was a lot of blood, but no pain. This time she drew her knees up to her chest and launched her heels into Lule's stomach, winding her assailant and pushing her towards the washbasins. As she reached out to stop herself from falling, Lule's right hand caught the door frame, dislodging the Beretta from her grasp. It clattered along the floor, then slid under one of the cubicles.

The brief lull was enough for Ardiana to regain her feet. She stumbled out of the cubicle and caught Lule with a wide-arching right to the side of her face, grabbing hold of Lule's hair as she dipped to try and lessen the impact of the blow. With a fistful of hair in each hand Ardiana dragged Lule's head down to meet her knee and heard a dull sickening thud as the two connected. Lule fell to the floor, pulling Ardiana down with her, both women scrambling and punching at each other. She managed to pull free and start crawling towards the gun, but Ardiana grabbed hold of her trailing leg and hauled her back. The marble floor provided no purchase for Lule's hands as she clawed at its slippery surface, trying desperately to break free again. The sound of Ardiana's phone cut through their breathless grunts and groans. Lule's gaze flicked towards the cubicle where Ardiana's handbag lay open on the floor.

With a growing realisation of what the vibrating phone meant, Lule let out a scream and kicked herself free, leaping to her feet and lashing out at Ardiana with renewed energy. She kicked her face and stamped the heel of her shoe into Ardiana torso, over and over, until Ardiana lay still, surrounded by a pool of blood.

Lule stood for a moment, panting for breath, exhausted,

sweat glistening on her forehead and tears running down her face. She snatched her gun from the floor and lifted the phone from Ardiana's handbag. Before she made for the exit she bent over the prone figure. 'If anything happens to the boy, I'm coming back to kill you.'

*

Keira was at the short end of her third sour when the bundle on the lounger next to her shifted and the boy sat bolt upright. His eyes immediately searched for Lule, then fixed Keira with an intense, distrustful stare.

Keira tried a smile, but got nothing in return.

In a soft, low voice she said, 'Ermir, *unë quhem* Keira.' Then, indicating what was left of the food, tried gesturing for him to eat something. The boy continued to stare. Keira pointed towards the hotel, then walked her index and middle fingers down the palm of her hand. 'Lule will be back in a minute.'

The boy's face was thin and drawn, carrying too much experience for someone so young in the folds of skin around his large eyes. Thin arms poked out of a pale, worn T-shirt and his skinny legs barely touched the sides of his oversized grey flannel trousers.

Ermir suddenly stood up and crossed to Keira. He then laid his head on her shoulder, wrapped his arms around her waist and nestled into the crook of her neck. The gesture was so unexpected that at first Keira didn't know how to respond. There was a scent of almond oil from the boy's hair and a faint muskiness from his soft brown skin. As his bony arms pulled her tighter Keira's instincts kicked in and she hugged him back, hoping that, for this moment at least, he felt safe.

Seconds later it was over; the boy slackened his embrace and turned away.

It crossed Keira's mind that Ermir was hugging her younger self, Niamh McGuire, the eight-year-old girl whose life was changed for ever the moment she picked up a gun and killed a man. Ermir was comforting a young girl longing for the father she never had. His act was simple and pure, but the impact on Keira cut deep.

Ermir moved to stand by the tray of food, then stopped. For a moment it looked as if he was staring out to sea, but when Keira followed his eyeline she spotted two figures – in silhouette – moving along the beach.

They were heading straight towards her and, even from a distance, it was obvious they posed a threat. She scanned the patio area for Lule and Ardiana, but there was no sign of them. Something was wrong.

Keira weighed her options. She could run, but she'd have to take the boy with her and he'd slow them down. Or she could stay and fight.

Keira picked a knife from the tray Xhon had left and tucked it into the sleeve of her blouse. The knife was too light to throw any distance, but it might be useful. The men were moving fast, no more than twenty metres away now, then suddenly they split up. One moved down the beach towards the shoreline, the other came a few paces closer then stopped; they were positioning themselves to block any escape.

Keira was already on the move. Without taking her eyes from them she grabbed hold of the boy's hand. 'Ermir,' she whispered, pointing up to the hotel, 'Lule is there.' The boy's large dark eyes stared back at her with no hint of fear. He looked across to where the men were standing then back at Keira. 'We need to go now, okay?' continued Keira.

Ermir offered no resistance as she moved off towards the patio. The lights of the hotel seemed much further away than they had just a few moments earlier. Keira checked over her shoulder. The men hadn't moved. As she made her way into the dim light of the roped-off section of the beach she realised why.

The tables in this area, previously occupied, were now free except for one. A lone figure slouched on a chair – his legs spread open and a gun dangling at the end of a limp arm – blocking the path back to the hotel. Keira kept walking, pulling the boy along with her until she was close enough to make out the features of his face. He was roughly the same age as her, with a crew cut and a sneer straight out of a grade-one acting class.

'Excuse me, I'd like to get past,' said Keira. 'My boy needs his bed.'

'Your boy needs his bed?'

'Yes.'

'Where is he?'

'Who?'

'Your boy.'

'Right here.'

'That's not your boy.'

'Okay, *this* boy needs his bed. Would you mind getting out of the way?'

'You are the lawyer?'

'No, I think you have the wrong person.'

'You are not the Keira Lynch?'

'No, I'm the Niamh McGuire,' replied Keira.

'Niamh McGuire!'

'That's right. I don't like to use my real name when things are about to get nasty.'

The guy did his B-movie sneer again.

'Things are about to get nasty?'

Keira let the knife hidden in her sleeve slip down into the cup of her hand.

'If you don't get out of the way . . .'

'You got any moves to back up all this tough-bitch-talk you're giving me?'

'My uncle was a hit man, taught me every move in the book.'

The guy laughed, then said, 'Your uncle is a hit man?'

'Was.'

'So, what moves he teach you?'

Keira's hand shot out and – with the snap of her wrist – flipped the stainless-steel knife she'd been holding through the air. It stuck point first, deep in the guy's right eye socket, and sent him sprawling backwards over the chair, squealing in agony.

Keira scooped Ermir into her arms and ran past him onto the boardwalk.

Seconds later she was at the metal gates leading up to the pool. Ermir's arms were wrapped tightly around her neck.

Keira glanced behind. The two guys on the beach were already closing in, weapons drawn.

As Keira turned for the stairs, she felt a sudden jolt. Her head snapped back and a searing pain burst through her skull. For a brief moment she thought she'd misjudged the opening and ran into the gatepost by mistake, but by the time she'd realised what had happened it was all over. She caught a flash of needle, small, glinting in the darkness and felt a sharp pain in her arm.

Her last thought, as the darkness closed in, was for Ermir: the look of fear on the young boy's face as she fell to the ground.

*

No one turned.

Mostly they were too engrossed in conversation – or staring intently, wondering what the other was thinking – to notice Lule as she picked her way between the tables. Even when she reached the edge of the poolside area and climbed onto an empty table to get a better view over the tall perimeter hedge, no one turned.

From this vantage point it was possible to see the lights of Golem shining in the velvet darkness to the east. To her right was the haunting, umber glow from the port of Durrës. It was also possible to see the row of empty loungers further down the beach, close to the water's edge where Keira and Ermir had been sitting just minutes earlier.

Lule started to scream.

Only then did the people turn.

They watched as the girl with the torn dress – blood glistening on her shoes and a handgun hanging limply by her side – screamed until her throat was raw.

Seventeen

Keira lifted her head and opened her eyes. Her vision was blurred, neck stiff, head throbbing, her face painful and tight. The swelling around her eye was up again: she wanted to touch a finger to it, but something was stopping her.

Keira sat for a moment trying to figure out where she was and remember what had happened.

Someone was breathing heavily, behind her or beside her, she couldn't tell . . . or was it the sound of her own lungs labouring to draw in air? The light was dim, barely enough to see by. She was sitting on a padded chair that was facing into the corner of the room and made a rustling noise when she moved. It appeared to be covered in dark plastic sheeting. When Keira tried again to touch her fingers to her face she realised both hands were bound together behind her back.

As her senses slowly started to return she saw that the floor was also covered in the same plastic: the walls too. She felt herself swaying gently from side to side, then noticed it wasn't just her that was moving but the room itself.

Someone spoke: a thick Albanian accent poached in alcohol that crackled, like whoever it belonged to needed to clear their throat.

'You knock out easily.'

The voice sounded vaguely familiar, but Keira couldn't place it.

She tried to turn her head, get a look at the guy, but the sharp pain in her head made her stop.

'I'm better when my opponent faces me off rather than goes for the sneaky-shit option. The first punch winded me, and there was no way I could raise my hands to stop the asshole with the syringe because I was holding a child.' Keira could hear the slur in her voice.

'How is your head?'

'Sore.'

'You would like some painkiller?'

'If you're offering. And something for motion sickness; the room won't stop moving.'

'We're on a boat.'

'Swell.'

'If you want to get off alive you only have one thing to remember. If I am asking you to close your eyes, you will close them and keep them closed until I say you can open them again. I will cut you free from the binds and give you some medication, but if you attempt to turn around and look at me, I will shoot you in the head. Do you agree to the rules?'

'Would a blindfold not be easier?'

'This makes it a little more of a game. It gives you the power to choose your fate. You can decide whether you live or die, and is better, I think.'

'What have you done with the boy?'

'For the moment, the boy is safe.'

'For the moment?' repeated Keira.

'Yes.'

'Can I see him?'

'No.'

'He's hungry. He hasn't eaten anything since this morning.'

'You have brought food for him?'

'No.'

'For the moment he is safe.'

'He'll be scared.'

'Are you not scared?'

'This isn't my first time.'

'You are an expert?'

'No. But I know what the boy will be going through. I know what he will be feeling. I've been there.'

'And you survived or you wouldn't be sitting here. So there is nothing to worry about.'

'I survived, but my captors didn't.'

'Now you are worried about me?'

'No.'

'Don't worry about me. This is not my first time either.'

There was movement behind her: water being poured into a tumbler, the sound of a blister pack being opened followed by the rustle of plastic underfoot as the figure approached from behind.

'What's with the black plastic?' asked Keira.

'It's not for you.'

'What's not for me?'

'Sometimes the conversation does not go as well as you would hope. It gets messy. I paid half a million for this boat and I like to look after it. Cleaning bloodstains is a pain in the ass. The plastic catches the spills and can be rolled up and thrown away without the need to redecorate. But I think you are not going to give us any trouble . . . close your eyes.'

Keira did as she was told. She could feel the cold steel of

a blade slip between her bindings then the warm rush as the blood flowed again into her arms and wrists: a tingling sensation in her hands. It was an unpleasant feeling but she flexed her fingers, forcing the muscles to recover some movement. She could sense the figure behind her: up close.

'You are flying home tomorrow?'

'Supposed to be.'

'When does the trial start?'

'What trial?'

'Keira, you're a lawyer; a job you don't get if you're dumb. So I'm going to assume you are smart and in return I would like you to do the same for me. I only have a few questions to ask. Answer them honestly and I will make sure you are at the airport tomorrow in time to catch your flight home. Does this sound reasonable?'

'Sure,' replied Keira, figuring she had no option but to agree. 'Can I have the painkillers first?'

'Soon as we finish our conversation! When does the trial start?'

'First thing Monday morning.'

'And you are the main witness against Engjell E Zeze?'

'Yes.'

'I already know the answers to these questions; I'm just making sure you are not trying to bullshit from the start. What happens if you don't show up?'

'If I don't show up the court will issue a summons for me to appear, then if I still fail to show they might issue a warrant for my arrest and possibly look at charges of contempt.'

'And what would happen to the charges against Engjell E Zeze – they would drop them?'

'The prosecution would look to the other evidence against him – of which there is plenty – and try to construct a case based on that.'

'So the trial would still go ahead?'

'Yes.'

'If you were defending him, what would you do to get him off?'

'Stick the barrel of a gun in between his teeth and pull the trigger.'

'I need you to be serious.'

'I am being serious.'

'What would happen if the main witness contradicted all the evidence, said she couldn't remember, made out what she'd said might be wrong, sowed in some doubt . . . what would happen then?'

'I'm the main witness.'

'I know.'

'You want me to go in there and throw the case?'

'What would happen? Could you damage the case enough . . . that Engjell walks?'

'I'd be doing something known as "falsifying an affirmation to tell the truth concerning matters material to an official pro-ceeding". Most people call it perjury.'

'I don't care what the fuck it's called, I'm asking what would happen.'

'It's a gamble.'

'For you?'

'For everybody. The Crown has a lot of other evidence it could use, but this would certainly blow a big hole in the case. Chances are – if I was convincing, no signs of duress – then the case might collapse and E Zeze would be free to go. But I think you've got the wrong girl here. I want to see that little fuck hang, not walk free. I could have killed him twice in the past and I didn't because I believe in the law. But there are certain people I would make an exception for and he is one of them.'

'S'that why you stuck a piece of cutlery in one of my *mik*'s eye sockets?'

'I believe in the rule of law, but I was cast in Newry and forged on the streets of Glasgow. I know when to run, I know when to call for help and I know when – no matter what I say or do – someone's getting a slap. I was taught – "even if you know you're going down – throw the first punch". Your *mik* wasn't there at the beach to go swimming, so I made sure I got in first. If I had my chances over again with E Zeze, I wouldn't hesitate. It was a mistake – one that I won't make again. Why d'you want him out? Or her. Is it a 'he' or a 'she'? By the end I couldn't tell.'

'Engjell E Zeze is not of this earth. The Watcher is a demon that lives below the ground and survives on the souls of his victims, it can be male or female: whatever it chooses.'

'The guy's a psychopath.'

'Engjell – the Watcher – carries the lifeblood of the Clan: a symbol of our power. It's not good for business to have him rotting away in a cell like an ordinary mortal. It's bad PR.'

'Why don't you wait till he gets sentenced then break him out of jail? You'd be in with a better chance.'

'We don't want there to be any doubt that he is a free man and that the reason for his release is legally sound.'

'And what will the story be over here? He vanished from his prison cell after devouring the soul of his guard, then, with the help of some fellow demons, dug a tunnel all the way back to Tirana?'

'Something like that. People here are very superstitious.'

'All this to spring a fucked-up contract killer?'

'Why are you come to Albania?'

'Are we changing the subject? I was enjoying the conversation about the demon that can't use his supernatural powers to escape from Barlinnie.'

'You going to start getting tricky again?'

'Well, ask me a real question. You already know why I'm in Albania . . . to help the boy.'

'And it never occurred to you that this would put you in danger?'

'No.'

'I'm thinking you are naive.'

'I'm thinking the same.'

'Your eyes are still shut?'

'Yes.'

'Hold out your hand.'

Keira extended her arm and felt two small tablets being placed into the palm of her hand. Whoever had given them to her then grabbed hold of her wrist and guided a glass of water into her other hand.

She heard him walk to the other side of the room. 'You can take the painkillers now.'

'Did I pass?'

There was no answer.

Keira palmed the painkillers into her mouth and swallowed them. The water tasted strange, but it was cool and she was thirsty.

'The fate of the boy Ermir is in your hands. If you want to help him, you know what you have to do.'

'If it all works out and Engjell E Zeze walks, or flies or whatever the hell he does, how do I know you'll let the boy go?'

'You don't.'

'And if it all goes wrong, what happens then?'

'To him or to you?'

'To the boy.'

'Before, we would have taken him into Europe through Greece. The borders between our countries are very porous. He would be traded on to an individual or group of individuals who like to fuck young boys, then when they got tired of his screaming and wetting himself – 'cause that's what they do, you know: the little fuckers wet themselves all the time – they would dispose of him and come looking for something fresh. But now, because of all the shit in Syria and Afghanistan, Europe is awash with young children. They are too easy to come by so there is no money any more. When there is a glut in the market you have to sell cheap or dispose. With Ermir, we would probably just dispose of him.'

There were lots of things that Keira could have said in response, but she'd come across enough people who were beyond reason to know that there was no point in telling them where they were going wrong. Just as the law was there for the protection of the law-abiding, reason was there for the benefit of the reasonable.

'Will you give me your *besa* that no harm will come to Ermir while he's with you?'

'If it makes you feel better.'

Keira was so thirsty she finished off the rest of the water.

'This water has a strange taste.'

'Who said it was water?'

141

Eighteen

The sound of a creaking door felt like a nice touch – a small accent to the dream playing in cinemascope inside Keira's head; the juddering sensation too. That was before she realised that someone's hand was on her shoulder shaking her awake.

'Okay, you got to get up now, we here . . . We here, lady.'

Keira opened her eyes a crack to see a taxi driver staring back at her: a blur of objects moving behind him. Slowly the images pulled into focus: a straggle of commuters all heading in the same direction towards tall glass doors that slid open and shut, swallowing them whole.

The yellow cab had pulled up outside Rinas International Airport in Tirana.

Keira stared up at the slope of glass that spanned the entire front of the terminal building. It was six a.m. and the airport was already busy.

She swung her legs onto the pavement and – with the help of the taxi driver – pulled herself unsteadily to her feet.

'You okay?'

Keira felt like shit, but still replied, 'Yeah, fine.'

'You stand there. I get your bag.'

He lifted a small cabin bag from the boot. 'You want I take into airport?'

'Thanks. What happened to the boat? How did you get my case?'

The driver looked puzzled, so Keira tried again.

'My bag – where did it come from? Did you pick me up from a boat?'

'From hotel.'

'Who booked the taxi? Was it me, because I don't remember ordering a cab.'

The driver squeezed his lips together, while he tried to figure out what she meant and said, 'I get call on radio, taxi from Hotel Shkop to airport. I come to hotel and take to airport. You book it, someone else, I don't know.'

'Okay, sorry, I'm a bit confused, because I don't think it was me, but that's fine. I need to be here, so . . . how much do I owe you?'

'Is already paid.'

'By whom, do you know?'

'Lady, I pick you up, I drop you off. This I know. Who booked, who paid . . . I have no idea.'

*

It took Keira just under thirty minutes to reach the head of the queue. In that time she'd managed to drink two litres of water and the painkillers she'd bought from the newsagent's were just starting to take effect. Her head was still sore, but nowhere near as bad as when she'd first arrived at the terminal. The girl behind the ticket desk nodded for Keira to step forward.

'Passport and ticket, please. Where are you travelling to?'

Keira felt a knot in her stomach, 'I'm flying to Gatwick, then connecting through to Glasgow, but I've just remembered I

143

don't have my passport, it was stolen . . .' She was about to go into some lame explanation when the girl interrupted.

'I'm afraid I can't do anything without a passport. You didn't get a temporary visa?'

'Someone was supposed to meet me here this morning, but I'm late . . . I wasn't thinking . . .'

The girl was staring back at her now, checking out the bruises and swelling on her face – making a decision. 'I'm afraid I can't do anything here. If you go to our customer service desk they might be able to help, but I can't check you in without a passport, I'm sorry for this.'

'I can't miss this flight. Will I need to join the queue again?'

'Maybe, maybe not, customer services will try to help you.'

Halfway across the busy concourse Keira thought she heard someone calling her name. She stopped to look around, then spotted Pavli heading towards her.

Keira's relief was tainted by a sudden unease: she had no idea what to tell him about the night before. As he made his way through the crowds she decided to say nothing until she had figured it out herself. Pavli looked serious: maybe he already knew.

'Are you okay?'

'Yeah.'

'Sorry I'm so late. But we are okay on time for the plane, I think.'

'Yes.'

'What is happen to your face? It looks worse. It is infected maybe?'

'Maybe.'

Keira was puzzled. The voice that had called a moment

earlier didn't belong to Pavli: it had been a female voice.

He noticed that her focus was elsewhere.

'You are looking for someone?'

'No, no one. Sorry. Thanks for coming, Pavli. I was at the front of queue before I realised I didn't have my passport. I don't know what I was thinking.'

'Rough night?'

'You could say.'

Pavli pulled an A4 envelope from the police-issue rucksack he had slung over his shoulder.

'Here are your papers. You have to sign them in front of an official; that would be me, and a witness – that will be the girl at the desk. Come, we go over.'

Pavli led Keira back to the ticket desk and straight to the head of the queue. His uniform ensured that there were no objections to them cutting in.

'This is my friend. I will sign her papers then you will sign as a witness then she will get on the plane, yes?' It was more of a command than a question. Pavli signed the documents and handed them over to the girl, who in turn signed them and handed them back.

'You have an executive lounge?' asked Pavli.

'Yes,' replied the girl, who was frowning now, 'But Miss Lynch's ticket—'

'Make sure my friend can go in there,' said Pavli, cutting across her.

The check-in clerk smiled a tight one and said, 'Of course, officer.'

Pavli turned to Keira. 'You have time for kafe turke?'

'If we're quick,' replied Keira.

*

The café was busy. Keira waited by a table whose occupants were just about to leave while Pavli went to the counter.

The table was in the corner with a view past a souvenir shop through into the check-in hall.

Keira slipped in behind the departing couple and sank into the chair. The seat was still warm. She rested her elbows on the table, closed her eyes and cupped her forehead in her splayed fingers. Blurred images of the previous night's events flashed through her mind. She remembered everything up to the point she'd taken a hit to the solar plexus and had a needle stuck in her arm. Everything after that played out in a series of snapshots with no freeze-frame. The images were strange and disturbing, but Keira couldn't hold on to them long enough to analyse or absorb what they meant.

'I bought you a few tullumba as well.' Pavli was back with the coffees. 'If you don't feel better after this then it must be the hospital you are needing.'

'Just sitting on a seat warmed by another person's arse has made me feel better already.'

'You are okay?'

'Just trying to piece together what happened last night.'

Keira picked a tullumba off the plate and bit into it. The sweet syrupy sponge worked well with the thick, gritty bitterness of the coffee.

Pavli continued, 'I got a call from my father saying you disappeared from the beach.'

Keira wondered what else Xhon had told his son, but she was still reluctant to say too much.

'He tried your room, but there was no answer. I think he was worried.'

'Yeah, I took some sleeping pills and had an early night.'

'So you missed all the fun?'

'What fun?'

'The girl on the table with the gun.'

Keira's heart was doing double time against her ribcage as she replied, 'I must have been upstairs at that point.'

'Stood there covered in blood, screaming like she was trying to push the waves back with her voice alone.'

Keira could feel Pavli's eyes on her as she asked, 'What was that all about?'

Pavli shrugged. 'Couple of the staff tried to talk her down, till she raised the gun on them then ran off.'

'Who was she?'

'No idea.'

'Your dad didn't say who it was?'

'Why would he know?'

Keira had watched too many witnesses foundering through their interviews with the police, tying their story in knots and blowing the defence wide open. That's what she was doing right now, but she couldn't help herself. She knew she'd been drugged the night before: her brain was way off its personal best. She made an attempt to answer Pavli's question.

'It might have been one of the guests. He was on duty last night, I thought he might know . . .'

'He was washing out the ladies' toilet at the time. One of the diners had reported a big mess down there.'

'What sort of mess?'

147

'Blood everywhere, like there had been a fight: nasty one. You didn't see this?'

'Am I under caution?'

'What is caution?'

'Is this Xhon's son Pavli having a conversation or officer Pavli Variboba conducting an investigation?'

'You're about to get on a plane. No crime has been reported to me, no one is arrested. This is Pavli having the chat with you. Although the fact that you asked, makes me think maybe there is something you are not telling me.'

Keira was annoyed with herself. She didn't want Pavli to think she was holding out on him, but now more that ever she needed to get on that plane. If she told Pavli what had happened – or what she remembered of it . . . 'I didn't see anything. I was in my room.'

'I think even if I did arrest you now you wouldn't tell me anything: also the fact that you haven't asked about the girl at the apartment.'

'Ask what about the girl?'

'Anything! You identified her as the girl you were looking for – Lule – but it wasn't her, it was her flatmate. I think maybe you knew this. I think – for some reason – you still don't trust me.'

'I'm still trying to make sense of it all myself. You were the only person who knew the address where Lule lived. It was a bit of a coincidence that there were people waiting for her when she got back.'

'You think I called someone and told them the girl Lule's address? Why would I do that? You were with me the whole time. Did you see me call anyone?'

'No.'

'But, what you are saying is, you don't trust me.'

'I'm not sure what I'm saying.'

'Eliza Kastrati knew the address as well. She was in the car when I called it in. How do you know it wasn't her?'

'Her name is Ardiana, not Eliza. She works as a hooker. That's why she didn't want to give you her real name.'

Pavli shook his head. 'And *you* don't trust *me*!'

'She was trying to help me.'

'So am I.'

They sat in silence for a moment, then Pavli said, 'You are coming back to Albania?'

'Yes . . . I have to.'

'Have to or want to?'

'Both.'

'We can go for that drink maybe?'

Keira didn't hear Pavli's last question. She'd spotted someone amongst the crowds staring over at her – a fleeting glimpse, then the figure was gone. The female voice she'd heard earlier calling her name was no delusion.

Pavli was speaking again, but Keira's attention was elsewhere, searching the throng, scanning the faces of every passer-by hoping to see her – hoping to prove that she'd not been mistaken.

Then she caught sight of her again, heading towards the toilets, looking back to where Keira was sitting, imploring her to follow.

Keira was already on her feet, moving away from the table when she stopped and turned to see Pavli staring after her.

'I'm sorry, I think I should go through to the gate now. I have to go to the bathroom first, so I'd better get going. We should probably say our goodbyes just now.'

Pavli pushed out from behind the table. 'Don't forget your case.' He pulled Keira's flight case from under the seat and handed it to her.

'Also, you left these behind in my police car. I thought you might want to take them.' Pavli lifted the small, grubby toy from his bag along with the framed photograph of the boy.

'Thank you.'

She extended her hand and caught the look of bemusement on Pavli's face.

'That's it?' he asked.

'That's it,' replied Keira.

Nineteen

The queue to get into the Ladies straggled out the door and onto the concourse. As Keira slipped in alongside Lule she noticed the bloodstained tape wrapped around her swollen knuckles.

'What happened?'

'Where's the boy?'

'His name is Ermir. Call him by his name.'

Lule shot Keira a look and repeated her question. 'Where is he?'

'I don't know . . . He's been taken.'

'Where?'

'If I knew that I wouldn't be standing here.'

'Why are you standing here? Ermir has disappeared and you are catching a flight home – running away? What the fuck is this?'

'I'm not running away. I have to go back. I have no choice.'

'You have come looking for him and brought with you nothing but trouble. I fucking told you to leave us alone.'

'Lule, not here.'

'Who has taken him?'

'I don't know.'

'Is your cop friend going to help?'

'I haven't told him what happened.'

'You're right not to trust him, but I know now it wasn't him that gave out my address and got my friend Nikki Shyri killed. It was that bitch Ardiana. When I follow her into the bathroom she is on the phone: setting us up. I gave her a smack on the side of the face as she came out of the cubicle, but she was high: doesn't even feel it I think. Started fighting back like a crazy cur, but I've got crazy to spare. I left her on the floor and ran to warn you guys, what is going on, but I am too late. If I hadn't screamed myself hoarse and had to escape the hotel I would have gone back and shot her in the fucking head. S'what I should have done with no hesitation. I told you to leave us alone. They've got the boy; now they will come after me.'

'They didn't mention anything about you. They're trying to get at me.'

'If they are for getting at you, why would they keep him and let you go?'

'It doesn't matter. The only thing that matters is to get Ermir back safe. That is all there is.'

'You need to go in here, to the toilet?'

'No.'

'Me either. Where will we go?'

'Walk with me to the gate.'

The two women set out across the concourse towards the security booths.

'Why these people are after you?'

'They need me to do something for them, and while that's the case I think Ermir will be safe.'

'What thing?'

'It's complicated, but not something for you to worry about. The point is, you should be safe too. You're not even on their radar, but I still think it would be better if you kept out of the way. Do you have your passport with you? I could buy you a ticket. You could get on a plane right now, come with me.'

'It's back at my apartment. I went last night after I left the hotel, but it's still crawling with cops. If it is true what you say that they are after you, then I will stay here and look for the boy. I will find that bitch Ardiana and make her tell me who she's been talking to. She will know who has Ermir. She will know where he is.'

They'd reached passport control.

'If I don't go through now I'll miss my flight. Keep out of the way, Lule. Don't try to fix this on your own. I *will* be back and I will get this sorted out. How do I get in touch?'

'Give me your number. I'll call you.'

'Take this.' Keira pulled a business card from her bag and handed it to her together with an envelope full of cash. 'And this too. This'll keep you going for a few days.'

'I'll be okay.'

Keira lifted Lule's hand from her side and pushed the envelope into it. 'I don't want you to be okay, I want you to be safe. Take it.'

For a brief instant it seemed as if they would hug, but the moment passed.

'Eat, stay healthy, keep your head down and your Beretta in your bag.'

Keira turned and made her way into the taped-off channel that led through to the security checkpoint.

Lule shouted after her. 'I believe you.'

'Believe what?' replied Keira.

'When you say everything is going to be okay . . . I believe you.'

The bus was already boarding. Lule had waited until Keira disappeared through into the departure area – then headed straight out of the terminal building and across to the bus terminus.

She climbed aboard, paid 120 lek and sidestepped her way along the narrow aisle to the back of the coach and a seat next to the window.

Aside from a few backpackers near the front and some shift workers from the airport the city-bound bus was all but empty. Even though there was plenty of room, Lule stayed clenched in a tight ball, her far-off gaze registering little of what was happening on the other side of the tinted glass.

A few minutes into the journey Lule flipped open her bag and peered inside. The back corner of the magazine floor-plate on her Beretta was pressing through the canvas and digging into her thigh. Lule lifted the bag clear of her legs, let it settle again in a more comfortable position, then dipped her hands in and pulled open the envelope that Keira had just handed over. She riffled the bundle of notes. Without having to take the money out and count, it was easy to see there was more than enough there to keep her out of trouble for a while.

Lule had every intention of heeding Keira's advice to eat, stay healthy and keep her head down, but there were a few things to take care of first.

Twenty

It wasn't until she got home to her apartment and examined herself in the mirror that Ardiana realised just what a mess she was. The injuries were mostly superficial, but there was a lot of blood. Taxis had pulled over when she hailed them, then as they drew nearer had sped off. She'd been forced to walk halfway home before one stopped and the driver let her climb in the back.

After cleaning herself up as best she could, Ardiana sat naked on the small balcony outside the kitchen and smoked joints until her brain stopped receiving messages from the bits of her that were sore. At one point she looked up and saw the old guy on the top floor across the street staring over with his hand on his dick. Ardiana waved across and let her legs fall open a little to give him a better view.

It wasn't the first time she'd caught the old guy. One day she'd found herself standing next to him in the grocery store and tapped him on the shoulder. 'You keep playing with yourself on my time I'm going to have to send you a bill.'

The old guy came straight back at her with, 'Who you kidding, lady? I'm the one putting on a show for you.' Ardiana had laughed so hard she had tears running down her cheeks when she left the store.

When she was numb enough on weed not to care any more she'd gone to bed, but hadn't slept well. It had been too hot through the night: humid enough to threaten thunder, and the street outside was noisy with music playing into the early hours.

By morning the air had freshened. Ardiana left the dark humidity of the living room, her eyes half shut against the bright sunlight streaming into the hallway and fumbled her way to the bathroom.

She'd left the balcony doors open overnight and could feel the cool air caressing her naked body as she padded barefoot across the wooden floor. Ardiana groaned as she clicked on the light in the bathroom and heard the extractor whir overhead, the noise of the fan sounding louder than usual. Her mobile lay on top of the cistern where she'd left it the night before.

She squatted over the toilet. Everything was sore again. Her legs were a mess of bruises and there was one the shape of a continent on her right thigh. Her ribs ached so bad she guessed a few of them must have cracked when she'd hit the floor of Hotel Shkop's toilets.

Ardiana lifted the phone and pressed the on button with her thumb, then frowned at the display. It showed a screen full of missed calls from Fatjo: most of them from last night, but a couple already this morning. It wasn't even eight a.m.

As soon as Ardiana had made a coffee and smoked a spliff she'd call Fatjo and give him the bad news: this pussy was out of action and probably would be for the rest of the week.

She wiped and washed then headed to the kitchen, lit a ring on the stove, filled a pot with water and added three heaped teaspoonfuls of Skënderbeu, her favourite brand of coffee. Just before the water came to the boil she lifted the pot off the stove and stirred the brew, repeating this process three times until the murky water began to form a head of tan froth.

The doorbell rang.

'Fuck off.'

Ardiana took her time pouring the coffee into a mug, then made her way out into the hall and over to the videophone.

The buzzer sounded again. 'Shit.' Fatjo's big round face filled the screen.

He'd buzzed again before she pressed the key symbol to let him into the building.

Ardiana left the front door off the latch and took her coffee out on to the balcony.

She was lying back on the lounger with her eyes closed when Fatjo found her.

'You want some coffee, it's in the pot.'

Fatjo filled a mug then pulled up a stool and sat just inside the glass doors, sheltering from the sun. He was wearing the same suit as always and sweating worse than usual.

He wiped his forehead on his sleeve. 'S'too hot. You got anything cooler?'

'Maybe a beer in the fridge.'

'It's a quarter after eight in the morning.'

Ardiana gave Fatjo a look that had 'I fucking know that. What you doing here so early?' wrapped up inside.

'Go put some clothes on. I'm trying not to look at your pussy sitting there staring back at me, but it's all I can see.'

'Close your eyes.'

'Here, cover yourself with this.' Fatjo stretched behind, lifted a dishcloth from the handle of the stove and tossed it over to her. 'What happened last night? Where the fuck did you go? You wouldn't even pick up. I tried calling.'

'I just saw your messages this morning.'

'What happened to your hair? It's all caked to your head.'

'It's blood.'

'Did one of your clients beat up on you? What the fuck happened?'

'I wasn't working last night.'

'Weren't working?'

'You didn't get the message from Vedon.'

'Vedon! What message? Why would the *krye* want to call me?'

'To tell you I had the night off. Or maybe I was to call you – I can't remember. Someone was supposed to call someone.'

'What's he have to do with it? What the fuck does Verbër Vedon got to do with giving you the night off? You're working for me.'

'I told him I should call you, but he was like, "Don't worry, I'll let him know."'

'Let me know what?'

'That I had the night off.'

'So you're working for him now?'

'No.'

'So what the fuck is going on?'

'I did him a favour . . .'

Fatjo was chasing her down now, interrupting her. She could see the beads of sweat break out on his forehead then race each other all the way down to his chin.

'What kind of favour?'

'Relax, Fatjo . . . Honestly, it was nothing.'

'What was nothing? If it's nothing, then fucking tell me.'

'He wanted me to contact him if we found the boy.'

'Why? Are you trying to cut me out of the deal here with the lawyer?'

'Of course not.'

'I hope you're not fucking with me, Ardiana.'

'Jesus! Relax, Fatjo. Vedon didn't tell me why. He just told me to let him know if we found the boy. What the fuck would he want with the finder's fee? Like he's going to chisel you out of a few grand? Think about it, Fatjo! He's the boss. What's he need with that sort of loose change? My guess is he's got something much bigger going down and the lawyer or the boy or both of them – how should I know – have something to do with it. But you'll get your money, so calm yourself for fuck's sake.'

There was a loud bang from the end of the hallway that made Fatjo turn. Ardiana sat bolt upright and looked out through the kitchen. 'Shit, that made me jump. Did you close the front door?'

'I might have left it open.'

'You want to go check?'

'The wind's just closed it. You want me to go check it did it properly?'

'You didn't close the door when you came in?'

'I closed it over. Maybe it didn't click. You want me to go see?'

'I'll go.'

'You lie there and keep that pussy covered. I'll check.'

Fatjo poked his head into the hallway and checked the front door.

'It's closed.'

'Go check.'

'I don't need to go check. I can see the fucking thing is closed.'

'It should be locked.'

Fatjo made the few short steps to the end of the hallway and tried the door. It was shut tight. He flicked the snib over and heard it snap into place.

'Door's closed and locked. You want me to take a photo on my phone to show you?'

Ardiana didn't reply.

Fatjo stopped at the kitchen sink on his way back and filled a glass with water. He drank it down then refilled his coffee. 'So what happened last night then that Vedon tells you to have the night off?'

'I found the boy.'

Fatjo stood for a moment trying to think his way round this one. Eventually, he repeated, 'You found the boy?'

'I stopped by the Hotel Shkop for a drink with the lawyer and the boy was lying there, fast asleep on a lounger down at the beach. I couldn't believe my fucking eyes. They're all sitting around having a drink and eating dolma, like this is what they do every Saturday night.'

'Who's all sitting round?'

'The lawyer, the boy and some bitch. I think she's the one looking after the kid. His mother maybe: I don't know. I'm all confused.'

'I hope to fuck it isn't his mother . . . she's dead.'

'That's right. Not his mother, but she looks after him. Anyway, she was on to me straight away, but what she doesn't figure on is, I know where her mom lives. That whore's getting a call-back soon as I'm fit again. She's the one gave me the bruise the size of Alaska on my thigh. Messed me up. Came into the toilets when I was on the phone to Vedon and fucked everything up.'

'You phoned Vedon before you phoned me.'

'You were next on the list, but she messed with the schedule. I stepped out of the cubicle and *bam!* I get a right hook nearly knocks me out. Bitch's holding a gun too. I'd done a few lines so at first I'm a little dazed, but I'm not feeling too much in the way of pain, but she's going at me like some crazy demon and then we're scrambling around on the floor for, like for ten minutes until the bitch gets another one in that does knock me out. When I come around she's gone, but I figure I shouldn't hang about till she gets back and finishes the job. And that's what happened. I came back here and tried to smoke the pain away, but I'm hurting all over.'

Ardiana lifted the flap on her pack of cigarettes and pulled out a ready-made joint.

A moment later it was lit and a jet of blue-grey smoke streamed through the tight circle of her pursed lips. After another deep draw she offered the roll-up to Fatjo. 'Want some? A sprinkle of Thai temple ball, but mostly tobacco.'

'It's too early.'

'For what? What d'you mean it's too early? Life never stops being a bitch. It doesn't have a timetable of when it's easy and when it's going to fuck with you. It just tries to fuck you up all day long, every day. So why do you have to have a timetable for easing the pain? Levitate a few feet off the ground, is all, not fly to the moon. Marijuana is armour for your mind. Listen to me, Fatjo, I'm an expert. "Too early"! You got to take a big deep lungful of this shit and fight life off for as long as you can, before it's *too* late.'

Fatjo liked Ardiana. They had history together. But when she got stoned – which was happening more and more often – she could be a pain in the ass. After her no-show the night before, he was in no mood for any lip.

'What happened to the boy? Where's he now ... and the lawyer? Did they escape?'

'I've no idea. Vedon was sending round some *miks* to pick them up, but I don't know what happened.'

'You haven't called him already to find out?'

Ardiana lay back with her eyes closed letting the 'Marijuana armour' work its magic. 'Back off, Fatjo. You're acting like you need your goddamn nappy changed. I'm telling you everything that's going on. If you're worried about the finder's fee, call Vedon. You know what he'll say? "What finder's fee?" I'd bet you the whole amount again he isn't even aware there is one.'

There was another loud bang from the direction of the hallway that made Ardiana start and the hairs on her arms stand up. 'Jesus fuck, Fatjo! You just threw coffee all over me. Go close the goddamn front door.'

Ardiana stopped when she saw the look on his face. Slowly she swung her legs over the side of the lounger and sat upright. Glancing down, she realised that it wasn't coffee splattered all over her torso. Fatjo's hands were clasped around his throat, trying to stem the flow of blood seeping from the exit wound made by the bullet that had just passed through the back of his neck and out via his windpipe.

Ardiana watched in stoned silence as Fatjo's bulky frame slumped heavily to the floor.

Twenty-one

The coach turned off of Rruga Adria, into a large square filled with buses parked at a slant, and drew to a halt adjacent to the main railway station: the final destination on the Tirana to Durrës route.

The pneumatic doors hissed open allowing a draught of cool air in.

It was early Sunday morning so the motorway between the two cities had been much quieter than usual and the bus had made good progress: a relief for the overheated travellers on-board.

'What time do you leave again for Tirana?' Lule asked the driver as she waited for the elderly couple in front to man-oeuvre themselves down the stairs holding a clutch of cases.

'Five – ten minutes. I have a coffee, a cigarette, load up and go.'

'And the next after that?'

'There's one on the hour, every hour.'

'Will the next one have air-con?'

'They all do. I get too cold, so I don't turn it on. S'it hot back there?'

'I've dropped a dress size.'

'Shoulda asked. Locals complain it gets too cold, then the tourists complain it's too hot. Can't win.'

The older couple in front finally made it out onto the

tarmac. Lule jumped off behind them and stood in the sunshine with her eyes closed, letting the small beads of perspiration evaporate from her face. It was just before eight a.m. According to the map on Lule's phone the address she was heading for on Rruga Mili Goga was just over a kilometre away: a ten-minute walk or a two-minute taxi ride. Lule figured an hour would give her plenty of time to do what she had to do and still make it back for the nine o'clock bus.

She was in no hurry so decided to walk. Hoisting her bag over one shoulder, she made her way between the stationary buses, heading north towards a pedestrian bridge that spanned the four lanes of Rruga Adria.

On the opposite side of the road a street barista was setting up stall from the back of a three-wheeler Piaggio Ape. He was in the process of laying out the syrups on a small table to the side, but the smell of warm coffee already filled the air. Lule ordered a kafe turke, then smoked a cigarette while she stood watching him prepare it.

'Don't usually get a customer this early on a Sunday. You're my first. Cool breeze, but the sun is already warm. I think it's going to be a good day.'

'Do people drink lots of coffee even when the weather's warm?'

'Sure. I do iced as well, but mostly they take it hot.'

Lule could see him checking her out: staring a bit too long at her taped-up hands, but still smiling the dumb smile guys do when they want to let you know they're interested.

The coffee was almost ready. 'You want any syrups? I got caramel, vanilla, mocha, everything.'

'Just nude,' replied Lule. 'No adornments.'

'You on your way home or on your way out?'

'Visiting someone who's dying.'

'Shit. I'm sorry to hear that.'

'D'you ever wake up in the morning and wonder what it would be like to know this was your last day on earth?'

'Never,' replied the guy, accepting the offer of a cigarette.

'You don't walk around thinking this might be the last time I look out at the sea or feel the sun on my face,' continued Lule, 'or hear a human voice, or smell the scent of wild jasmine? The last of everything.'

'I wake up in the morning and think about water. Nothing in this world grows without water, nothing in this world works without water. I buy my beans from a guy that sells the good stuff. I get the best quality I can afford, but doesn't matter how good the coffee beans are if you don't have the aqua. It's only a small tank I can fit in here. Sometimes I sell so much I run dry and I have to pack up and go home. So most of the time I don't think about dying, I think about having enough water. Some people take coffee as it comes, some people try to make it a little sweeter, some people have the same thing every day, some people mix it up a little: have it a different way, it's like life ... and then there's those that like Earl Grey. They don't count.'

The barista handed Lule her coffee in a small glass. 'In return for the smoke, and as you're my first of the day, this is on me.'

'Thank you.'

'Does your friend know he's dying?'

'It's a she, and no.'

'Shit. How long does she have?'

Lule checked her watch.

'Not long.'

Ten minutes later Lule was standing in the shade of a tree, across from number eight Rruga Mili Goga, staring up at the top-floor balcony, wondering how she was going to get into the building, when a car pulled up outside and a fat guy with a neck like a bull got out and headed for the front door.

He stood with his finger on the buzzer, waiting to be let in.

Lule crossed towards him, pretending to search her bag for keys.

She timed the cross just right. As she closed the last few steps towards him the main door buzzed open and Lule was able to follow him through into the lobby. He even held the door open for her.

'Thanks. Saves me hunting for my keys,' added Lule lamely.

He pressed the button to call for the lift.

'You going up?'

'I'll take the stairs, but thanks,' replied Lule.

As she headed for the stairwell Lule was sure she could feel the guy staring after her, but it didn't matter.

She was in.

Lule climbed the concrete staircase to the top floor and had just started to push through the fire door onto the top landing when the lift arrived. She stepped back and peered through the long rectangle of glass in the centre of the door.

The big guy got out of the lift and made his way over to an apartment at the far end of the hallway. It looked like the door had been left open for him. Just as he was about to disappear inside, the fire door next to Lule slammed shut. It was only a few centimetres of travel but it let out a metallic clanking sound that echoed down the landing and caused him to turn and look over.

Lule ducked back against the wall.

She waited a few minutes – until she was sure he'd gone inside – before she risked poking her head round to check. Lule cursed under her breath as she saw the number on the door and realised it was the same apartment that she was heading for. She checked her watch. It was already a quarter past eight. If she wanted to make the next bus back to Tirana she'd have to start making her move.

Lule slipped the bag off her shoulder and reached inside. The rubber grip of the Beretta was cool to the touch. The guy she'd bought the gun off said they were 'custom fitted for comfort'. Lule wrapped her fingers around the handle and squeezed. The guy had been right; it felt good.

Lule leant in and pressed her ear against door. There was a faint mumble of voices from somewhere deep inside. She pressed a little harder, then stepped back as the door suddenly sprang open.

Lule thrust her hand into the gap between the edge of the door and the frame to stop it from closing. She stood frozen, holding her breath, straining for any sign that the occupants had heard the click of the latch, but their conversation continued.

Lule edged through the narrow opening into the apartment, then reached down to close the door quietly behind her. In the same moment a draught of air pushed down the hallway and slammed the door closed.

The voices stopped.

Then footsteps.

Someone was coming.

Lule ducked into the nearest doorway and found herself in the bathroom. She tucked in behind the door, clutching the Beretta across her chest with her finger through the trigger guard. A shadow passed in the hallway. Then a voice: 'Door's closed and locked. You want me to take a photo on my phone to show you?'

Lule watched as the shadow passed the other way, waited till she could hear the conversation start up again, then cautiously made her way back into the hall. In just a few steps Lule was standing at the entrance to the kitchen. On the far side the big guy was blocking the doorway out onto the balcony, with his back to her, a mug in his hand. Beyond him – naked on a lounger – lay Ardiana. Lule couldn't see her face, but she recognised her voice. She was discussing what had happened the night before, giving the big guy some mouth, like she was calling the shots. She mentioned 'the boy' and a name that Lule had heard before: Vedon.

Verbër Vedon – the boss of the Clan. If he was the man behind Ermir's kidnapping and everything that had happened to the lawyer over the past few days then Lule knew that what she was about to do was dumber than dumb.

She raised the Beretta, aimed it at the back of the big guy's head and pulled the trigger. The bullet exploded from the end of the barrel with a deafening crack. Lule could hear ringing in her ears as she watched the big guy drop to the floor and saw Ardiana sitting up, her breasts and torso spattered with blood.

Both women watched Fat-Joe Jesus twitching on the floor as a large pool of blood spread out beneath him. It took several minutes for him to die and in that time their eyes never left him. Finally, the gurgle of air from his lungs hissed to a stop and it was over.

Ardiana looked up to see Lule staring at her breasts.

Lule said the first thing that came into her head.

'Are they real?'

Ardiana stared back, eyes bloodshot, just starting to come up on the Thai temple ball. 'What?'

'Your tits. They look good. Are they real?'

'Got them done a few years ago, before they discovered it was the same silicone they used for mattresses. Though I tell you this, no guy's ever seen these and wanted to go to sleep.'

'They look good,' repeated Lule.

Ardiana held out what was left of her joint. 'You want some of this? Might chill you out a little.'

'Got a bus to catch.'

'So?'

'So, I don't have time.'

'How did you know where I lived?'

'Word of mouth.'

'Would that mouth have belonged to a bitch called Helena, lives not far from your mom?'

'That would be the bitch.'

'You just killed Fatjo Jesus. You know who he works for?'

'I heard you talking.'

'Verbër Vedon's going to chop you into little pieces and feed you to his dog when he gets hold of you. He don't even own a dog, but he'll go buy one specially for the occasion. If you want I can talk to him: say it was a misunderstanding. Tell him Fatjo was cleaning his gun and shot himself or some shit like that. Although you'd have to explain why the bullet caught him in the back of the neck.'

'Where would Vedon have taken Ermir?'

'Who the fuck is Ermir?'

'You're involved in this game and you don't even know the main player's name?'

'Ermir's the boy?'

'Where would they take him?'

'You ever heard of the *Dhi Gondolë*?'

'No.'

'Chances are he's on that.'

'What is it?'

'Vedon's got a boat tied up in the port down there. You can't miss it: it's the only privately owned yacht that's allowed to moor in the whole goddamn harbour: what does that tell you? Might be a good place to start.'

'And it's called the *Dhi Gondolë*?'

'That's just its nickname. They fill the boat full of kids they've stolen off the streets then sail them down to Greece and sell them to heavy-shit paedo gangs. You might as well go buy yourself a lifetime supply of tissues, go home and start grieving. If your boy's on there it's already too late.'

'So what's the boat's real name?'

'I don't know. It's some Greek bitch. A goddess or something: I can't remember. There's a party on the boat every Thursday night. Local dignitaries, high-ranking Clan members, that sort of thing. Dress up a bit smarter and you could get yourself on board. You let them fuck you in the ass, they'll let you go ashore again. Otherwise they'll fuck you anyway and throw you into the dock with a stone tied around your neck. If you're lucky they'll send you overseas.'

'Yeah, I have some experience of that.'

'You do? Well then, put the gun away. We're practically sisters.'

'What happens to the kids?'

'Those with slightly less conventional tastes get to go below-decks and take their pick. If you're lucky you might get to see your boy one last time.'

'D'you ever wake up in the morning and wonder what it would be like to know this was your last day on earth?'

'All the time.'

'What do you see yourself doing?'

'I'd roll a big fat joint and sit right here on this balcony and stare up at the sun until my eyes burned out. That way I'd no longer be able to see what I was missing.'

'You want to take a big deep lungful of that shit and fight death off for as long as you can, before it's *too* late?'

Lule was quoting something Ardiana had said earlier.

Ardiana corrected her. 'It's not death you fight off with this shit, it's life.'

Lule put her straight with three bullets.

The first knocked Ardiana backwards against the balcony railings, the second punched a hole just below her ribcage and the third bullet ripped a hole in her right breast that started oozing industrial silicone.

Lule checked her watch. If she wanted to make the nine o'clock she'd have to run.

She looked up and caught an old guy on the balcony oppos-ite staring over. Lule dropped the Beretta to her side and waved across to him. He didn't wave back.

Twenty-two

Jak Greco's doughy face grimaced as he tugged the joint from his mouth then reached across and turned the music down. He sat listening for the dull thump to come again.

The cops had been crawling through the building all night long and the banging from the flat below had only finished about an hour earlier. The noise from downstairs had kept him awake most of the night so he was feeling the need to relax. As far as Jak was aware, they'd been in collecting evidence and were all done, but maybe they'd forgotten something and come back. He frowned, hoping it wasn't about to start again.

Then he heard it: not from below, from down the hallway – someone at the front door.

Jak scrambled to extinguish the spliff, then slid open the balcony door to waft out the smoke. The cops had already been in: some guy called Variboba asking all the questions. They'd taken a statement, wondering what, if anything he'd heard, but luckily he'd been out at the time of the murder and couldn't tell them a thing; asked him how well he knew the dead girl. Jak had stumbled over that one. He used to drop her in a bag of weed now and again and he'd tried to screw her flatmate Nikki one night at a party in their flat, but Jak didn't go into any of that. He told the cops he didn't really know her at all, which was kind of true: started babbling about them saying hi to each other in the lift or if they bumped into each other at the corner store, but just because he lived above her didn't mean they were best of friends. He knew her name was Lule, but didn't know her well. Said she was a head-turner, although she didn't give much away: dressed down, like she didn't want the attention. Also, she had a son. Told the cop he'd heard her kid crying in the middle of the night; it had woken him up a few times. Sure it had pissed him off, but not enough to want to beat her to death. They asked how did he know she'd been beaten to death? The old guy in two-twenty told him the girl had screamed and cried like an animal: he'd heard every sickening smack of fist on flesh as they'd beat her, the walls being no thicker than a cereal box: the old guy said it was the worst thing he'd ever heard.

By the time the cops left, Jak's paranoia had kicked in. He felt like he'd talked himself into becoming a suspect.

Jak checked the whites of his eyes as he passed the mirror in the hallway.

He looked stoned.

He felt stoned.

First view through the fisheye peephole showed the hall outside was empty: then Jak caught a movement. Relieved it wasn't the cops, Jak slipped the latch and opened up.

'You supposed to be dead.'

'Cops got it wrong.'

'So who is dead?'

'Nikki.'

'You stopping in for Sunday lunch?'

'Just passing. You mind if I come in?'

Jak swung the door wide and ushered Lule through. Before

closing it again he checked the hallway outside. 'Where's your son?'

'Been kidnapped . . . and he's not my son.'

'He your lover!'

'Not even funny, you sick fuck.'

Jak stared after her as she strode down the corridor and into the lounge.

'What you been smoking?' asked Lule, sniffing the air.

'You can still smell it?'

'All the way from the lobby.'

'Shit. There are cops all over the building. I put it out when I heard the door. You want a blast?'

'I'm on rakia.'

'Got some in the fridge. You on for some more?'

'I'll take a shot if you're offering.'

Lule stepped out onto the balcony. The car park below had emptied except for a few of the residents' cars and one police vehicle over by the entrance.

It felt strange to look out over a scene that was so familiar knowing it wasn't just the viewpoint that was different: everything had changed.

Jak was behind her with a glass of rakia filled to overflowing and the joint fired up again.

'They had a recovery truck attach a line to your green Mercedes. Pulled it onto the tilt-tray this morning and towed it away.'

'It's not my Mercedes. It belonged to Nikki. Thought of driving it across the border into Macedonia or maybe even down to Greece.'

'Would have been a dumb idea. Car's too distinctive.'

'Yeah.'

'Do the cops know you're not dead?'

'Yeah.'

'They looking for you?'

'I guess so.'

'How'd you get past them?'

'They're only guarding the third floor and the entrance. There's no one out back or on any of the other floors. I walked in.'

'I think they're in your apartment. At least they were. I haven't heard anything down there for a while.'

'That's what I'm here to check. I need to get something.'

'They've definitely got someone posted outside your front door. What you going to do, climb over the balcony and break in?'

'No, you are.'

'Me? Why the fuck would I want to do that?'

'I've got cash.'

'So have I.'

'I'll pay you.'

'I don't want your money.'

'You haven't heard the price.'

'There is no price.'

'Say a figure.'

'I'm not interested, bitch. Haven't done that climb for a while now and I'm coming up on this Royal Afghani. Only way I could do it was if I flew.'

'What, then?'

'What d'you mean, "What, then?" I'm not fucking interested. If you want to buy a bag of shit I'll take your money, but this gun ain't for hire. I'm not some dead bitch's fucking earthly errand boy.'

'"Earthly errand boy!" Where d'you come up with crap like that?'

'On board the Royal Afghani express.'

'Have you still got the camera in Nikki's bedroom?'

Jak made a face like he was confused, but didn't say anything.

'The pinhole camera you put in the light fitting. You still jerking off watching her get dressed in the morning?'

'What the fuck are you talking about?'

'Nikki knew you'd done it. She used to lie down on her bed and rub herself knowing that you were upstairs watching. I think it gave her a kick. Does it have sound? You got any of last night's action on there? You might have recorded her getting murdered.'

'C'mon, get the fuck out of here before I shout down and get the cops to arrest your ass. You're putting shit in my head I don't even want to think about.' Jak made to grab the glass of rakia from Lule's hand, but she was too quick for him. She sidestepped, downed the contents and handed it back with a coy smile. Getting all girly on him now. 'I'll blow you.'

Jak made another face. Lule was a good-looking girl. She didn't pay much attention to what she was wearing most of the time, but on the few occasions Jak had seen her made up he couldn't take his eyes off her.

'If I climb down and get whatever you need from the flat, you'll blow me?'

'Yeah.'

'You gonna show me them titties too?'

'Sure.'

'What d'you want me to get?'

'There's a floorboard under my bed, it's loose. If you pull it up you'll see a box of nine-mil shells and my passport.'

'That's all?'

'There's a few other things in there, but that's all I need.'

*

Pavli watched her walk straight across in front of his unmarked police car, heading for the rear of the building. A few minutes later and he would have missed her.

After he'd left Keira at the airport he'd slipped in behind a pillar and watched her join the queue for the toilet. He wasn't sure what he was hoping to see, but Pavli didn't have to wait long to find out. Keira had started up a conversation with a young woman. Pavli figured it straight away: it was obvious they knew each other. The two females left the line and were deep in conversation as they made their way over to security. By the time they parted, Pavli was in no doubt that this was Lule, but there was no sign of the boy.

He followed her out of the terminal and watched as Lule boarded the Tirana-bound bus. That was when it crossed his mind to drive back to the apartment block off of Bulevard Gjergj Fishta and wait for her to arrive. He was certain that was where she was headed. That's how he'd come to be sitting there in the car park when Lule walked right in front of his car. He'd expected her to arrive sooner, and for a moment thought he might have missed her, but that didn't matter: she was there now.

Keeping a watchful eye on her as she strolled past the two

uniforms sitting in the patrol car, Pavli felt for the leather safety strap looped over his service revolver and unclipped it. His radio crackled into life.

'Been a double homicide up in Durrës, did you hear? Fresh out of the wrapper, this one: big guy in a suit and a chick with no clothes on. They're waiting for an ID but rumour is the big guy's connected.'

'I haven't been listening,' replied Pavli.

'You want us to stay here or head up and see what's happening?'

'No, I need you here. You see the girl's heading around the back?'

'Sure.'

'She look dead to you?'

'Maybe a bit pale, but she's definitely still breathing.'

'She's the girl's supposed to have been murdered last night.'

'Got some balls. She smiled at us as she walked past. What d'you want us to do?'

'Stay in the patrol car. She'll be watching to see if you're going to follow her. Leave her for a few minutes until she thinks she's safe. When I get out and head in through the front, you two go around and block the rear.'

*

Jak clambered over the guard rail and lowered himself until his feet were resting on the top railing of the balcony below. From there – even though he was stoned – it was an easy manoeuvre to jump down. He checked the patrol car over by the entrance. The cops were still sitting inside, but they were on the blind side of the balcony, so there was no danger of being spotted.

Jak slotted the key Lule had given him into the sliding door then eased it open just wide enough to squeeze through. At first he wondered what the kitchen chair was doing in the centre of the lounge, then he got it. It was obviously where the attackers had tied Nikki up while they beat her. The plastic tie-wraps used to restrain her lay on the floor underneath. The area around the chair was spattered with bloodstains highlighted by circles of chalk. Everything else in the room looked the same as usual, but a few shades darker. Jak looked for a light switch to fight off the gloom, then realised that they were already on. The idea that someone had died there just hours earlier was freaking him out.

As Jak moved further into the room he caught the reek of disinfectant. He didn't want to hang around – also, there was a cop right outside the front door who could walk in at any moment.

Lule's bedroom was a mess: the contents of her chest of drawers and wardrobe had been emptied onto the floor; there were clothes scattered everywhere. Jak lifted the corner of the valance then cleared some shoes and magazines from under the bed. Lule had described which floorboard to pull up, but he'd already forgotten. He rapped the floor gently with his knuckles until eventually a hollow sound told him which one to lift.

With his arm at full stretch under the bed, Jak's fingers played inside the cavity. At first there was nothing, then – tucked down at one end – he felt the box of shells and the passport. Jak pulled the objects clear and headed for Nikki's bedroom. As he made to cross the hall Jak changed direction and walked silently towards the front door, his heart pounding as he leant forward to peer through the fisheye lens at the cop standing guard in the hallway.

A banging noise from behind made him start. Jak checked his watch. He'd only been down there for five minutes and already the bitch upstairs was getting impatient.

*

Lule was staring at the full-colour image of Nikki's bedroom on the monitor in Jak's lounge. She stamped her foot on the floor again and saw Jak's big droopy frame appear in the doorway. He stepped onto the bed and held the passport and box of bullets up to the lens waving up at her and smiling at the same time. Lule wasn't in the mood.

She crouched down and hissed, 'Hurry up, you fucking prick.'

Jak's left hand was already wrapped around the bottom of one of the railings, steadying himself as Lule made her way out onto the balcony. He reached up and placed the box of nine mils on the balcony floor then pulled the passport from inside his belt. Lule caught a movement out of the corner of her eye. The cop she'd seen earlier talking to Keira in the airport had just stepped out of a car and was heading for the entrance of the building.

Lule crouched down out of sight and hissed at Jak, 'Give me the passport, there's a cop coming.'

'Yeah, and I've got dumbfuck tattooed on my forehead. I put this up there and you'll slope off without keeping your side of the bargain. I'm at least three steps in front of your plan, babe.'

He was leaning out from the balcony, holding the passport

in front, dangling it between his thumb and forefinger. 'You gonna do anything more than just blow me?'

'Stop fucking about, Jak. Give it to me.'

'Who's fucking about? What else you gonna do for this?'

'Whatever you want, Jak. Please, just give it up to me. There's a fucking cop on his way.'

'I'm gonna keep it with me until you fulfil your side of the agreement.'

Lule knew there was no time. 'Give me the fucking passport right now, you prick.'

Jak was looking straight up at her, his puffy, round face smiling as he tried to put the passport back in his pocket. 'It stays in my pants until you come and get it.'

Lule knew what was going to happen before it did. Her brain was so far ahead of the event it was as if she was watching in slow motion.

The passport slipped from between Jak's fingers and fell to the ground – spiralling and flapping like a wounded bird. Instinctively Jak reached out and tried to grab it, but as he leant out further from the balcony his grip on the railing started to unravel. His trailing hand shot upwards, clutching for another railing, but missed. As he started to fall backwards Lule screamed and lunged forward to try and grab hold of his wrist, but it was too late.

*

Pavli jumped back just in time to avoid the body landing on top of him. He'd noticed the passport fall to the ground and stopped to look up. There was a scream and he caught sight of the girl stepping back from the edge of one of the balconies.

Pavli recognised the face of the guy on the ground: he'd interviewed him the night before about the girl's death. Scanning the balconies overhead for any further sign of movement, he tried to count which one the girl had been standing on. Then, with his weapon already drawn, he raced into the building.

Taking the stairs three at a time, he soon reached the third floor. The officer on guard outside Lule's apartment pushed upright off the wall when Pavli burst through from the stairwell.

'Get this door open,' barked Pavli. 'And get on the radio: call for an ambulance.'

The officer fumbled a set of keys from a loop attached to his belt and unlocked the door as quickly as he could. Pavli marched through the hallway, checking the rooms off until he came to a halt in the lounge. There was no sign of the girl anywhere. The only thing out of place was the open balcony door.

Pavli was standing next to the chair in the centre of the room when he heard a door slam in the apartment above and realised he was on the wrong floor. He was back in the corridor in seconds. As he passed the officer Pavli yelled at him, 'Tell the guys in the patrol car, no one is to leave the building. No one.'

He crashed through into the stairwell and stopped dead, tilting his head to one side as he tried to get a fix on the hollow echo of footsteps. The harder he listened, the more it was obvious that they were not heading down as he'd first thought, but up.

'Wait,' shouted Pavli, 'I just want to talk.'

*

Lule heard the cop shouting to her; the words distorted as they reverberated between the walls of the stairwell. She was already on the seventh floor with only one more to go and her lungs were burning. Lule made the top landing and burst through the fire door into the 'drying green' – a large open-plan area at the top of each block residents used to hang their washing.

Lines of laundry stretched from one side to the other, billowing and fluttering in the warm breeze blowing through the wire-mesh fencing that enclosed the entire area. Lule sprinted headlong into the tangle of clothes, pushing her way between lines of drying sheets and dripping T-shirts until she reached the far end. She fumbled in her bag, looking for the key to the large metal connecting door that led through to the adjoining block of flats.

Lule screamed in frustration.

The key was hooked on the set she'd given to Jak.

She pulled the Beretta from her bag and pointed it at the lock, but figured straight away it wouldn't help. The idea had been to lock the door behind her and stop the cop from getting through, but if there was no lock . . .

Lule was trapped. The last thing she wanted was to get into a gunfight with a cop, but if that was the only way out, then that was what she'd have to do.

The fire door on the other side creaked open and Lule knew the cop was there: listening, waiting for her to make a move.

*

Pavli was breathing hard as he stood staring at the sea of washing rippling and twitching silently in front of him, knowing that the girl was somewhere on the other side. He let his breathing settle then said, 'Lule? I know you're up here. I just want to talk. There's a lot going on here I don't understand, but what I do know is this: for whatever reason, Miss Lynch, the lawyer, is trying to protect you, and if I'm right about her then there must be something she sees in you that's worth protecting. I know you're carrying a weapon, but let's not go there. I'm going to place my gun on the floor and kick it out of reach so you know I'm serious. I have no reason to harm you. I have no wish to harm you.'

Pavli lay face down on the rough concrete floor searching underneath the washing. He slid the gun out of reach, then stayed flat to the ground, watching for any movement – listening. As he lay there the distant sound of sirens could be heard over the sound of fluttering laundry, but that was all.

There was no response from the girl.

After a minute or so, Pavli got to his feet, retrieved his weapon and pushed his way through the hanging laundry to the far side. When he reached the connecting door leading to the next building he tried the handle, but it was locked.

Pavli checked the ceiling for hatches and scanned the area for any other hiding places, but the drying area was a featureless box with no hidden nooks or recesses.

Just as he was about to give up Pavli noticed a gap in the wire mesh to his right. The mesh had been bent back. The hole was barely big enough to squeeze his head and shoulder through. On the other side of the mesh was a metre-wide ledge that ran around the entire perimeter of the building. The apartment block fell away in a sheer drop. Pavli could see the two patrol officers standing sentry at the rear exit door.

He ducked back inside and ran to the opposite wall. Through the mesh he could see down into the car park of the apartment block next door.

Pavli slammed the palms of his hands against the mesh in frustration.

Whether Lule heard it or not he couldn't tell, but she turned, looked up and smiled as she picked her way between the parked cars, then headed out onto the Bulevard Gjergj Fishta.

Twenty-three

It was early Sunday evening when Keira's aircraft finally touched down at Glasgow International. The prevailing winds blowing in from the Atlantic pitched and tossed the aeroplane all the way to the end of the runway. The drop in temperature forced Keira to pull her jacket closed around her as she exited onto the air stairs.

Including stopovers in Fiumicino and London, the journey had taken close to twelve hours.

Plenty of time to think.

Keira was surprised to see her new secretary Kate McMaster waiting for her as she emerged from the baggage reclaim hall into arrivals.

'Everything okay?' asked Keira.

'Thought you might want a lift.'

'It's the weekend.'

'Nothing on telly and I've finished my book.'

'I could easily have got a taxi.'

'I doubt you'd squeeze that fat lip into a taxi. You didn't do it justice on the phone. I thought you said the swelling was going down.'

'It took a few more knocks last night.'

'I was starting to get worried when I didn't hear from you.'

'Things got a bit out of hand. Still not sure exactly what happened, but I couldn't get to a phone.'

'Looks like you're chewing a bag of marbles. Will you be okay for tomorrow?'

'The High Court's seen worse than this.'

'How did you leave it with the cop guy?'

'Told him I'd keep in touch. He was very helpful, but I'm still not sure I trust him.'

Keira was looking over Kate's shoulder.

'You okay?' asked Kate.

She had spotted a man with a close-shaved scalp coming towards her holding an envelope.

'You are Keira Lynch?'

The guy spoke with an Albanian accent and had a large tattoo of an eagle that covered one side of his neck.

'Are you asking me or telling me?'

'This is for you.'

'Who from?'

'Is a present to welcome you home.'

The guy handed her the envelope, then turned and headed out of the terminal.

'What happened there?' asked Kate.

'No idea.'

'D'you know him?'

'No.'

Keira tore a strip off the top of the envelope and tipped out the contents.

A passport fell into her hand.

She flipped it open and checked inside.

'Who does it belong to?' asked Kate.

'Me.'

'What's he doing with your passport?'

'It's the one they stole from my hotel room the other night – from the safe. Someone's flexing their muscles. Sending me a message.'

She slipped the passport back into the envelope and put it away in her bag.

'Are you sure you want to keep going with all this? From the outside looking in it's starting to get a bit messy.'

'I need to help the boy.'

'If you can find him.'

'I have found him. It is getting messy . . .' replied Keira as they headed out of the terminal towards the car park, '. . . but I've got a plan. Let's go for a drink.'

'Early start tomorrow,' replied Kate. 'Patrick Sellar wants to see you first thing to run through your witness statements and let you in on the prosecution's line of attack.'

Keira lit a roll-up and took a long draw on it. 'Are you okay to have a drink?'

'Yeah. It's the class A I have to steer clear of – that was a one-sided love affair.'

'I feel like some food. Something good. The stuff on the plane looked like it had already been eaten.'

'I've got a full fridge. Why don't we go back to mine and while you're having a soak I'll fix a carbonara. None of your creamy shite. Just egg yolk and good pancetta. Don't go back to the office. You can stay the night and I'll drive you over to the court in the morning. You can wear something of mine, if you need to. D'you like rum?'

'I drink whisky.'

'Not once you've tasted a Larchmont: white rum, curaçao orange, lime juice and syrup. You'll think you're sitting in the

Gannet. It's one of theirs.'

They'd reached the car.

Kate had been driving Keira's old BMW while she was away but it looked different.

'What have you done to the car?'

'Cleaned it. Inside and out. Got it serviced too,' said Kate as she started the engine. 'Sounds more like a car now.'

'Did Patrick Sellar mention a time?'

'Nine a.m. He's spitting blood that he hasn't been able to get a hold of you: been ringing the office every day. Creepy wee bastard dropped in last week looking for you, like he was trying to catch me out or something. I don't think he believed me when I told him you were away: got an expression on his coupon like the west of Scotland weather: changes every two minutes and you don't know what's coming next.'

'He's creepy, and he's dangerous. This is a big case for him. He's got designs on becoming a QC, so he'll be doing everything he can to ensure that it goes well and he can take silk asap. The newspapers will be all over this one and there is nothing Sellar likes better than seeing his face on the front page.'

*

Below the surface, the warm bathwater stung the back of her head and the side of her mouth where the skin was broken. Keira lay with her head underwater, listening to the dull rhythm of her heart pulsing in her ears, and for a moment the world was quiet.

Two Larchmonts in and almost at the point where the voices in her head had nothing else to say, her lungs started screaming for air. Keira fought against it for as long as she could, then surfaced. Kate was standing in the doorway holding a highball glass in one hand and the framed photograph of Ermir in the other.

'You sticking with the Larchmonts or d'you want to switch back to your old ways?'

'I'll stay with the rum. It's a bit sweet, but it's doing the job.'

'Pasta's nearly ready. D'you want the next drink in here?'

'No, I'll get out.'

Keira was aware of Kate staring at her body, but there was no awkwardness.

'Your scars are much sexier than mine. I've only got a few of the white ones left on my arms and thighs. Apart from the Russell's signs on my hands, most of the others have disappeared. Just those and the mental scars left now.'

'We've all got those.'

Keira stood up and reached for a towel.

'I've emptied your bag and put on a wash.'

'You don't have to do all this, Kate.'

'I know, but it makes me feel good. I'll get bored of it soon enough so make the most of it.' She held up the picture frame. 'Is this the man cub?'

'That's him.'

'He looks happy in this one.'

'Hopefully we'll get him to a place where all that's left are the white scars.'

'Poor wee soul.'

Keira finished drying herself, then wrapped the towel around her chest and headed to the bedroom to get dressed holding the fresh Larchmont Kate handed to her as she passed.

'You can borrow anything you like from the right-hand wardrobe, but avoid the left. It's full of party gear and stuff I'm hoping I'll be small enough to fit into one day: I know I'm dreaming. Everything else is fair game. What are you, an eight, a ten?'

'I buy an eight, but I'm really a ten.'

'Same here. Tens are in the right-hand wardrobe. Don't even open the left. It'll depress the shite out of me if you try something on and it fits,' said Kate as she headed back to the kitchen.

Keira called through, 'Food smells good.'

'That's the pancetta.'

'Bacon with an Italian accent.'

'Yeah. You want some wine with it?'

'Might as well.'

'Red or white?'

'Red.'

'I chucked Hathi into the wash as well. He was in a bit of a state.'

Kate drained the pasta into the sink and was about to mix it with the pancetta in the frying pan when she became aware of Keira watching her from the kitchen door.

'What did you just say?'

'Red or white?'

'The other bit.'

'Hathi. He was manky, so I threw him into the washing machine. S'that all right?'

'How do you know about Hathi?'

'Everyone knows about Hathi.'

'I don't.'

191

'I've read the book about a million times.'

'What book?'

'*The Jungle Book.*'

'What's a Hathi?'

'It's not a what; it's a he.'

'It's the only word that Ermir ever says. But no one knows what it means. He keeps repeating it over and over again.'

'Have you never seen the film, or read the book? Colonel Hathi's an elephant.'

Kate's mobile started to ring. She picked it up from the coffee table and checked the number. 'A redirect from the office,' she said as she thumbed the green button to answer. 'Hello . . . No, I'm her assistant. Can I help? Hold on a second and I'll see if I can reach her.' Kate pressed mute. 'Lule in Albania . . . wants a word. Sounds like she's been drinking, but it's a shit line . . . What'll I say?'

'I'll take it,' replied Keira reaching for the phone. 'Lule!'

Lule's voice was difficult to hear: masked by interference and too much rakia. 'Are you there?'

'Your voice is faint, but I can hear okay,' replied Lule. 'I know who has taken Ermir . . .'

Keira mimed to Kate to bring her a pen and paper.

'. . . Is a guy called Verbër Vedon.'

'Verbër Vedon?'

'This is not good. Vedon is crazy motherfucker. He is the *krye*: the boss man. Also, I know where they are keeping Ermir. He has boat—'

'Don't do anything on your own, Lule. It's too dangerous for you and for Ermir. Engjell E Zeze's trial could last for weeks; Vedon won't do anything to Ermir until it's over. We have time to figure out what to do and get help. Don't do anything on your own.'

'When you have done whatever Vedon has asked of you he will kill the boy and then he will kill you. There is no time. That bitch Ardiana told me everything. She is working for Vedon. She all the time is lying to you and fucking with you, but not any more. After I leave the airport I visit her and the boyfriend Fat-Joe Jesus and she has told me everything, and also paid for her mistakes.'

'What does that mean? What d'you mean, Lule?'

'I have been back to my apartment also, but your boyfriend has taken my passport so I have to stay here in Albania. Even if I wanted to leave, this I cannot do now. It is a sign from Kaltrina that I cannot go anywhere until I save her boy. This is what I promised. I know where they are keeping Ermir and now I will get him back. But for now I must go. I will call you again when I have him.'

'Wait . . . Lule, no!'

The line went dead.

Keira looked down at the name Verbër Vedon scribbled on the notepad and asked. 'What's your dad doing for dinner tomorrow night?'

'My dad? Shit. Why do you want to see him? Can't you just phone him instead?'

'I need a face-to-face.'

Twenty-four

The sun on the McLennan Arch cast little in the way of shadow as midday rang out from a distant bell. Keira walked through the centre of the arch towards the pure Doric portico at the front of the original High Court building, where a crowd of reporters and photographers had gathered on the edge of a cordon manned by a handful of police officers. They stood at the end of Mart Street, which in turn led to Jail Square and the new entrance at the rear of the courts. The order seemed to be 'snap everything that moves, interview anything that talks'. Keira picked out Patrick Sellar's rat-grey hair in amongst a bask of journalists as she ducked under the blue-and-white perimeter tape and was immediately challenged by one of the cops on guard. Keira flashed her citation at him and was waved on.

Patrick Sellar acknowledged her with a nod as she passed in front, then excused himself from the group and followed her along the street into the reception area.

Keira had awoken early that morning and taken her time over breakfast. She was now too late for Sellar's proposed 'run through', but in plenty of time for the start of proceedings.

'The eye is naturally drawn to the colour red. In the theatrical world the wearing of red is a deliberate ruse practised by insecure actors to draw attention to themselves on stage. Are you hoping to draw attention to yourself today, Miss Lynch?'

Sellar was commenting on the bright red cowl-neck dress

Keira was wearing. She'd borrowed it from Kate along with a black woollen cardigan.

'What does the theatrical world have to say about mud-brown tweed?'

Sellar looked like he wanted to respond, but thought better of it.

'Must be strange to be on the other side of the fence?'

Sellar was trying his best to come across as friendly.

'In what way?' replied Keira.

'Standing in the witness box rather than on the floor.'

'Haven't given it much thought.'

'There's no time to brief you now. I assume you'll be happy to go straight in?'

He assumed she'd worn red to attract attention, assumed she'd feel strange about being in the witness box, assumed she'd be happy to go straight in – Sellar made a lot of assumptions, but Keira replied with a simple, 'Sure.'

Keira was wary of Sellar, but not afraid: she saw him more as an irritation than a threat. It was Sellar who'd opposed Kaltrina Dervishi's application to join the witness protection programme on the grounds that it was too expensive. It was Sellar who had signed the bail documents allowing Kaltrina Dervishi to walk out of HMP Cornton Vale and on to the knife of Engjell E Zeze. It was Sellar who'd tried to stitch Keira up by feeding the press misleading information about traces of heroin found in her apartment.

Keira had been surprised to see his name down on the citation as the prosecuting lawyer in the case against E Zeze. In her opinion it was Sellar who was responsible for this whole goddamn mess.

'How was your break?'

'Eventful.'

'I came looking for you last week, but to no avail.'

Keira stared back at him wondering what the angle was, then said, 'Yeah, I was on a break.'

'What happened to your face?'

'Lots of things.'

Sellar eyed her with suspicion. 'Let's hope you're a little more guileless when you get into the witness box.'

'Let's,' replied Keira as she spotted Kate making her way along the corridor towards her. 'No more delays?'

'Not that I'm aware of. I heard a rumour that the Americans were considering applying for extradition. I believe that was why the trial date had been moved several times for no apparent reason. But I think it's just that – a rumour. They've suddenly gone very quiet on the proposal.'

'Extradition? To where?'

'One would presume the United States.'

'Why would they want to extradite E Zeze to the States? Has he committed any crimes over there?'

'Not as far as I'm aware, but I get the sense from some of the communications I've received that there's some political element to all of this that I am, as yet, unaware of. I've had some very strange conversations with some very strange people who – to my mind – have nothing to do with any of this.'

'What sort of people?'

'That, my dear, as they say, is none of your concern.'

Kate joined them.

'This is my new secretary, Kate.'

'Yes, we met last week.'

Sellar didn't offer to shake her hand so Kate didn't either.

'I can't rid myself of the feeling that I know you from somewhere. Where else might I have seen you?'

'I used to be a stripper,' replied Kate.

Sellar didn't react to the comment in any way except to ignore it. 'Where do you live?'

'Bearsden.'

'I'm out that way myself. Maybe I've seen you in the area.'

'Maybe.'

'What's your second name?'

'I'm sorry, I don't date older men.'

'When one spends most of one's time dealing with facts it's very easy to find flippancy instantly tiresome. You, my dear, take it to a whole new level. I'm not after a date, I can assure you. I'm simply asking for your second name. Are you capable of answering a straight question with a straight answer?'

'Sure. My second name is none of your fucking business. Straight enough?'

A court officer appeared over Sellar's shoulder. 'Advocate Depute, they're ready for you in court.'

Sellar's expression gave nothing away as he turned on Kate to deliver his exit line. 'I don't think the legal game's for you, my dear. You lose composure too easily under pressure. Looking good is a virtue, sounding good is a skill. I think your talents are possibly more suited to a vocation where being able to string a sentence together is unnecessary. If you still have contacts in the world of exotic dance, maintain them.'

*

197

While the jury were being sworn in and the public gallery opened, Keira was shown to a room set aside for witnesses.

Kate was seated alongside her, but hadn't said anything since the encounter with Sellar.

'Before you do that, there's a few things I want you to do for me,' said Keira cutting through Kate's thoughts.

'Before I do what?'

'I've been through enough with you to know how this works. You're good at giving the ballbuster routine, but it doesn't take much to throw you off balance. You're sitting there letting that little shit's words run around with a razor inside your head. He's taken a slice out of your confidence and now you're figuring how to minimise the damage.'

'When Sellar finds out who my dad is he'll be all over it. I don't think me working for you is going to do your reputation any good.'

'I don't give a shit who your father is or how it looks to the outside world. If anything, I'm envious that you even have a father. I'd give up a year of my life to spend five minutes with mine. But I didn't employ you out of pity because your dad was a crim. I employed you because you'd be better at doing this job than anyone else I know. Stop thinking like a loser and get your boxing gloves on. If you *are* sitting there wondering what you can do to make this all better, here it is. I need an airline ticket to New York as soon as possible. Last thing tonight, preferably – first thing tomorrow morning at the very latest. Also, when Lule contacts you again tell her I need a photograph of her. Straight head and shoulders, no smiling. I need her to do this today if she can.'

'What if she doesn't call today?'

'She will. Did you give me back the keys to the safe or have you still got them?'

'I've got them.'

'Good. You head back to the office and sort the flights out. Empty everything out of the safe. I'll pick you up at the end of the day and we can head over and have a cup of tea with your dodgy dad.'

Kate pointed at Keira's red dress. 'Is that one of mine?'

'You said I could borrow whatever I wanted.'

'I didn't say you could look better in it than I do.'

'I've got a reputation to uphold.'

'When d'you want to fly back from New York?'

'It's one way.'

*

An hour after Kate left, the court officer poked his head round the door of the waiting room.

'Ms Lynch, if you'd like to follow me, I'll take you through. The scene-of-crime officer's just finished taking the jury through the pictures of the murder scenes.'

'A lot to work through.'

'Aye, sorry about the delay, there was plenty of it.'

A short walk along the corridor brought Keira to the entrance of the courtroom. The witness box was situated on the far side, opposite the jury. The press gallery behind was crammed full of reporters and the public gallery, over to the left, the busiest she had ever seen it.

At a table just a few yards from the witness box and flanked by two armed officers sat Engjell E Zeze, his thin, drawn face softer and more feminine than Keira remembered. The tailored suit he was wearing looked sharp, his shoes polished to a shine. E Zeze kept his gaze fixed on the wall opposite, staring straight ahead, his expression somewhere between cool and uninterested.

Keira wasn't prepared for the knot in her stomach and the sudden spike in adrenaline. The last time she'd seen him was on the pontoon at Rhu marina with the waters of the Gare Loch dripping from her sodden clothes as she stood over him pointing a gun at his head, her finger on the trigger.

Aware of her presence, E Zeze raised his eyes and shot Keira a thin smile that hit her like a blow to the stomach. Then she remembered the look of fear on E Zeze's face as her finger tightened around the trigger and Keira smiled back.

She made her way past the clerk of court – sitting at a desk in front of Judge Granville – and climbed into the dock.

George Granville was an establishment figure: one of the top judges in the judiciary and known for his fiery temper. He was an old-school drinker whose mood improved by the glass. The cons called him 'Happy Hour', because, before all-day opening, no court session ever ran beyond pub opening hours.

As Happy Hour made some introductory comments to the jury Keira found her mind drifting – estimating the distance between the witness box and E Zeze's table. Measuring from the heel of her right foot, she figured it to be no more than four metres. No wrist movement, just a simple throw. The knife would make one and a half turns in the air and stick in the centre of the target's throat.

The judge was talking at her, but Keira's focus was elsewhere. She'd spotted a face in the public gallery that she recognised:

the stocky guy with the eagle tattoo on his neck.

She could ask to have him removed from the court, but that might spoil things for later.

'Are you all right, Miss Lynch?' asked Judge Granville in a tone intended to let her know this wasn't the first time he'd asked.

'I'm fine, yes.'

'Oath or affirmation, then?'

'Affirmation.'

'If you could repeat after me: "I solemnly, sincerely and truly declare that I will tell the truth, the whole truth and nothing but the truth."'

Keira rubbed her wrists together behind her back and repeated the sentence.

Patrick Sellar rose from behind his desk and smiled to show the jury that he was the good guy, but his opening question signalled that he was going straight in for the kill. The evidence was stacked against Engjell E Zeze and everyone was watching. Sellar pulled a stopwatch from his pocket and held it aloft, then made a play of pressing the start button.

'Miss Lynch, how many bullet wounds do you have?'

'Three.'

'Someone shot you three times?'

'Yes.'

'Were they trying to stop you from doing something, did they miss another target and accidentally hit you? What d'you think the person that shot you was trying to do?'

'Kill me.'

'You had a client, a young girl by the name of Kaltrina Dervishi, whom you were defending in a trial, is that right?'

'Yes.'

'Can you tell us what happened to her?'

'She was murdered.'

'Are you able to tell us how she was murdered?'

'She was stabbed repeatedly, then shot in the head, execution style.'

'Is it true that she was carrying a child at the time: that she was pregnant?'

'Yes.'

This got some jury members shaking their heads.

'Did the baby survive?'

'No.'

More head shaking.

'Your assistant at the time was called David Johnstone. Without wishing to make this too arduous for you would you mind telling the jury what happened to him.'

'He was shot and killed.'

'Murdered?'

'Yes.'

Sellar stopped the watch and turned its face towards the jury. 'We are just over one minute into this case – seventy-three seconds, to be exact – and so far we have an attempted murder, the death of a young mother-to-be and her unborn baby and the murder of a young professional man. Before we get into the detail of each of these cases and before we even start to look at another three murders – which include a serving police officer and a nurse on duty, caring for the sick, can I just ask you, Miss Lynch, were you present when David and Kaltrina – and, of course, her baby – died?'

'Yes.'

'You saw them being murdered?'

'Yes.'

Sellar took his time asking the next question. The courtroom was already under his spell. There was not a sound anywhere: no cough, no rustle nor ringtone to break the solemn mood. First impressions were all that counted and his opening salvo would leave the jury wanting more. He wanted to tip Engjell E Zeze and his defence team off balance as quickly as possible and keep them that way. He dreamed of crafting an opening move that other prosecutors would learn from and employ for themselves in the future. The 'Sellar' would be defined in legal textbooks as 'a knockout blow with the first punch'. The fastest prosecution in legal history.

'Just before we move on, I have one more question,' continued Sellar, revelling in the moment. 'Can you tell us if there is anyone in the courtroom who was also there at the time these murders were committed?'

Keira shook her head.

Patrick Sellar stared at her.

'Just to be clear, Miss Lynch,' intervened Happy Hour. 'Are you saying in response to the Advocate Depute's question that you *cannot* see anyone in this courtroom who was also present at the time the murders were committed?'

Keira nodded. 'Yes.'

*

Patrick Sellar had immediately pushed for and been granted an adjournment. The last thing he wanted was for the E Zeze defence team to get a hold of Keira. If she didn't start playing ball there was every chance the case against E Zeze could collapse: an outcome that would have seemed unthinkable just a few hours earlier when he was outside with the press, playing it cool, confident in the knowledge that this was a show trial and he was all for playing the lead. Sellar had put a lot of time and effort into his prosecution: it was the case he'd been waiting for. It would show him at his analytical, methodical and logical best. It would guarantee his move up the judicial ladder. Any outcome other than a conviction on all counts and a lengthy sentence would – in his eyes – be a failure.

E Zeze walking free was not an option.

He'd asked Keira to follow into an interview room then slammed the door behind him.

Sellar's tone was low, each word spat through clenched teeth, but as hard as he tried he couldn't keep the threat from his voice.

'What was that all about?'

'What?'

'Don't start playing ignorant with me, Ms Lynch. I've been in this game long enough to know when someone is trying to blow a hole in a case, so don't insult my intelligence by throwing down the coy card. Let me warn you now, if you start backtracking on your statement I will rip you to fucking pieces professionally.'

Keira could feel her temperature rising, but still managed to play it cool on the outside, 'What are you talking about?'

Sellar pulled a pen he was white-knuckling from his pocket and for a moment looked as though he was going to stab Keira with it. His face twisted and contorted until finally he managed to rein back from assaulting her. The struggle to control his rage was playing out right in front of her.

Then, as if a switch had been flipped, he was back in command of himself. 'I will put today down to pre-trial nerves: a blip in the prosecution case due to . . . jet lag. You can have a copy of the statement you gave to the police at the time of the murder to take home and read tonight. If that doesn't spur your memory I'll have you dismissed as a hostile witness. I advise you to think very carefully about your next move. You know full well I can get your statement adopted, and it will then become the evidence used in the trial anyway. You can vacillate as much as you like, Miss Lynch, it makes no difference, but if you do . . . I promise you this: not only will I have you up for contempt but I will do everything I can to prove you are guilty of perjury.'

Twenty-five

Keira's new office was a fifteen-minute walk from the High
Court, along Bridgegate to Gorbals Street, crossing the murky
waters of the Clyde, then down past the Sheriff Courts into the
cobbled road and Yorkstone pavements of Carlton Place.

The office was one of many in a yellow sandstone terrace of
Victorian properties fronting the river. Two rooms sat on the
top floor with views along the seven arches of Glasgow Bridge
that stretched across the Clyde to Jamaica Street, where the
Procurator Fiscal's old offices in Custom House sat abandoned
on the opposite bank.

As she stepped up to the front entrance of the building Keira
looked over her shoulder. The guy with the eagle tattoo had left
the High Court at the same time and was making no attempt
to disguise the fact that he was following her. He stopped to
light a cigarette when he noticed Keira staring at him.

A few seconds later she was heading in his direction.

'I'm only going to be in here for a short while,' started Keira
as she drew up beside him. 'Then I'm going to run my assistant
home – you might want to write some of this down – she lives
in Bearsden. After dropping her off, I'll head to the airport
and catch a flight to New York. I'm still waiting to find out if
I'm good to go this evening, but I'm fairly certain I'll get on a
plane.'

The guy didn't respond so Keira kept going.

'You might want to go get something to eat, have a coffee or something: have a break. If you give me your number I can call you – let you know what time the flight is and just meet you at the airport: save all this fannying around. I don't know you well enough to tell whether you can understand what I'm saying or if you're just ignoring me, but give it some thought. Who is it you work for? Is it Vedon in Albania or are you one of the guys left over from Abazi's gang in Glasgow that used to do all that prostitution-and-drug-lord thing? What happened? You don't hear much about him these days. I was told he wound up dead in a posh hotel in Paris. Is that true? Did he retire? Can you guys retire? You don't really meet that many older criminals, do you? Short life expectancy – one of the pitfalls. My assistant and I were wondering what the hell that is on your neck. Is it a bruise? An ink stain? A birthmark, maybe? The marks on my face will go, but yours are so distinctive, they'd be very easy to identify in a line-up when you get arrested for intimidating a witness and God knows whatever else they'd hang on you. Anyway, I love our little chats, but I have to run: plane to catch. New York. Don't know the time yet, but I'll let you know as soon as I find out.'

Without waiting for a response, she turned and headed back.

*

The small office space was stacked with shipping boxes full of past case notes and legal documents still to be unpacked. For a brief moment, while she was sitting by the pool in Albania at the Hotel Shkop, Keira had been able to forget about how much of the mundane there still was to deal with back home. A couple of months had passed since E Zeze had been arrested and charged with multiple counts of murder. Still recovering – Keira hadn't really worked since he'd attacked her – most of her time had been spent trying to track down Ermir, but in the intervening weeks she'd also resigned from her old practice and set up on her own.

Three of the murders committed by E Zeze had taken place in Keira's old apartment: she couldn't face going back there, so most nights were spent sleeping on a foldaway bed in the office. It was supposed to be a temporary set-up, until she could sell the apartment and find somewhere else to live, but Keira was getting used to the simplicity of it. There was a shower in the toilet and a microwave on top of the fridge if she wanted hot food, although she mostly ate out. Weekends were spent down on the west coast at her mother's house in Scaur. What few possessions she owned had been packed up and shipped there too: everything but the Mick Rock photograph of David Bowie, which now hung behind Kate's desk on the wall opposite, positioned there so that Keira could see it without having to crane her neck round to look.

Today the boxes and scattered paperwork were acting as a reminder of all the shit that still had to be done.

Kate caught her expression. 'Don't worry; in a few weeks we'll have this place sorted. Needs a few soft furnishings, a bit more storage and the inevitable *touche de rouge*, but you can leave all that to me. And you can stay at my place as often as you like. It depresses the shit out of me thinking of you sleeping on the floor in here. It's starting to smell like a bedroom. It's also against the tenancy agreement. Flight's booked for eight thirty tonight. You need to be at the airport by six, so if you want to see my dad, we'd better get a move on. What kept you?'

'I was going through my itinerary with the tat guy. He doesn't give much away.'

'Your coffee's gone cold, d'you want me to make a fresh one?'

Kate got up from behind the desk and made her way over to the kettle sitting on top of the small fridge in the corner.

'No, I'm good,' replied Keira.

'How'd it go?'

'Adjourned until tomorrow morning.'

'What'll they do when you don't show up?'

'Issue an arrest warrant, charge me with contempt, who knows. Hopefully I'll be back in a few days and get everything sorted out then. Did you hear from Lule?'

'Not yet.'

'I really need to talk to her.'

'I got the number she called from last night. It came up on the office phone system. I've tried it a few times, but no one's picking up. D'you want me to try calling it just now?'

'Yeah.'

Kate leant across and picked the receiver up from the desk.

She pressed redial and waited. 'It's gone to voicemail; d'you want to leave a message?'

Keira took the phone from Kate.

'Lule, it's Keira Lynch. Something has come up and I have to fly to New York tonight, but as soon as I get back, we're going to get everything sorted out – I promise. In the meantime, I need a passport photograph of you. Talk to Kate here in the office and sort that out, but I need it quickly. Also, can you be at Bar Fiktiv tomorrow lunchtime. It's on Rruga Taulantia in

Durrës. When you get this message call to confirm. If I don't hear back I'll keep trying you on this number, but – if you can – be at Bar Fiktiv, between 1 p.m. and 2 p.m. There'll be a delivery for you.' Keira dropped the handset back onto the cradle. 'Let's hope she picks up the message.'

'The cop guy, Pavli, has phoned about twenty times. He wants you to contact him as soon as possible. Says it's urgent. Something to do with Lule, but he didn't say what.'

'I'll call him when I get to the airport.'

'Your flight bag's in the boot of the car.'

'Did you get everything out of the safe?'

'There was a brown envelope with an out-of-date airline ticket to Niagara and some photos inside, a USB stick and a small sample bottle of what looked like treacle. If that's what you mean by everything, then yes: it's in my bag. Sorry, I wasn't being nosy, but the envelope wasn't sealed, I was just checking what was in there.'

'It's fine.'

'The two guys in the photos have got the dodgiest eighties mullets I've ever seen. The taller one was your double. Same eyes. Was he your dad?'

'I think so.'

'You think so?'

'I only met him once. Couple of days later he was dead.'

'In all the time I've known you, you've never been with a guy.'

Keira threw her a look, 'What's your point?'

'You're beautiful and funny and smart. You should be in a relationship.'

'If I was with a guy would that make me more beautiful, funnier and smarter?'

'Course not. I'm just saying, you should be having a bit of fun. Give Pavli a try. Is he interested?'

'Who knows.'

'He's a guy – of course he's interested. Maybe the whole dad-leaving-you thing is why you don't like men.'

'I do like men.'

'But you don't trust them.'

'Even men don't trust men.'

Twenty-six

'I could sort out the boy's passport in a few hours, Keira darlin', but you'll be gone by then. And obviously there's nothing I can do about the girl's until you get me a photograph. Once I've got that, it's easy.'

'Even though they're Albanian passports?'

'Anything you want. Syrian, Turkish, Afghan, American – whatever . . . although you probably wouldn't want an American passport these days.'

Keira was sitting at the kitchen table in the Holy Man's house in an affluent neighbourhood of Glasgow.

'I need them to be good,' continued Keira.

'Doll, I use this guy myself. I cannae go anywhere outside the UK travelling as Jim McMaster without getting pulled over by Customs and a couple of fingers stuck up my arse. But I still manage a wee holiday every year as Mister David Robert Jones and nobody bats an eyelid.'

'You travel the world using Bowie's name?'

'God rest his soul. Ziggy fuckin' Stardust even owns a wee property on Antigua for when things go tits up. Straight on a plane, boom I'm sunning my wrinkly old cheeks in the Caribbean. You could show these things in a gallery. These'ur nae just passports, they're works of fuckin' art.'

'How will I get them?'

'When you get to New York call Kate and tell her the

address; I'll get them couriered out to you or anywhere you want. If you need them to go to Albania, that's fine. I'll send them express. And thanks again.'

'For what?'

'Looking after my girl.'

'I'm not looking after her, she's looking after me.'

'I'm serious. She's changed. Even just in the last few weeks I've seen her confidence grow. She's like a different person.'

'Kate's the same person she's always been, you've just never seen it before.'

'I'm trying to pay you a compliment here for fuck sake.'

'Well, don't. It's Kate that's done all the hard work; pay her the compliment. All I did was hold her hand once in a while . . . you should try it.'

'See if a guy talked to me the way you do I'd knock his teeth out.'

The Holy Man's wife popped her head around the door.

'Hi, Keira.'

'Hey, Gillian, how's it going?'

'Good, all good. Jim, there's a guy parked across the road. Been there for a while now: keeps looking over at the house.'

'Aye, he's an acquaintance of Keira's,' replied Jim. 'I'm gonnae drop Keira at the airport, then if he's still hangin about I'll have a word with him. No worries, Gill.'

'Where's Kate?' asked Gillian.

'Upstairs getting changed.'

'Is she staying for dinner?'

'No just you and me, doll,' replied the Holy Man. 'I'll pick up a takeaway on my way back. Where did you park the people carrier?'

'The garage.'

'Cool.'

'D'you want me to bring it around the front?' asked Gillian.

'No, I'll get it. No worries, doll.' The Holy Man eased back from the table and stood up. 'Ye ready?'

Keira stood as well. 'All set.'

'What's going on in New York?' asked the Holy Man.

'None of your business,' replied Keira.

'You're asking for it, doll, I promise you. You're fucking asking for it.'

*

The expression on Esad Seseri's face didn't change when Keira Lynch waved across the street to him as she climbed into the passenger seat of the people carrier. Esad started the engine of the Mercedes and pulled in behind as it drove off. After ten minutes it was clear that the lawyer was heading for the airport, just as she'd told him. Esad turned on the radio, lit a cigarette and settled in for the ride. The brief was to keep an eye on her during the trial; make sure she was doing as Mister Vedon had told her. No one had called back yet, to tell him what to do if she got on the plane.

Flying off to New York wasn't part of the script.

Twenty-five minutes later he turned off the M8 and circled down to the roundabout leading into Glasgow International. The airport was busy. A queue of cars had formed waiting to pull into bays at the drop-off point. Esad switched lanes and drove into the short-stay car park, then quickly made his way towards the terminal. He made the end of the walkway just in time to see Keira – still in her red dress – disappear inside. Esad held back, waiting to see if she would re-emerge. When he was satisfied that she wasn't coming out again he crossed the slip road and entered the terminal building and headed for departures.

The only plane leaving for New York that night was a British Airways flight. A few passengers were in line to check in and none of them was Keira Lynch. Esad pulled his wallet from his trouser pocket and made his way over to the desk, running so that he arrived out of breath.

He cut in front of a passenger hauling a bag onto the conveyor belt. The check-in clerk shot him a look.

'Please, I am so sorry. My fare, she has left this wallet in my taxi.'

Esad made a big deal of reading the name inside. 'Keira Lynch. Is all her money, I think. She is flying to New York. Has she checked in already or am I in time to catch her?'

The clerk looked down at her screen then back at Esad, uncertain whether to confirm the passenger's name on the list.

Esad caught the look of uncertainty. 'Please, I run after her?'

The clerk looked him up and down then said, 'If you're quick, she might not have gone through security yet.'

'I am go catch her, if not I can come back here and you can get it to her on the plane?'

'We're not allowed to do that, but if you come back and see me I'll sort something out.'

'Thank you,' said Esad over his shoulder as he ran towards the escalator and up to the first floor.

He arrived at the security gate just in time to see Keira leave the line and enter one of the full-body scanners.

Esad thumbed a number into his phone and wrote a text message.

Lawyer checked in. 20:30 flight GLA–JFK. What now?

The response was immediate.

Visit secretary. Find out WTF is going on.

Esad decided to head straight over to the secretary's apartment. That's where the lawyer and she had ended up the night before. Maybe he'd break in and be sitting waiting for her when she got back: give her a fright. Sit quietly in the dark, let her get in and settled then say something casual, like, 'Nice place. If you tell me everything I need to know, I won't mess it up . . . get blood everywhere.'

Yeah . . . 'get blood everywhere' was good. Let her know he was relaxed, but not to be fucked with. Let her know he wasn't going to take any of the sort of shit the lawyer had given him outside her office. Standing there mouthing off to him and thinking she was smart. The only reason he hadn't smacked the bitch in the face was because of Mister Vedon. He'd been told to observe but not engage. Nothing physical as far as the lawyer was concerned. But Mister Vedon hadn't said anything to that effect about the secretary. She didn't have any such protection placed on her. She was a looker too: they both were. Esad started to imagine going back to the apartment and finding the two of them together in bed. He walks in and surprises them and everything is cool. They'd be like. 'We were just saying it would be great to have some cock.'

Esad grinned as he slid his ticket in the pay machine to validate it. He was still grinning as he rounded the corner and crossed out from under the canopy into the open air, heading towards the parking bay where he'd left the Mercedes. He stopped grinning when he realised that the car wasn't there. Esad took a moment to look around the other bays. Maybe he had come to the wrong part of the car park. Confused, he walked over and stood in the empty bay. No, this was definitely where he'd left it.

The rain had turned heavy. Large droplets bounced off the tarmac. The sound of an engine on the far side of the parking area caught Esad's attention: a car, headlights on full beam pointing straight at him. The car started forward, slowly at first, then gaining momentum until it was hurtling through the rain towards him. Esad tried to shield his eyes from the glare of the headlamps, at the same time slipping his hand inside his jacket and rolling his fingers around the grip of his battlefield-green Glock 19.

The car was less than ten metres away.

Just as he was about to draw his weapon and open fire the car changed direction and drove up to the exit barrier. As it passed, Esad saw an old man at the wheel with a white barrier ticket pressed between his lips. Peering through the rain, into the darkness again, Esad could just make out the silhouette of another vehicle parked behind the bay the old man had just pulled out of. He couldn't be sure, but it looked like his Mercedes.

With the Glock hanging by his side, Esad made his way through the rain. As he drew nearer he realised he was right: it was his car, but couldn't figure how it had moved from one side of the car park to the other. Esad slowed his approach. From where he was standing the car appeared to be empty, but his time in the army had taught him to be cautious. Having walked around the whole vehicle and checked underneath for any signs that the car had been tampered with, Esad tried the handle on the driver's side; the door opened. He was relieved to climb in out of the rain, but still puzzled as to what the hell was going on.

A glint of something metal caught the corner of his eye. On the passenger seat next to him sat a Mass card for the dead on top of which lay a small crucifix. On the front of the card was an image of Christ on the cross. On the flipside was printed the words 'The Holy Sacrifice of the Mass will be offered up to include the repose of the soul of ——' with a space left blank. Beside it – scribbled in pen – someone had written 'Your name here'.

A movement outside made Esad turn, but there was no time to draw the Glock and fire. The front end of a dark-coloured people carrier rammed into the side of the Mercedes. The window exploded, sending shards of glass flying through the air as the driver's door caved inwards. Esad's legs and hips were shunted to the left while the upper half of his torso jackknifed towards the crush of twisted metal that used to be the door. His head smacked off the top of the crumpled door frame with a dull thud, smearing the leading edge with blood. The crucifix Esad had been holding spun through the air, appearing to hover in front of his eyes momentarily before it disappeared into the darkness.

*

Everything was pissing Milot Gjokaj off today.

Staring up at the arrivals board then back at his watch told him nothing he didn't already know. The flight from Glasgow should have arrived by midnight, but had been delayed for eleven hours by 'technical issues'. It was now gone 10.30 a.m. and the bags had only just arrived in the reclaim hall.

He'd received a call at 1 a.m. from the guy that was supposed to be covering this gig telling him he had to take over and to be at the airport for 8 a.m. The traffic from Manhattan out to JFK had been terrible and it was going to be even worse travelling back into town at this time of day. He'd also parked in the short-stay car park, so the flight delay was going to cost the best part of fifty bucks just for parking. Add to that the fifteen-dollar breakfast that tasted so bad he wished he'd eaten the twenty-dollar bill he'd used to pay for it instead.

Milot was on the verge of throwing something when the lawyer woman appeared on the other side of the glass security doors. Because she wasn't carrying any luggage she was one of the first ones through. Milot had studied the photograph of her so many times he didn't need to look again. She was wearing the red dress, just like he'd been told, and there was bruising all down one side of her face. Once she'd cleared the security gates Milot watched the lawyer lady head straight for the restrooms over by the ATM.

Keeping one eye on the restroom door, Milot moved towards the ATM to cash up his wallet, pressed his card into the slot and punched in his PIN code. As he stood waiting for the money to appear two females came out the toilet. An older woman in conversation with a younger one, the younger one wearing jeans and a jacket: dragging a large heavy case behind

219

her. When Milot's cash arrived he slipped it into his wallet and pulled out his phone. He dialled in a number then after a few rings said in Albanian, 'Hey it's Milot. I'm still at JFK. Shitload of traffic on the way here and the fucking flight was delayed even more. The lawyer has arrived, she's just taking a piss. Call me back if you want me to follow her, see where she's headed. Only problem is I'm on my own, so I'd have to leave my ride here and follow her in a cab, get someone to pick it up later. Cost a fucking kidney to leave it at the airport, so I'd rather not, but let me know.'

A mother and daughter were the next ones into the toilet. No one else had come out. After ten more minutes had passed Milot was getting impatient. The mother and daughter were in and out along with maybe four more females, but no sign yet of the lawyer in the red dress. Milot looked at the sign above the entrance wondering if maybe there was a shower or something in there.

An old woman was heading into the restroom. 'Excuse me lady,' said Milot. 'My girlfriend went in a while ago. Said she was feeling sick after the flight: she hasn't come out. Would you mind just checking on her, make sure she's okay. Her face is all beat up on one side. She's wearing a red dress.'

'Sure,' replied the old woman.

'Thank you.'

A few minutes later the old lady reappeared. 'There's no one in there, sir.'

'No one wearing a red dress?' asked Milot.

'No one at all,' replied the old woman. 'Restroom's empty.'

'She tell you to say that?'

'Who?'

'My fucking girlfriend! She tell you to say the fucking toilet is empty?'

The old woman started backing away. 'No one told me nothing. There's nobody in there, mister.'

Twenty-seven

'I have no option but to postpone the trial, Patrick. I can't let it run indefinitely, though, you know that. The whole bloody thing could collapse.'

'I know.'

'The rumour is, she boarded a plane bound for New York last night.'

'It's not a rumour, George; I have a friend who works for the intelligence services at Glasgow International. He confirmed to me that she was on the plane and that she disembarked at JFK.'

Advocate Depute Patrick Sellar and Judge George Granville were sitting in the judge's chambers just off the main courtroom, Granville cradling a large glass of Glenfiddich.

'D'you want one?' he asked, nodding towards the bottle.

'Too early for me, George. I'll need to keep my head together until I can figure out what to do.'

'I've granted a warrant for her arrest. As soon as she steps off that plane on the way back, they'll grab her. What the hell is she up to?'

'I've no idea. The trial couldn't have got off to a worse start. There's more than enough evidence to convict E Zeze, but without that bitch standing up and corroborating it, his defence team could tear the case to shreds. This type of behaviour just confirms what I've always felt about Keira Lynch . . . she's unstable. Very suspect family history . . . daughter of a republican terrorist, no less. What does that tell you?'

'Where did you hear that?'

'I have my sources. I hesitate to mention it because it seems so trivial, but my guess is this whole charade is a personal slight against me. Some comments I made to the press around the time the circumstances of this case were coming to light were misinterpreted and it appeared as if I was attacking her. Traces of heroin were found in her apartment at the time the murders took place. I was asked a straightforward question by a journalist – "If the drugs were found to belong to Keira Lynch would she be struck off?" To which I gave a straightforward answer, and these were my exact words: "Heroin was indeed found, and if it was proven that the drug belonged to Miss Lynch then she would face disciplinary charges, but at this stage in the investigation it is far too early to draw those kinds of conclusions." Of course, that appeared as the headline *Drug lawyer could face charges*. And I was credited in the ensuing article as having given an interview to the effect that she was a dealer. I don't think she has forgiven me for that and this is her slightly twisted way of exacting revenge.'

'Patrick, Miss Lynch is a very good if somewhat unconventional lawyer. I know she doesn't always toe the line and she's had her run-ins with the Law Society, but surely she wouldn't jeopardise her entire career over a personal spat with yourself. It must be in her interests to see this E Zeze character put away, surely?'

'Nothing would surprise me any more. I visited her new offices last week . . .'

'She's no longer with McKay and Co.?'

'No, she's set up on her own. Opened an office in Carlton Place.'

George Granville raised an eyebrow. 'Carlton Place?'

'Exactly. She hasn't been able to practise for the last three or four months, and she was never a partner at John McKay's outfit, but she can still afford to set up shop in Carlton Place . . . on her own? I visited the premises last week looking to run through the prosecution's line of attack and make sure she was up to speed with what areas of her evidence I would be focusing on et cetera, and I met her new secretary. I thought she seemed familiar, and I was racking my brains to think who she reminded me of. Then yesterday I saw her in the corridor alongside Ms Lynch and it came to me. I'll give you a hundred if you can guess who it is.'

'I wouldn't know where to start.'

'You're more likely to know the girl's father, actually.'

'One of us?'

'Other side of the fence.'

'A criminal's daughter?'

'Not just any old criminal. Jim McMaster. Lynch's new sidekick is Kate McMaster, the daughter of the infamous Holy Man. I'm guessing she wants to become a lawyer.'

'Maybe her father's looking for ways to cut down on his legal bills? Interesting choice, employing the daughter of that nasty wee bastard. Sailing a bit close to the wind, is our Miss Lynch. I can think of a number of situations where this relationship might be deemed to compromise the integrity of her office.'

'Exactly.'

'She's leaving herself vulnerable to criticism and questions over her impartiality. As a casual observer I'd counsel against it – a dangerous liaison. If the papers got hold of that information it could be all over for Miss Lynch. It's dog-eat-dog out there, Patrick. They'd tear her to shreds.'

'It is a dog-eat-dog world indeed, George,' replied Sellar, agreeing with the old judge, 'and Keira Lynch is the bitch.'

When Judge George Granville smiled at the 'bitch' line, Sellar knew he'd done enough. All he had to do now was plant the story with a suitably dodgy journalist and Keira Lynch would be the main focus of the press should the trial flounder and fail.

Everything was set up.

*

As Lule eased onto the bar stool she caught her own reflection in the mirror behind the bar and for a brief instant wondered who the girl staring back at her was. With her make-up done and the short black asymmetric bob she hardly recognised herself.

The girl doing her hair at the salon had tried to talk her out of cutting it too short. She'd also tried to convince Lule to keep it the same colour, but had reluctantly given in. When it was finished the girl had commented, 'Your boyfriend gonna think he's dating someone else.' Lule had replied, 'Wait till he finds out it's me that's dating someone else.'

Lule had used some of the money Keira had given her to buy some new clothes and thrown the old ones in an alleyway dumpster. Everything had changed for the girl looking back at her from the mirror: not just her appearance.

The Bar Fiktiv was already starting to fill up. Most of the lunchtime clientele came from the surrounding offices, but there were a few tourist types sitting at the tables out front, sweating it out in the Albanian sunshine.

The barman appeared. 'If I looked that good I'd be staring at myself as well.'

'I've just had my hair cut; trying to decide if I like it or not.'

'If you ask me it looks great.'

'I didn't ask you.'

'I could come by yours later and comb it into different styles for you, if you like?'

'A kafe turke is what I'd like.'

'You staying for lunch?'

'Just a coffee for now.'

'You meeting someone? Boyfriend? You want me to fix you a table?'

'I'm happy at the bar. Has anyone been in, left anything for me?'

'What kind of thing?'

'I don't know . . . a package kind of thing.'

The guy made a show of looking around and under the bar and said, 'No, can't see anything, but I've got a package you could open if you like.'

'Kafe turke, thanks.'

'Be right back.'

It was warm. Lule moved a few seats down to sit under the overhead ceiling fan, then checked the time on her phone. It was almost 1.30 p.m. The bus from Tirana had got stuck in traffic and arrived into Durrës station half an hour later than scheduled. A quick scan of her fellow patrons revealed nothing; no one was looking over at her or trying to attract her attention. The message Keira had left had been too vague: Lule had no idea what she was supposed to do. Was she meant to wait for someone to drop the package off? Was the package hidden somewhere and she would get a message to tell her where? All she could do was wait and hope that something would turn up.

The barman was back with the coffee. Just as he placed it down on the counter Lule caught a movement behind her. She glanced in the mirror and saw a figure settling into a table in the far corner. Lule turned and stared, waiting for the moment of recognition. It took a few seconds before Keira Lynch finally recognised her, but when she did a smile spread across her face and she immediately rose to her feet, beckoning Lule with a nod of her head to come and join her.

*

'What happened to New York?'

'Nothing. It's still there.'

'I thought you were there too.'

'I am. At least my passport's there, and so is my secretary Kate – looking a lot better in a red dress than I ever did. She should be taking off and heading back to Scotland any minute.'

'As Keira Lynch?'

'As Kate McMaster: and while everyone else is trying to figure out where Keira Lynch disappeared to, hopefully we can go find Ermir.'

'What about the trial, and E Zeze?'

'One thing at a time. I can't get over your new look. It's like talking to a different person. First thing we have to do is get a head-and-shoulders shot and send it to the guy that's forging your new passport. You'll need a new name, too.'

'I need to be someone else. A lot has happened since you have been away. It feels like weeks.'

The waiter appeared carrying the coffee Lule had left on the bar. He placed two menus on the table and said in Albanian, 'Have a look at these if you want to eat anything,' then to Keira. 'Would you like a drink?'

Lule translated for her.

'Just a coffee please,' replied Keira.

When he was out of earshot Lule said, 'I didn't think you were ever coming back.'

'I had to return to Glasgow to show my face, buy us a little time. I was always coming back. When I was eight years old I was in a similar situation to the one that Ermir is in right now. I know how scared he'll be. I know the effect it had on my life and I'm not prepared to see the same thing happen to anyone else. Kaltrina told me a story about a friend of hers. They were both caught up with this asshole called Fisnik Abazi: the guy ran the prostitutes in Glasgow. Most of the girls were trafficked there, Kaltrina and her friend amongst them. Abazi took their passports and put them to work, got them screwed up on heroin, the usual story. Kaltrina's friend got caught with a few dime bags and some cash and was dragged from her room in the middle of the night then beaten like a dog. Kaltrina heard her friend scream until she was dead then stayed up most of the night, too afraid to leave her room. In the morning she saw a trail of blood along the corridor where they'd dragged her friend from the bedroom. She was devastated – wondered how she would manage to go on without her. In a strange way – without realising it, though – her friend had done Kaltrina a favour. Because of what happened that night, Kaltrina decided it was time to get out of there.'

Lule's next words were only just audible, 'Kaltrina ended up dead. How can this be a favour?'

'The first time I heard the expression was from Kaltrina. Fisnik Abazi used it to scare the shit out of the new girls when they first arrived in Glasgow. They were already scared, but he'd show them photographs of a corpse in an open grave and tell them, "You can leave any time you like: the grave's already dug." The only other time in my life I've heard that expression was the other evening sitting outside your apartment block, in the back of a police car. You repeated it almost word for word. Then there's your voice. You speak English with a Scottish accent ... When I asked you to come with me at the airport on Sunday you said you didn't want to go somewhere that would fuck with your head. You wanted to go somewhere that would give you good memories. Kaltrina told me her friend's name was Tulla. I figured out on the plane home that must be you. Tallulah is sometimes shortened to Tulla, right?'

'First time I ever met Kaltrina she got my name wrong. It kinda stuck. She was the only person who ever called me Tulla. No one else.'

Keira reached across the table and took Lule's hands in hers. 'I'm here to help you too.'

Lule sat with her head bowed, staring at the table, struggling to hold it together. Her voice cracked as she spoke, 'I wasn't into drugs, but they are pushing the gun into our heads and forcing us to take that shit till we were so wasted we didn't know what was the year. Once they think you're hooked they leave you alone. I'd save mine up, hide it: sell it to the girls that got fucked up on it. It was hard to do this, they are always watching. I knew one day I was going to escape so I'm always trying to put a little money aside. Kaltrina she was the same. She wasn't into that shit either. One of the girls screwed me over, though. Said I'd cut the bag with talc, then told Abazi's guys what I was doing. They beat me so hard I can't hear anything on my right side. I knew they were going to kill me anyway so I played dead. Let them drag me down to car and then, just as they are lifting me into the trunk, I kick and I scratch and I gouge my way the fuck out of there. I fight so hard to stay alive I nearly killed myself, but I got away. I escaped. That's why – when you showed up – I thought they'd found me again. I thought you were one of them. I've been living with all this shit hanging over me for so long I don't know what's real and what isn't any more. I thought you were Clan. I am sorry to Kaltrina and I am sorry to you.'

'You have nothing to apologise for, Lule. Don't feel guilty for surviving. If Kaltrina's looking down on you just now she'll be delighted that she was wrong. She'll be more than happy that you survived that night. And she'll be grateful for everything you've tried to do for her son.'

'She ended up dead. Will she be grateful for that?'

'She ended up free. If Kaltrina was here, she would thank you.'

Lule's head dipped and it was a long time before she was able to say anything else.

Twenty-eight

A two-metre-high perimeter fence ran the full length of the Rruga Doganes and separated the busy service road from the freight dock beyond. From their vantage point on the steps of the Church of Apostle Paul and Saint Asti that sat atop a small hill overlooking the Port of Durrës, the two women could see the entire stretch of the yard beyond, stacked with containers piled three or four on top of each other in long rows that shielded most of the ships in the harbour from view.

'The *Persephone* is on the other side of the blue containers in the middle,' said Lule.

'How do you know?'

'I walk down here last night. The passenger terminal is at far end of the dock. I buy a ticket for the ferry and get onto the quayside, but I can only glimpse the boat from there. It is too far away to see what is going on. The boat is known also as *Dhi Gondolë*. Ardiana told me this. It is not a good thing.'

'What's *Dhi Gondolë*?'

'They are making fun with the words, but it is nothing to laugh at. *Dhi Gondolë* is translated directly as the Goat Boat, but they are not meaning the goat, they are meaning like the English word kid. Is a baby goat, yes?'

'Yes.'

'The Goat Boat is how Vedon traffics the children out of Albania.'

'Where to?'

'I don't know for sure, but Greece is further down the coast: I think maybe there. Ardiana mentioned this as well.'

'Are you sure it's the *Persephone*?'

'Yes, sure. I couldn't see the name, but it's a luxury yacht. The only private boat that is allowed into this bit of the port.'

'Let's go check it out.'

'Then what?'

'Call the cops.'

'You still don't get it, do you? Vedon has a party on the boat every Thursday night. The Chief of the Policia is probably one of the guests.'

'So what are you saying?'

'I think we should try and get onboard.'

'Then what?'

'I don't know. See what happens.'

Keira shot Lule a look, 'You must have been up all night thinking up that one.'

'It's a better idea than calling the cops.'

'Let's go check it's the right boat first; then we'll come up with a proper plan.'

They waited for a break in the traffic, then sprinted across the road. With little effort both women climbed the wire-mesh fencing and dropped down into the container yard. Three stacked rows of the large metal boxes ran in parallel lines for the full length of the yard. Sticking close to the nearest they travelled a hundred metres or so then tucked into a gap between containers when they heard the voices of men approaching along the corridor on the opposite side. When the voices had faded and they were certain that the men had passed, Lule and

Keira squeezed through to the other side, then ran along the next alleyway of containers looking for another gap that would lead them to the dockside.

A security camera – high on an overhead gantry – turned towards them. Keira grabbed Lule's sleeve and pulled her to a halt. 'You ever been on the street and someone's running towards you? You're immediately wondering what's going on. If they were walking you wouldn't even notice them. We've got to stop running.' Keira gestured towards the gantry. 'We may be too late.'

The unbroken line of containers stretched in front of them as far as they could see. 'We'll be up at the far end before we can get through to the other side. I can't see any gaps. You think we should head back the other way?'

Keira turned to check how far they'd come. That's when she saw the Port Authority patrol car turn in at the southernmost end of the corridor. The span between the containers was not much wider than the car. As it started to pick up speed, Keira spotted a container with nothing on top of it and gestured to Lule. 'Up there.'

They broke into a sprint, but the patrol car had already covered half the distance between them. Keira leapt onto the side of the container and grabbed for the rolled metal edge on top, but her fingers slipped off and she fell back to the ground. With her first attempt, Lule managed to grasp onto the rolled edge, but had no strength in her arms to pull herself up. Keira grabbed Lule's foot and guided it onto her shoulder, allowing Lule to clamber onto the corrugated roof of the container where she dropped flat onto her stomach and reached her arms out to Keira.

As the patrol car screeched to a halt fifteen metres away, Keira made one last effort. This time she managed to get purchase and with Lule's help hauled herself up onto the roof. The driver crashed the gears and started reversing.

Keira joined Lule on the other side of the container and sat with her feet dangling over the edge. Before them was the port of Durrës. The quayside teemed with dockers loading and unloading cargo. A fleet of fishing vessels was moored on the far quayside and at the north end of the dock, two huge passenger ferries sat side by side in the calm waters, waiting to depart. All around the air was filled with the sounds of activity: men shouting, engines revving and horns blowing.

Keira sat for a moment taking in the scene before asking, 'Where is Vedon's boat?'

'Don't know,' replied Lule. 'It must have sailed this morning. It's not here.'

'Where did you see it last night?'

Lule gestured towards a gap between two cargo vessels. The space appeared small, sandwiched between the huge ships, but it was big enough to fit a sixty-metre yacht.

'It should be right in front of us.'

The Port Authority car drew alongside the container and the two officers jumped out. They were armed, but kept their weapons holstered. Both men were in their mid-forties and carrying too much weight around the gut; too dumb to do anything other than low-paid shift work for the private company brought in to run the security contract. They spent most of their time driving up and down the length of the dock, talking small about big events and waiting for something to happen.

The driver was the first to speak, addressing the women in Albanian.

'You enjoying the view?'

'The ships look a lot bigger when you see them up close,' replied Lule. 'It's amazing how something like that stays afloat. How long is it?'

'Ship's four hundred metres; so's the other one. You ever heard of Michael Johnson?'

'Can't say I have.'

'American runner. He could run the full length of that ship there in a spit over forty-three seconds. That's the world record.'

'It'd take me all day just to walk that far,' said Lule.

'You seemed to be going pretty fast when you spotted us over the other side of the container.'

'Thought you might be cops.'

'Well, I guess in a sense we are. You know this is a restricted area? You're not allowed in here without a pass. You got a pass, lady?'

'No.'

'What about your friend there?'

'She doesn't know what you're saying, she's from Scotland.'

'She got a pass?'

'No.'

'How'd you get in here?'

'Climbed the fence.'

'If you want to look at the boats you can go up the passenger terminal. They've got a viewing gallery on the first floor.'

'We were looking for one boat in particular.'

'Yeah? Which one?'

'The *Persephone*.'

Keira caught the officers exchanging a glance.

'Why you looking for her?'

'Friends with the owner. Got invited to a party there Thursday night and he told us to come down and check it out.'

'He tell you to climb the fence to get in?'

'We were running late. Didn't want to miss anything.'

'Boat's gone, I'm afraid. Fuelled up about an hour ago and set sail.'

'Any idea where to?' asked Lule.

'Why don't you call the owner and ask him? Him being such a good friend.'

'He sees my number flash up on his screen, he's not going to pick up.'

'Does he owe you money or something?'

'Kinda. My friend and I are supposed to be working the boat Thursday night. He said we'd make some good cash. Got bills to pay like everyone else . . . we need the job.'

'Yeah, what work d'you do?'

'Cleaners.'

'S'that right?'

'Yeah, cocks, mostly: bit of spit and polish until they're gleaming.'

Keira had no idea what Lule was saying, but the two Port Authority guys had big dumb grins all over their faces.

'Cleaners!' continued Lule. 'Of course we're not cleaners, we're fucking hookers and we're supposed to be on that boat. You gonna tell us where they're headed? Do you know?'

'Yeah we know.'

'Where?'

'Come down off the container and we'll tell you.'

'Tell us first, then we'll come down.'

'You've got to come off the container. We'll escort you off the quayside, then we'll tell you.'

'Tell us, and I promise we'll get off.'

'Party's maybe happening in Vlorë.'

'Thursday night?'

'Tonight. They brought it forward.'

'You ever been to the party?'

The guys were smiling again. 'We don't move in those circles.'

'But I bet you do some favours for the owner. He a friend of yours too?'

'Sometimes. Earn a little bit on the side doing security.'

'So they're sailing down to Vlorë, then they sail back here?'

'No. It's a place called Orikum: got a marina there. Just the other side of Vlorë.'

'Orikum Marina?'

'Only marina in the whole of Albania.'

'Then they head down to Greece, that's right, 'cause Mister Vedon asked if we wanted to meet him down there, but it's too far.' Lule dropped Vedon's name in to make the whole thing sound more authentic. It worked.

'Usually the boat heads down to Igoumenitsa for a few nights, yeah. Drop off whatever friends they got staying on board, pick up some new friends, then sail back. You gonna come down from there now?'

'Not only that, but when we get back from Vlorë, my friend and I are gonna climb that fence again and meet you two guys for a spot of cleaning.'

'So what's the plan?'

Lule and Keira were walking back to the car, the sound of the dockyard fading behind them, swallowed by the noise of traffic.

'We need help,' replied Keira. 'Even supposing we got on to the boat, what would we do then? We can't just take Ermir. If there are other children we can't leave them behind. Have you got your phone?'

'I'm in way too much shit, I haven't even told you yet. I can't call the cops if that's what you're thinking.'

'I can.'

Twenty-nine

Pavli Variboba's computer screen pinged a message notification onto the screen marked urgent. He clicked it up full size. The subject read: 'You looking for trouble?' A tag from the receptionist who had fielded the call read: 'Received by phone. No Name. No caller ID.'

The message read:

Party invite. The Persephone – this evening. Orikum Marina, Vlorë. Mister Verbër Vedon requests the pleasure of your company to celebrate another successful voyage on the Dhi Gondolë. Come inspect the cargo before it's moved to its final destination. Bring your friends.

Postscript: I might let you buy me a drink. K. X

Pavli picked up the desk phone and called dispatch. 'I need a raiding party: four squad cars and two support teams – full battle dress. Call me when they're ready and I'll meet them out back.'

'You want them now?'

'Right away.'

'Where you headed, boss?'

'The coast.'

*

It was rush hour when Keira and Lule hit the town of Vlorë. Keira had imagined it as a small seaside village, but in reality it was almost as big and overdeveloped as Durrës. Its huge port – at the crossroads of the Adriatic and Ionian seas – supplied the south-eastern end of Albania with virtually everything it needed. By the time they'd negotiated the early evening traffic the sun was almost gone from the sky.

Once through and out the other side they continued to follow the coastline until they saw signs for Orikum. The number of vehicles they passed started to tail away until soon theirs was the only car on the road. To the left, mountains rose out of the darkness and disappeared into the night sky, their ragged ridgelines obscured by a flotilla of storm clouds gathering over the summits. To their right the Adriatic stretched as far as they could see.

There were no street lamps and all the signposts they passed had weathered beyond legibility. Eventually Lule said, 'We must have passed it.'

'D'you think it was those lights further back?'

'I think maybe yes. I was expecting somewhere bigger.'

Keira slowed and bumped the car down onto the hard, stony verge. The narrowness of the road made turning difficult, but eventually she was able to manoeuvre round and start back in the opposite direction.

After five kilometres they saw the lights of a building sitting on its own on the right-hand side and pulled over. The property had a large field of compacted earth that doubled as a car park to one side. The field was deserted except for two other cars parked alongside a wooden lamppost set in the middle. Keira steered the car slowly over the undulating ground –

avoiding the potholes – until she came to a halt just outside the dim pool of light.

Both women stretched as they got out of the car, then made their way through the darkness to the front of the building.

An unlit sign above the entrance read PIZZERIA.

The lights were on inside and music was playing, but when Keira tried the door she found it locked.

Lule was standing further along the wooden veranda, peering in through the window. 'There's a guy inside.'

She rapped her knuckles on the pane of glass.

The guy – wearing a baker's hat and striped apron bearing the words PIZZERIA FAMOUSA – made his way around the counter and headed over to unlock the door. 'We don't open for another half an hour,' he said as the door creaked ajar.

'We're looking for Orikum Marina,' said Lule.

The guy pointed back along the road in the direction they'd just come from. 'Just the other side of that rise. A hundred metres there's a turn-off leads right down to it. Everybody misses it. Can't see it when you're driving along, even in broad daylight, but if you cross the road here and look down you'll see it along on the left. Got to know what you're looking for. There's a bar called the Cabrestrante down there and a seafood restaurant, but they won't be open yet either. If you want I'll fire up the oven and fix you whatever you want . . . look.'

The guy flicked a switch just inside the door and a canvas-covered terrace on the opposite side of the road lit up. 'Go grab a table and I'll bring you something to drink. If you sit shore-side you can look down to the water – nice view.'

'Can you see into the marina from there?'

'Sure. You'll be looking right into it. Like I said, it's just along on the left.'

'Guy wants to know if you want some pizza?' said Lule turning to Keira and translating.

'I'm hungry. Yeah,' replied Keira. 'Any kind'll do.'

'You want wine?'

'Beer. Cold, times two.'

'Looks like we're on,' said Lule to the guy in Albanian.

The terrace was built on stilts rising out of the shallow rocks below. It was large enough to accommodate eight tables and had a balustrade on three sides – the road side being left open. The women chose a table in the far left corner. There was an ornately carved wooden gate set into the balustrade that opened onto a set of rickety wooden steps. The steps descended haphazardly to a small shingle beach. A hundred metres further along the shoreline – hidden from the road – was Orikum Marina. The *Persephone* – too large to enter the shallow bay – sat pointing out to sea, anchored near the mouth of the harbour, its stern moored to the farthest end of the quay.

The Cabrestrante bar they'd been told wasn't open was filled with people, its tables spread all along the quayside, the hypnotic crackle of traditional Albanian music floating across the bay towards where Keira and Lule were sitting.

'D'you think we've been conned?'

'I'll decide once I've eaten the pizza.'

'I grew up listening to this music: Lab Polyphonic Group. Never thought I'd grow to appreciate the magic. This track is called 'Qanë e motra per vëllane' – A sister is crying for her brother.'

'I like it. It fits the moment, but I think listening to this type of music at home wouldn't sound the same.'

'Not as good?'

'Not better or worse, but it's memory music ... something you'd hear in later life and it'd transport you right back to this moment.'

'What is this moment?'

'The lull before the storm.'

The guy arrived with the pizzas and placed them on the table.

'I thought the Cabrestrante was closed,' said Lule, shooting him a look.

'That's where the tourists go. You sit here for another half an hour this place is gonna be jumping: locals only, though. You wouldn't get a table if you showed up then. I charge you Albanian prices too, not rip you off, like the crook that runs that shithole down there. One bite of my pizza and you'll realise you done the right thing.'

'Who owns the big boat?'

'Not sure. It stops in here every now and then. There's usually a party goes on till late, but it's off limits. Most of the time the guests arrive on another boat – trying to be discreet, but everyone round here is wise to what's going on. You know it's party night when the coachload of girls arrive at the yard on the other side of the main building. Aside from my pizzas it's the only excitement there is around here. I'll go get you some more beer and let you enjoy the view.'

Lule waited till the guy was out of earshot then said, 'What'll we do if the cop doesn't show?'

'He will.'

'What will I do?'

'You can stay here, or wait in the car if you don't want him to see you. I'll head down to the marina when he arrives and check out what's going on.'

'Where will you go with Ermir if you get him off the boat? We should arrange somewhere to meet.'

'What about your friend Helena in Dushk? Is Dushk far from here? I think I could probably find her house again if I drove around a bit. You could take the car and I'll see if I can get a lift with Pavli.'

'She lives at the bottom of the hill from my mother.'

'Ardiana drove all around, I thought it was miles away.'

'No. It's close to my mother's, but I think Helena would not be happy for us to show up. She's not really a friend: I haven't seen her in years and Ermir would go crazy if you took him back to Dushk. I don't think this is good idea. Also, Dushk is maybe an hour away from Vlorë. Maybe we should ask Mister Pizza Famousa if there's somewhere around here.'

'It'd only be for one night. In the morning we'll head south and wait for the passports to arrive. We'll book a ticket out of Tirana under your real name to throw them off the trail. If they're watching for you it might just buy us enough time to get out while they're looking the other way.'

'You sure you are a lawyer?'

'You're the one who'll be breaking the law, not me. I'm just speaking my thoughts out loud and you happen to be in earshot.' Keira nodded for Lule to look over her shoulder. In the far distance a convoy of blue flashing lights could be seen speeding along the coast road. 'You better eat up.'

By the time the police cars were passing the pizzeria the food was almost gone. They followed the stream of blue lights as the vehicles turned off the road and swept down towards the marina, sirens wailing noisily into the darkness. Moments later the quayside was filled with armed officers. Muffled shouts and cries filled the air as they secured the area. A six-man team broke away from the main group. Even at this distance Keira could make out Pavli with his distinctive limp amongst them. With weapons drawn they crossed the metal gangplank onto the boarding platform on *Persephone*'s stern.

'I'll make my way down,' said Keira as she pushed back from the table. 'Are you going to wait here?'

'I'll watch and see what happens,' replied Lule. 'As soon as I see you have Ermir, I will leave.'

'. . . and go where?'

'I'm just thinking they will probably take the children back to the police station in Tirana. They may not let you take Ermir right away. If this happens I will follow you and wait outside. If you are allowed to take him now, then I will wait here for you, but you'll need to lose the cop.'

Lule watched Keira climb down the wooden stairs towards the beach.

In a loud whisper she called after her, 'The first thing you do is tell Ermir I am here, please.'

Keira's reply came out of the darkness.

'I forgot to tell you – I know what Hathi is.'

Lule didn't quite catch it. 'What did you say?'

Keira's response was drowned out by the sound of gunfire echoing around the bay.

*

Keira ducked instinctively and hurried as best she could over the pebble beach towards the near end of the quayside, her progress hampered by the darkness and the uneven surface underfoot. Eventually, she reached a set of coarse concrete steps that led from the beach onto the northern end of the marina. She'd counted three shots. Then nothing.

An officer challenged her as she approached the bar area.

'*Më vjen keq, por ju duhet të prisni këtu.*'

'I'm sorry, I don't understand.'

'*Ju duhet të prisni këtu.*' He held up his hand, indicating for Keira to stay where she was.

Keira pointed to the boarding deck at the stern of the *Persephone*. 'Pavli Variboba... I'm here to meet Officer Variboba.'

The cop either didn't understand or didn't care, but Keira wasn't going any further.

The patrons of the Cabrestrante restaurant had all turned and were staring at the large yacht. No one spoke. The only sound came from the Lab Polyphonic Group, still playing in the background.

A row of officers lined the top end of the quayside, weapons trained on the *Persephone*.

Looking back along the coastline, Keira could see the lights of the pizzeria's wooden terrace. The platform appeared to be floating above the rocks and for a moment she thought she saw Lule waving, but she couldn't be sure.

There was a commotion on the yacht: muffled shouts and angry voices, as the officers climbed back onto the quayside. Pavli was at the head of the group. He looked agitated as he waited for the others to join him. He barked some commands and his men dispersed in groups of three or four to search the rest of the marina and the surrounding area.

Pavli was heading to the Cabrestrante when he spotted Keira. He immediately waved to her to join him – shouting at the cop barring her way with an instruction to let her through.

'Told you I'd be back,' said Keira as she approached.

'Yes, you are full of the surprises. I didn't think you meant so soon. What can I get you?'

'A young boy called Ermir off the boat.'

'He's not on there. I meant, what I can get you from the bar.'

'You searched the entire boat?'

'Bow to stern,' replied Pavli. 'There's some crew and a very pissed-off Mister Vedon on board, that's all. No Ermir, no other children.'

'What was all the shooting about?'

'Three shots . . . We always fire three shots: it's like a warning. Do a lot of shouting as well. It lets people know we are not playing games.'

Pavli and Keira reached the bar and pulled up two stools.

'You would like a Korça?'

'I don't know. This was not quite how I was expecting the evening to go.'

'The boy is not on there, Keira. I am sorry.'

Pavli ordered two beers anyway and asked for a menu. 'I haven't eaten since this morning. You are hungry?'

'I've just had pizza,' replied Keira.

'You mind if I eat?'

'Go ahead.'

The beers arrived quickly. Pavli held out his glass and waited for Keira to do the same.

'What are we drinking to?' asked Keira.

'Two things: One is – I am finally managing to buy you a drink, and the other is a toast to the end of my career.'

'Why's that?'

'I head up an anti-corruption team in Durrës Policia. We are not exactly popular. We are supposed to work in secret, but everyone knows who we are. A lot of people want to see us fail and tonight will give them enough to make that happen. There are no children, no call girls, no drugs or even guns on board Mister Vedon's boat. If I didn't know better I'd say he knew we were coming.'

'Shit.'

'Yes. Is shit.'

Keira took a sip of her beer and said, 'Vedon's on board right now?'

'Yes.'

'He's the reason I was late for the flight on Sunday morning. I was taken on to a boat – probably the *Persephone* – on Saturday night when it was anchored in Durrës.'

'I thought you were having early night at the hotel?'

'I told you that because I didn't want to make a scene.'

'What is "make a scene"?'

'I didn't want to make a fuss. I knew I had to get on that plane Sunday morning ... so, I just told you that, but I was taken from the hotel and held on that boat.'

'You were kidnapped?'

'Yes.'

'You think Vedon had you kidnapped?'

'I know he had me kidnapped. I was tied to a chair. I spoke to him, or rather, he spoke to me.'

'You can describe to me what he looks like?'

'I didn't see him, but I'm pretty sure I would recognise his voice.'

Pavli shot her a look.

'The story sounds a bit lame, but it's the truth. I'm certain it was Vedon. And I know he has Ermir, hidden away somewhere.'

Pavli made a play of wiping the condensation from the neck of his beer bottle, but didn't say anything.

'You don't believe me?'

'I don't know what I believe any more.'

Keira paused to take another drink and give herself time to think. 'After all the shit I've been through, getting beat up, robbed . . . all the rest of the crap, finally here's something that actually hurts – words. Nothing physical, just words, and it stings. Weird, eh?'

'I'm not saying I don't believe you, it's just . . . ever since you arrived, I think you have not been always honest with me. It's difficult to know what is real and what is not.'

'When will you be finished here?'

'I'm finished.'

'Can you give me a lift?'

'How did you get here? You are not driving the car?'

'I got a lift.'

'From who?'

'Does it matter?'

'There you go again. It's not that I don't believe what you are saying, it's that you don't tell me anything I can believe.'

'There's something I want to show you.'

'Can I get something to eat first?'

'Sure, no hurry.'

'Where do you want a lift to?'

'I need to go pay for my pizza, up the hill.'

'That's it?'

'Then I want to go to Dushk to show you where this all started and why it matters. And prove to you that this is all very real.'

'Then what?'

'Then we'll come back here and arrest that son of a bitch Vedon, get him to tell us where Ermir is and you'll be able to keep your job.'

'What's in Dushk?'

'A crime scene.'

Thirty

The terrace area of the Pizzeria Famousa was now packed with locals, just like the guy had said. When the police car pulled up across the street Lule sank lower in her seat and peered between the diners as Keira jumped out and disappeared inside the main building. When she left, Keira climbed into the cop car and drove off without looking in Lule's direction.

The owner was standing at the side of the table holding up another beer. 'Your nice friend sent you this. Said to tell you she was heading to Dushk: she'll meet you there.'

'She'll meet me there?'

'I'm pretty sure that's what she said.'

'She say anything else?'

'Yeah, I didn't catch the words too well. I don't speak good English, but she mentioned something about *Dhi Gondolë*.'

'What about it?'

'Something like it was empty, if that makes sense. Yeah, that was it, "*Dhi Gondolë* is empty."'

'Thanks.'

'You all done?'

'How much do I owe you?'

'Your friend already paid.'

'D'you need the table?'

'Not till 10 p.m. You're good for at least another half-hour. After that if you want to keep going, the Cabrestrante's open till late. You want a coffee or maybe I'll bring you some rakia, yes?'

'I'm good, thanks.'

'I saw her get into the cop car. Is your friend a cop? Or maybe she's under arrest?'

'No, she's a lawyer,' replied Lule.

'I missed the whole thing. Was in the kitchen: didn't even hear the sirens, nothing. Something going on in the marina I think, but nobody knows what.'

Lule wasn't really in the mood for small talk, but the guy was just being nice so she played along as best she could without encouraging him to pull up a chair.

'Yeah, I watched it all from here, but nothing really happened.'

'Cops should have stuck around and gone to the party.'

Lule knew the answer to her next question, but asked it anyway. 'There's a party here tonight?'

'Not here, on the boat . . . It won't start for a while yet. Stick around for long enough, you'll see the guests sailing round the headland,' said the guy. 'Cops were too early.'

Lule was on her feet.

'You sure I can get a drink down at the marina? They've locked the gates.'

'Still full of all the people got the moorings: they don't go back to their boats till they're ready to fall in the sea.'

'You think they'd let me on?'

'To the big boat?'

'Sure.'

'You got an invite?'

'Sort of,' lied Lule. 'I'm supposed to be meeting someone on-board.'

'So long as you got an invite: but if I was you I'd have a few more drinks then head back into town 'n' crash someone else's party. If the people on that boat don't know you, they'll shoot you dead and throw your body in the sea before they'll let you eat one of their canapés.'

*

Pavli popped the boot lid open and after rummaging around inside appeared at the passenger-side door holding a torch. Keira climbed out and stood beside him. In contrast to the cool freshness of the coast, the air inland was warm and sticky. They were parked on the verge opposite Kaltrina Dervishi's house. Street lamps and houses scattered along the floor of the valley and surrounding hillside twinkled in the darkness, but up on the hill it was pitch black.

'You'll need something to cover your mouth and nose,' said Keira, whispering under her breath.

'Why are we talking so quietly?'

'Instinct, I guess.'

'D'you think there's something lurking out there, listening to us?'

'There are plants in the garden that witches use to make themselves invisible.'

'Shit sake. I'm a city boy. Even if the sun were high in the sky this place would give me the creeps. What are all those shapes?'

'Old garden machinery. Tractors and a horse-drawn plough all rotting away. The garden's full of them.'

'When I was thinking "first date", this is not what I had in mind.'

Keira's face was difficult to read, but her lack of response told Pavli all he needed to know.

They walked behind the beam from Pavli's torch as it traced a route along the path and up to the front door of the cottage. The building looked bigger: more imposing than it had in the daylight.

'You okay?' asked Pavli.

'Yeah, It's just, I know what's behind the door. I'm not in any great hurry to see it again.'

'Would you rather stay in the car?'

'No, let's just go in, take some photographs, then get the hell away from here.'

Pavli pressed a handkerchief to his mouth, placed his hand on the doorknob and twisted. The door gave way much more easily than it had done a few days earlier. As it swung open the heavy wooden door clattered against the side wall, the noise reverberating loudly in the stillness.

Keira stood – with her hand clamped over her mouth and nose – watching over Pavli's shoulder as the torch beam searched the interior: first the small vestibule behind the door then through into the kitchen area. Just as Pavli was about to step inside, Keira pulled her hand free of her face and grabbed him by the arm.

'Wait.'

'What?'

'Something's wrong.'

Pavli stared back at Keira, waiting for her to continue.

'There are no insects. When I was here the other day it was swarming with flies.'

'So, they must have all flown away when you opened the door.'

'It's not just that: the stench from the dead bodies was over-whelming. We wouldn't have been able to stand here and have a conversation without gagging.' Keira took the torch from Pavli and stepped inside. Within a few strides she was standing in the middle of the kitchen.

The table and chairs were still in place. Everything, except for the area between the table and the cooking range, looked exactly as it had before.

The bodies had been removed.

Keira flicked the torch beam around the rest of the room, checking for any signs of what had happened, but nothing else appeared to have been touched.

Pavli flipped a wall switch by the doorway and a shaded bulb dangling from the ceiling flickered into life. He took a few moments to look around.

Keira crouched and ran her fingers over the rough, terracotta surface of the floor tiles, then touched them to her nose. 'Disinfectant . . . This is fucked up. Just a few days ago there were two dead bodies right there. Kaltrina Dervishi's parents: what was left of them. Someone's been in. They were right there. This floor was stained with a big pool of dried blood, now it smells of bleach.'

'Is this where you came on Saturday when you were with the hooker girl, Ardiana Kastrati?'

'Yes.'

'You should have told me at the time. We could have come and looked then.'

'Yeah, well, there was a lot going on. How did you know she was a hooker?'

'You told me at the airport.'

'D'you think maybe she came back here?'

'I doubt it.'

'So why d'you mention her?'

'To see how you'd respond.'

'How I'd respond to what?'

'Me mentioning her name.'

'How did I respond?'

Pavli didn't answer.

There was short silence between them, then Pavli said, 'There's a bug in New Zealand called a weta, gets frozen in the winter then thaws out and comes back to life. Maybe that's what happened here. A resurrection.'

'We're not in New Zealand.'

'I could show you a real crime scene.'

'Shit, Pavli, what are you talking about? This is a real crime scene.'

'Your friend Ardiana.'

'What about her?'

'Someone took a dislike to her and her pimp. A guy called Fat-Joe Jesus: I was at the poor girl's apartment checking out the three bullet holes she had in her chest and the one that missed Fat-Joe's mouth and tore him a new opening in his throat. Guy across the street said he saw a woman pull the trigger. Said she was pretty. Even took the time to wave across to him. And turns out, Fat-Joe was the guy took you back to your hotel room after you fainted down on the beach. My dad recognised his face.'

'So. What are you suggesting? That I had anything to do with it?'

Pavli made a face, like he couldn't be sure.

'When did this happen?' asked Keira.

'Late Sunday morning.'

'I was on a plane to Glasgow. You met me at the airport and gave me my travel documents. I mean, Jesus, Pavli!'

'Where I saw you talking to the girl.'

'What girl?'

'The one you call Lule. I followed her back to her apartment and the next thing, the dope-dealer guy lives up above her, takes a dive from his balcony and breaks his neck.'

'And while he was learning to fly, I was over at Ardiana's apartment with a gun putting holes in her and Fat-Joe Jesus? Is that what you're insinuating? I was on a plane to Glasgow.'

'Yesterday you were on a plane to New York and look where you ended up. What happened, did the pilot get JFK mixed up with Tirana?'

Keira felt a jolt of adrenaline and stared back at Pavli for a moment. Then she said, 'So where are we going with this? Why have you waited until we get all the way out here to come at me with this? Why didn't you mention it over a beer at the Cabrestrante?'

'I'm just saying that, with you, nothing is adding up. You're looking for a boy that's disappeared who has dead grandparents that got up and walked away . . .'

'They didn't get up and walk away,' interrupted Keira. 'They'd been shot. Executed. They couldn't get up and walk away because they were dead. Someone's been in here and moved them.'

Pavli was talking over her, '. . . and all this while around you people are getting murdered. I don't know where I'm going with this, but I don't see it's going to end well.'

'You're starting to make me feel uncomfortable.'

'I am not meaning to do that. I have jigsaw in my head, but someone has stolen some of the pieces. You know what I'm saying?'

'Yes. Nothing adds up.'

'Nothing adds up.'

Keira could see that Pavli was agitated and wanted to calm things down, 'Look, Pavli, I don't know what the hell is going on here either. I have no idea why someone would all of a sudden go to all the effort of clearing a crime scene that's been left untouched for months. All I want to do is help a young kid out. That's all I'm here to do. I want to find him and give him some money and hopefully make his life better in some way. That's it. I didn't ask for any of this shit. I didn't kill Ardiana or Fat-Joe Jesus. I didn't ask someone to break into my hotel and steal my passport or get involved with some fucking gangster called Vedon, or any of this. But if we're going to make sense of any of it we have to trust each other. We have to work as a team . . . Do you agree?'

Pavli shook his head.

'I can't get used to this custom of yours. Are you shaking your head to agree or shaking your head to disagree?'

'I'm shaking my head to agree. We should work as a team.'

'We need to do some trust-building exercises.'

'We do?'

'I think I know one that will work.'

'You know how to make me trust you?'

'Yes.'

'How?'

Without taking her eyes off of him, Keira moved to the end of the table nearest to Pavli and leant back against it. She started to unbutton the front of her blouse, taking her time, button by button all the way down to the end, then let it fall open. The edge of the cotton caught on her nipples, exposing just the cup of her bare breasts and the flat, naked stomach underneath.

Pavli didn't move as Keira slowly undid the top button on her jeans and pulled them down just far enough to expose the top of her pubic hair.

'We are doing this here?' said Pavli.

'Here,' answered Keira. 'Let's make it a different sort of crime scene.'

'Are you serious?'

Keira shook her head from side to side, Albanian style.

'Your lips are not sore any more?'

'They're fine.'

Pavli stepped forward and gently pressed his lips to hers. He felt her tongue searching the warmth of his mouth and could taste the alcohol and tobacco on her breath. Pavli let his hand slide up inside her open shirt.

Keira squeezed her hands between their close-pressed bodies and started to unfasten Pavli's belt, undoing the top two buttons of his fly at the same time. Her hands searched around his waist as she started to pull and tug his trousers loose. With their mouths still pressed together Pavli hooked his thumbs under his belt in order to help.

He didn't feel Keira's fingers brush the leather safety clip looped over the Beretta holstered on the side of his utility belt.

He didn't feel the clip being flipped open.

He didn't feel the Beretta PX4 being lifted free.

It wasn't until the end of the barrel was pressed into his flesh that he realised something was wrong, but by then it was too late.

Keira whispered '*La Bête humaine*' in his ear before pulling the trigger.

Pavli felt the needle-sharp burn as the first bullet tore through his thigh. He staggered back against the sink and fell awkwardly to the floor, both hands clasped over his leg trying to stem the flow of blood. He immediately tried to get back on his feet, but his leg wouldn't support his weight and he crumpled back to the floor. The bullet had shattered his femur as it passed through his thigh and out the other side.

'Shit! What are you doing?' screamed Pavli.

'Where's Ermir?'

Pavli lunged for Keira, trying to grab hold of her legs, but she stepped easily out of reach and fired again, this time grazing his left arm just below the shoulder.

Pavli screamed again and fell backwards onto the floor.

Keira repeated the question. 'Where is the boy, Pavli? Why's he not on the boat?'

'You have lost your fucking mind?'

'No, I've lost my fucking patience. Before I ask you again I'm going to say one thing. If you tell me the truth I'll call for an ambulance, get someone here to fix you up. If I think you're bullshitting, I'm walking out that door and leaving you to bleed to death, d'you understand?'

'You are a fucking crazy woman. I'm trying to help you. All along I'm helping you, then you do this thing. What the fuck is wrong with you? You have lost your fucking mind, Keira.'

'My name is Niamh McGuire and if you knew anything about me you'd know just how much danger you're in right now. Answer the questions honestly and I'll help you, start fucking around and Niamh McGuire is going to kill you . . . Understood?'

'You are *di koka* . . . with two heads. The two personalities. You are fucking schizo.'

'I'm with Zola. Inside every human there is a beast. How did you know I was supposed to be in New York?'

'You told me earlier at the Cabrestrante. This why you shoot me? Because I ask about this?'

'I didn't tell you at the bar.'

'Okay, in the car on the way here, what does it matter?'

'I didn't tell you in the bar or in the car or anywhere. The only way you could have known that is if someone else told you, and I think that someone else was Verbër Vedon. I think the whole raid on his boat was a set-up: it was all for show. I think it was you who called ahead to say that you were coming.'

'Keira, Niamh, whatever person you are right now . . . You are wrong. You are both fucking wrong. You are crazy bitch.'

There was already a large pool of blood on the floor. Pavli lifted his head and stared at Keira, trying to focus, his voice suddenly faint. 'Please, you are wrong about me . . .' His eyes rolled back in his head and his voice was so quiet now that Keira could hardly hear him as he continued. 'Vedon doesn't have the boy . . . But . . . I think I know who does.'

His breathing was becoming increasingly laboured, his eyelids heavy and his words an incoherent mumble. Keira stepped closer and kicked the bottom of his shoe, 'C'mon, you son of a bitch. Where's the boy?'

Pavli opened his eyes briefly before his head tipped back and he passed out, his skull hitting the tiled floor with a crack. Keira stared down at him and cursed under her breath. She stooped to pick up the torch from the floor, then fumbled in his pockets looking for the car keys.

They weren't there.

Stepping over Pavli's prone body, Keira headed out of the house into the darkness. She made her way back along the garden path towards the police car, pulled open the driver's door and checked in the ignition.

The keys were nowhere to be seen.

As she turned to head back, a brief chink of light from the house next door caught her attention. The sight of an old woman's face staring out made her start; then, with the twitch of a curtain, the face was gone. As Keira moved back over the broken slabs towards the front door she had a flashback of Pavli clipping something to his belt – a keychain: chances were that the car key was on the floor trapped underneath him.

Keira crossed the threshold into the vestibule and stopped dead.

The kitchen was in darkness.

Keira reached in and flicked the wall switch, but nothing happened.

She trained the torchlight inside the kitchen.

The floor was empty.

Pavli was gone. In his place nothing but a mess of blood.

Streaks of red glistened in the darkness and marked the course he'd taken along the floor.

As Keira's gaze followed the lines of fresh blood she felt a tingle of fear run through her.

The trail of blood led along the kitchen floor towards the vestibule and underneath her feet.

She was already making the turn when she heard his voice.
'Now, you fucked up.'

Keira tried to duck the oncoming blow, but Pavli caught her hard across the side of her face with his fist and sent her sprawling into the kitchen, where she stumbled and crashed to the floor. Pavli's Beretta fell from her grasp and bounced along the tiles then skidded under the table, out of reach. The torch, too, clattered to the ground, smashing the lens and extinguishing the bulb. Keira twisted – hands covered in Pavli's blood – and tried to gain her feet, but Pavli fell on top of her, pinning her to the floor. She made a grab for his hair, but Pavli caught her hand in his left and delivered a right hook that connected with a loud smack to her jaw.

The blow stunned Keira, leaving her momentarily powerless to fight back. The weight of his body pressing down on her made it difficult to fill her lungs. Keira tried to roll him over, but her strength was already starting to fade. As she raised her free hand to strike, Pavli grabbed hold of it, wrenching both arms wide. She lay spreadeagled, unable to move with Pavli on top of her, his face just inches away now, close enough to feel his breath on her cheek and see the sweat glistening in his pores.

Keira drew on the last of her strength and butted Pavli in the face, her forehead connecting with the bridge of his nose with a sickening crack. He reared backwards, groaning in pain, giving Keira just enough time to pull her freed hands to her face and block the onslaught of blows that followed. Pavli was out of control, screaming and cursing in Albanian as his fists rained down on Keira.

The blows kept coming, one after the other, pounding at her face and head until eventually her arms fell limp and she lay motionless with her eyes closed, fighting against the wave of nausea sweeping up from deep in her stomach. She felt a sharp pain in her wrists, then heard a clicking sound as Pavli snapped a set of handcuffs on her.

There was a pause filled only with the sound of groans and heavy breathing. Keira could taste blood and vomit in her mouth as Pavli lifted himself up off of her. Her lips were split and oozing blood, the swelling around her right eye so bad it was difficult to tell if it was open or shut.

Pavli crawled to the other side of the room and sat propped against the wall holding the Beretta in his hand. Still panting, he said, 'Now we've got ourselves a crime scene.'

Keira lay flat on her back, unable to move, her head turned towards him.

'It was always a crime scene,' she replied in a barely audible whisper.

'Look where we're at now,' said Pavli. 'This is all fucked up.'

'Where's the boy?'

As he talked, Pavli ripped a piece of cloth from his shirt and started to tie it round his leg. 'Mister Vedon is finished with this game now. He has you down as naive: can't believe you came back to Albania rather than go to New York. For a moment he was not certain what you were up to. He thought you had the big plan – had him worried – but he laughed hard when I told him you'd come back here. It was not expected. He laughed hard because you are naive to think you can come back and make everything okay.'

'Where's the boy?'

'You were never going to get him back. Mister Vedon feels you may already have done enough to get Engjell E Zeze out of jail. The trial in Glasgow has been postponed... You and the boy have played your part. That is all he wanted. You know how all of this works... You have become incriminating evidence. No one wants you around to cause trouble in the future and no one wants the young boy to grow up looking for revenge.'

'And it's down to you to clean everything up?'

'We should just have fucked. I think we are attracted to each other. We could have fucked and you could have gone home and forgotten all about the boy and still be alive.'

'I am still alive.'

Pavli reached across and picked up what was left of his torch, then dragged himself along the floor, past Keira, to the doorway.

'You make things too easy for everyone. Mister Vedon thought he was going to have to find you in New York and have you killed there, but instead you came to him. He told me to take you somewhere quiet then – at the bar – you suggested coming here. Your client's house, where it all started... This will become the place it all ended too. It is poetic I think.'

Pavli used the wall and the table to brace against as he struggled to his feet. When he was certain he could support his own weight he lurched forward a few paces and stood over Keira, swaying unsteadily as he raised the Beretta and pointed it at her head.

'Where are the car keys?' asked Keira. 'I thought I saw you clip them to your belt, but they're not there.'

'You planning a trip?'

'Just curious.'

'Sun visor.'

'What's the Albanian for "do it now"?'

'*Beje tani.*'

'How do you say thank you?'

'*Faleminderit.* Anything else you'd like to ask – any last request – before you go?'

'I'm done. I'd just like to say, *beje tani.*'

'Okay,' said Pavli.

'I wasn't talking to you,' replied Keira.

There was a loud crack and the air filled with smoke as the shotgun blast exploded out through Pavli's chest in a mist of blood and gristle. He stared down at the gaping hole with a mixture of disbelief and shock, then slowly sank to his knees. The second blast caught him in the back of the neck and threw Pavli's headless torso forward with a jolt, as it landed heavily across Keira's legs.

Keira raised her head from the floor as much as she was able and said, '*Faleminderit,*' to the old woman standing in the doorway.

'*Je I mirëpritur,*' replied the old lady. '*Ti je vajza me mundi deri fytyrë që erdhi në derën time. Fytyra juaj duket shumë më keq.*'

'I don't understand,' replied Keira. 'I'm sorry.'

The old lady with the dry stacked hair dropped the shotgun to her side and pointed at her chest. '*Unë quhem Rozafa.*'

'Pleased to meet you, Rozafa. *Unë quhem* Keira.'

'Keira, you will bring my daughter back? My Lule?'

'I swear,' replied Keira.

Thirty-one

Lule glanced down at her phone buzzing on the table. It was a number she didn't recognise so she let it ring out, figuring they'd leave a message, and signalled to the barman to bring her another drink. A few seconds later the phone buzzed again: same number.

The third time the screen lit up Lule picked up the phone and answered in Albanian.

'*Kush është ky?*'

'Lule?'

'Who is this?'

'Keira. Where are you?'

'In the Cabrestrante, drinking much of the rakia. Where are you? Whose phone is this?'

'It's the cop's . . .'

'So where are you?'

'Still in Dushk, but I'm just about to leave. I'm in your house, sitting with your mum.'

'You and the cop are in my house, are you fucking kidding me?'

'Just me.'

'What's the cop doing? Did you show him next door?'

'The bodies are gone.'

'What? What do you mean?'

'Someone's fucking us around. I don't have time to go into it

267

just now, Lule, but I still think Ermir is on the boat . . .'

'The pizza guy reckons the cops got here too early. He said the party starts later.'

'Yeah, it's all screwed up. Pavli was lying. I'm going to leave in a minute and drive back to Orikum.'

'How long did it take to get there?'

'Just over an hour. Pavli had the lights and the siren on so it might take me a little longer. Wait for me in the bar.'

'Let me say hello to my mother.'

'She's upstairs. I'll get her to call you back.'

'I'm going to try get on boat.'

'No, Wait till I get there, Lule. I'll be as quick as I can.'

A horn sounded on the driveway leading down to the marina.

Lule turned over her shoulder and saw a furgon flashing its lights, signalling for someone to open the gates. One of the guys behind the bar made his way over to unlock them and wave the driver through.

'Something is happening. I'd better go.'

The minibus turned left into a service area that ran behind the main building of the marina. Lule fished in the canvas bag for her purse, left money on the table for the drink she'd just ordered, then headed towards the vaulted alleyway that led through to the service area.

Large flat-lid wheelie bins lined the rear walls of the Cabrestrante and the seafood restaurant, and there were a number of cars parked in an area reserved for staff. The furgon pulled into a gated yard at the far end and drew to halt. Lule sprinted across the open area and tucked in behind the furgon as the tall meshed gates slid closed behind.

The dimly lit yard, littered with fishing creels covered in discarded netting, opened on to the sea. A row of small yachts stood on stilts in a line that led to the other end of the yard where three empty cargo containers sat rusting in the sea air. At the end closest to the harbour three refuelling pumps stood silhouetted against the moonlit water beyond.

The minibus door creaked open and Lule heard the murmur of girls chatting as they disembarked.

She peered round the back end of the furgon and saw one of Vedon's men in a dark suit telling the young women to follow him. Lule counted twelve, all in their late teens or early twenties. She knew these girls well: knew how they worked, how they spoke, how they fixed their make-up to make their eyes look bigger and their lips more full; she knew how good they were at making a guy feel special even if he was a jerk. Joining this group of girls and sashaying on board would be easy.

Lule knew their story.

She used to be one of them.

The guy in the suit led the group through a narrow wooden gate that opened onto the quayside next to the stern of the *Persephone*. As she followed the girls onto the metal gangplank, Lule glanced back at the people sitting at the Cabrestrante. She saw the waiter lift the money from the table she'd been sitting at just few minutes earlier, then looking around to see where she'd gone. It struck Lule that she was looking into the past: staring at the world from a different dimension inhabited by a different version of herself. It would come as no surprise if the other Lule walked back to the table, sat down and ordered another rakia.

The girls were led across the gangplank onto the wooden

boarding deck and through into a large open lounge area with a bar at one end and a dance floor in the middle. Linen-clad trestle tables full of food – platters of fresh seafood, trays of meat cuts, displays of fruit laid out to resemble Giuseppe Arcimboldo paintings, hot servers steaming with curries and stews – were lined up along one side with uniformed staff standing behind, waiting to serve.

The girls were handed a glass of champagne by one of the many waiters milling around and told to follow the suited guy down to the lower deck, where they were shown into a large cabin and told to choose an outfit from the rack.

Everything was low cut, short or see-through.

Nowhere to hide a gun, thought Lule.

The cabin was kitted out like a high-end luxury hotel. Real wood and marble on every surface, deep pile carpet underfoot and a bed that was all mattress.

As the other girls started to strip, one of them caught Lule's eye. She looked younger than the rest and didn't appear to be having quite as much 'fun'.

'I didn't see you on the coach.'

'I made my own way,' replied Lule. 'This your first party?'

'Yeah. Seemed like a good idea at the time; now I'm not so sure.'

'You want my advice, don't drink the champagne. You'll wake up in the morning with a sore pussy, not knowing where the hell you are and your ass ripped open so wide next time you sit on sofa the damn thing'll disappear up it. If you really need a drink, go to the bar and watch the barman pour it. Don't take anything they hand you . . . not even the water.'

'Thanks. You done this before?'

'Only once. Woke up in Scotland.'

The girl smiled, then realised that Lule was serious. 'Was it this boat?'

'Different boat, same scam. If it all gets too much, dive overboard and swim to the beach. As long as you been acting drunk, no one's coming in after you.'

'What's your name?'

'Lule, yours?'

'Odeta.'

The girl reached across and shook Lule's hand.

'It's quite a boat.'

'Yeah, but don't get fooled, it's all a con. You don't get to own shit like this by being nice to people. The guy that owns this is a douche. There's no one you're going to meet tonight's gonna be looking for love: they're not gonna set you up for life or take care of you. All they want is to fuck some fresh pussy and grab your tits . . . after that, it's all over. They want to fuck about with you, but they don't give a fuck about you, you know what I'm saying?'

'Yeah.'

'How much they paying you?'

'Five thousand.'

'Lek?'

'Yeah.'

'That's just the basic. Guy wants to do anything more than squeeze your tits, tell him he's got to pay. They all carry bags of cash so don't let him pass you off with a cheque or an IOU: you'll never see the money. What time's the party start?' asked Lule.

'There was a hold-up. Meant to be here an hour ago, but

something was going on. I think the guests are supposed to be arriving on another boat any time now.'

The guy in the suit came back into the cabin. 'Okay, girls, hurry it up. Get your faces on, finish your drinks and let's get upstairs.' He stood waiting in the doorway running his eyes over the naked ones as they finished pulling on their clothes.

Lule thought about calling him out on it, tell him to stop being such a sleazebag, but didn't want to draw attention to herself.

When they were ready the girls formed a line and started to file past him out into the narrow corridor. Odeta stood at the back waiting her turn to leave the cabin. She glanced down and saw Lule lying on the floor next to the bed, tucked in as far as possible out of sight with a handgun clasped to her chest.

Lule winked at Odeta and held a finger to her lips. The young girl gave nothing away on her face, but Lule heard her say to the guy at the door, 'That's all of us,' as she left the room.

He'd counted twelve: everything was cool.

The door slammed closed and Lule was alone. She lay there for a few moments listening to the bass beat that had just started upstairs, trying to work out the tune: the artist was Adrian Gaxha for sure, but what was the name of the track? Lule pushed herself up from the floor then made her way around the bed and over to the cabin door.

She tried the handle: it wasn't locked. Easing the door open, Lule checked in both directions, then slipped out. The boat carrying the guests had arrived. The sound of voices shouting over the music filled the boat. The party had started.

There were five berths in all; two on each side and one in the middle to her right. Lule tried the door, but it was locked.

She walked the length of the narrow passageway checking the other doors and found they were all open, but the rooms were unoccupied. At the end of the short corridor a set of double doors led through what looked like a TV lounge to another set of doors.

As Lule moved through the lounge she noticed a large plastic box pushed in between the sofa and the wall and stopped dead.

A child's toy was pressing up against the lid, preventing it from closing. Lule lifted the lid. The box was filled to the brim with toys for all ages – boys and girls. As she knelt to look more closely she spotted an empty fun-size pack of Cocoa Crunch cereal under the coffee table that sat in front of the wall-mounted flat screen. The cereal was spilled out onto the carpet.

'What the fuck are you doing down here?'

The voice came from over Lule's shoulder.

Another one of Vedon's suited soldiers was standing at the entrance. 'You're supposed to be upstairs.'

Lule placed her hands on the floor and pushed up, slipping her Beretta out of sight under the sofa as she stood.

'I was sent down here to clean up the mess left behind by those useless fucking cleaners and to get the boy moved to one of the bedrooms.'

'Who sent you down?'

'The *krye*.'

'Is that right?'

Lule gave him one of her 'don't-fuck-with-me' looks and replied, 'Yeah, that's right.'

'What shit we talking about? I don't see any shit.'

Lule bent down and lifted the Cocoa Crunch pack from the floor.

'D'you want me to get the boy and you clean the shit up or d'you want to get him then go explain to Mister Vedon why this all took so fucking long?'

Lule could see the guy staring at her, trying to figure out if she was bullshitting or not. 'Where's the boy to go?'

'First bedroom on the right, next to the one the girls were getting changed in.' Lule threw the last bit in as an extra. If she knew where the girls were getting changed like she'd known about the mess on the floor and the fact that there was a boy, maybe she was legit.

In his mind it all stacked up.

'I'll get the boy,' said the guy as he crossed the room and rapped on the double doors with the fat part of his fist.

'Ibish?'

There was a muffled reply.

'Ibish, it's Kushtim, open up.'

Seconds later the guy Lule presumed was Ibish slid the doors wide and stepped into the opening. 'What's going on?'

'The *krye* wants the boy taken over to the bedroom.'

'Then what?'

Lule answered. 'Then you can take a break. I've to wait with him until his . . . date arrives.'

Lule was squatting by the coffee table.

'Yeah? And who the fuck are you?' asked Ibish.

'The kid's mom! Who the fuck d'you think I am?' replied Lule, giving him some of it back. 'Mister Vedon asked me to tidy up some mess and get the boy ready in one of the rooms. I'm just doing what I'm told. If you two did the same instead of standing around giving me shit then I could get upstairs and enjoy the party.'

Lule had no idea where this was going. The only line she was working on right now was to get Ermir out of the room and away from these two goons. After that, she'd figure out how to get the boy off the boat.

A thought struck her: as soon as Ermir saw her he'd react, say her name, run to her – blow it. She turned and busied herself with clearing the small nuggets of cereal from the floor, hoping that neither Ibish nor Kushtim would notice she was stalling.

Ibish disappeared through the double doors, spoke a few words Lule didn't catch, then reappeared almost immediately. Lule edged nearer the sofa. If Ermir did react to seeing her, she'd grab the Beretta and shoot the fuckers dead. Lule had her back to them – afraid to turn and look – as Ibish and the boy emerged from the room.

Out of the corner of her eye she caught sight of Ermir's skinny legs, his painfully wasted calf muscles: his feet, too big for his shoes.

Halfway across the room the big guy, Ibish, stopped.

'What suite is he going in to?'

Lule waited for Kushtim to answer, but Kushtim stayed mute.

'Lady, I'm asking what room,' repeated Ibish.

Lule was still play acting, cleaning up as her hand glided across the carpet and came to rest on the stock of the Beretta.

Kushtim finally spoke up. 'First on the right.'

She heard Ibish and the boy move off, then Ibish stopped and turned again.

'Lady, what's your name? I should introduce you to your kid.'

Lule had no option now but to turn. She slipped her finger through the trigger guard, ready.

She turned and said, 'It's Lule. My name is Lule.'

Ibish gestured to her and said, 'Come and meet the kid.'

Lule slid the gun back under the sofa and got to her feet. For a brief second she felt as though she was going to pass out. She stood a moment and waited for the room to stop spinning.

'You okay?' asked Kushtim.

'Fine. Stood up too quickly.'

Lule stepped forward with her arm extended ready to shake the boy's hand, knowing it was dumb, but she couldn't think what else to do.

There was no reaction at all from the boy.

It wasn't Ermir.

Thirty-two

The police-band radio broadcast an endless stream of unintelligible chatter against a background of hiss and crackle. Keira reached for the volume control and turned it to zero. Next she flipped the sun visor. The car keys slipped from underneath and tumbled into the dimly lit footwell. She groped around blindly before finding them tucked in under the clutch pedal. Her head was pounding and the flesh around her right eye so swollen she could no longer see out of it.

Lule's mother Rozafa had found a box of painkillers; a mixture of codeine and paracetamol, and given some to Keira half an hour ago along with a cup of strong muddy coffee: the pills and caffeine were just starting to kick in.

Rozafa, through a mixture of mime and gestures, had tried to convince her that driving was a bad idea, but there was no other option.

Keira turned the key in the ignition and watched the needle on the fuel gauge rise to just under a quarter-tank. The range was showing ninety kilometres. The onscreen instructions for the satellite navigation were in Albanian, but eventually after trying various combinations of button-press, she'd figured it out. Keira typed Orikum onto the screen and waited for the satellites cruising overhead to do their thing.

Ninety-five kilometres.

She would have to stop for fuel. After checking her pockets,

Keira remembered she'd used the last of her cash to pay for the pizzas and her purse – along with all her cards – was inside a travel case locked in the back of the hire car parked outside the Pizzeria Famousa.

She set off, hoping the gauge was wrong.

From her window Rozafa followed the glow of the headlights as the police car made its way to the top of the hill, turned and slowly trundled back down. In the darkness it was difficult to see, but Rozafa was sure Keira waved as she passed and the old lady lifted her hand to do the same.

Fifteen minutes later, having negotiated the narrow streets that laced the village of Dushk, Keira joined the SH4 highway heading south. She kept the flashing blues on for the entire journey and within an hour started to see signs for Vlorë and Orikum.

When she eventually hit the coast road south of Vlorë, Keira found a lay-by and pulled over. The pills had taken the edge off her aches and pains, but they had also made her drowsy. She wanted to lie back and go to sleep. Her ribs hurt when she breathed. Despite driving with the window down for most of the journey, beads of sweat clung to her brow.

As the car drew to a halt she threw the door wide, leant out and vomited onto the dry, sandy soil, clutching her ribs against the pain. When she'd finished retching Keira unclipped the seatbelt and stumbled out to sit on a large boulder sticking out of the verge. She sat with her head in her hands breathing heavily, spitting the acrid taste of bile out between her swollen lips.

When she'd recovered enough to stand, Keira walked around to the other side of the car, leant in and lifted Pavli's phone from the passenger seat. She thumbed in Lule's number, then – as she waited for her to pick up – looked across to the lights on the tail end of the long stretch of Vlorë bay towards Orikum Marina, still a fifteen-minute drive away.

When there was no answer, Keira closed the screen, threw the phone back in the car and headed for the driver's side via the rear end of the vehicle. An impulse made her stop and open the boot.

Two Heckler & Koch MP7s were strapped to the underside of the lid, both with extended 30-round magazines protruding from their pistol grips. On the floor of the boot sat three boxes of DM11 armour-piercing shells, a Kevlar body vest and an unopened package wrapped in clear cellophane. Keira figured the contents of this package were originally intended for her. Printed white, bold on the front in several different languages were the words BODY BAG.

Keira lifted a box of DM11s from the boot and emptied as much extra ammunition as she could carry into her pockets.

The Kevlar vest was heavier than it looked. Keira lifted it over her head and adjusted the various straps until it was a snug fit. Next she ripped the Velcro straps holding the machine pistols in place against the boot lid and freed both of them. Keira dropped the magazines out to check they were full then slotted them back into place. If there was any shooting to be done Keira was ready.

She took a moment to fill her lungs with the fresh sea air then climbed back into the driver's seat. The orange fuel light had been on for more than half the journey and the gauge was as far down as it could go, but the engine caught first time and seconds later she was speeding along the coast road with what looked like a grin on her battered face.

'Gonna have a hot time on the town tonight,' said Keira in a phony American accent.

*

Lule took the young boy's hand in hers. It felt light – as though the bones were made of dry twigs and the skin of paper. The boy stood rigid, his big blue eyes struggling to hide the fear as he stared up at her.

'What's your name?'

'Loran.'

Lule gestured for him to move into the corridor, then held the bedroom door open for him. 'Okay Loran, you head into this room here with me, while ... Damn it!' Lule clasped her hand up to her chest. 'Shit, my necklace has come off. Shit! You go into the bedroom and close the door, okay, while Ibish and Kushtim here help me find my necklace. I'll be with you in two minutes, but you mustn't come out, d'you understand? You'll be in trouble if you come out.'

Loran shook his head as Lule closed the door behind him.

'Where the fuck are you goin'?' asked Ibish as Lule brushed past him and walked back into the lounge.

'My necklace has come off, help me look,' replied Lule, heading straight for the corner of the sofa.

'I'll help the bitch look,' said Ibish, addressing Kushtim, who was still standing by the double doors like he had nothing better to do, 'You go get Mister Vedon, tell him the boy is ready.'

Lule crouched to the floor and immediately stood upright again, holding the Beretta. 'Found it.'

Her first shot punched through Kushtim's chest and stopped

him dead in his tracks. Shots two and three followed in quick succession and knocked him onto his back, his body falling dead – half in, half out – between the double doors.

Ibish was already drawing his gun, but Lule's fourth shot hit his shoulder, spun him against the wall and dropped him to the floor where he lay on his side, still scrabbling to unholster his weapon, aware that Lule had taken a few steps closer and was pointing the Beretta directly at him.

'Bitch,' he screamed, 'I'm going to fucking kill you, you cock-sucking fuckin' whore.'

Lule squeezed the trigger again.

The impact of the fifth bullet slammed his large, muscle-bound body back, hard onto the floor. She moved to stand over him as he lay moaning and cursing her. Lule knew the next bullet was the kill shot, but she had something to say first.

'A year ago, because of people like Vedon and the arseholes like you he employs, "cock-sucking fuckin' whore" would have been my job description ... That I can take, but only my best friends Kaltrina Valbona and Nikki Shyri are allowed to call me a bitch ... and they're both dead.'

Lule closed her eyes and squeezed the trigger. The Beretta bucked in her hands, spat out bullet number six and silenced Ibish's groans.

'Now you can call me a bitch.'

Lule's ears were ringing as she made her way back to the young boy. She needed to move quickly. Even with the loud music filtering down from the deck above, there was no way the shots would have gone unnoticed.

Loran was sitting on the edge of the bed when Lule entered. He noticed the gun straight away.

'I'm here to help you, Loran. Nothing is going to happen, okay. You're safe now, but you have to come with me. We're only going next door, but we have to move quickly. You have to trust me and come with me.'

Lule held out her hand, but the boy hesitated; too frightened even to stand up.

'I promise you, Loran, I'm going to help, but we must go now. Please, come with me. I know you're scared. Don't be. I'm going to make everything better. Come.'

Reluctantly, the boy placed his hand in Lule's and let her lead him next door to the bedroom the girls had used to get changed in. Lule made sure she shielded the view into the lounge from Loran as they shuffled along the corridor in the opposite direction. The last thing she wanted him to see was Ibish's corpse lying there with his head blown off.

'Are you alone?' asked Lule as they pushed through into the bedroom.

The boy shook his head.

'Are there others?'

Loran held up his index finger.

'Just one?' continued Lule.

He shook his head again.

'Is the other boy called Ermir?'

Loran shrugged his shoulders.

'D'you know where they're keeping the other boy?'

Loran thought for a moment. 'I think in the room at the end of the hall.'

He pointed in the direction of the room Lule had tried first, the one that was locked. 'I have heard him crying in the night,' whispered Loran.

'I want you to wait, Loran. I'm going to find the other boy and bring him back here. Then we're getting off the boat. Find somewhere to hide in this room and stay there until I get back. They might come looking for you, so stay hidden, okay?'

The boy's hands were trembling.

Lule put an arm round his shoulders and tried to reassure him.

'I won't let anyone harm you, okay?'

'Okay,' replied Loran, tears streaming down both cheeks.

'Can you swim?'

'Yes.' He hesitated, then added, 'Best in class.'

'Cool. Wait here. Everything is going to be fine.'

Lule poked her head out into the corridor. It was still empty, but she could hear doors slamming on the deck above and raised voices – men shouting to be heard above the music. A few steps and she was standing outside the room at the end of the corridor. She pressed her ear against the door and listened, but it was impossible to hear anything above the music. Lule tried the handle again and was surprised to find the door was now unlocked. Just as she started to push through the music stopped and everything fell silent. She turned her head to listen along the corridor, but there was no sound except for the dull thump of her heart beating in her ears.

She pushed the door just wide enough to poke her head through. The room spanned the width of the yacht: twenty metres from port to starboard. There were two sets of doors, one on either side of a huge king-size bed centred against the wall to the right of where she was standing. A large sofa sat beneath two portholes on the far wall and a polished metal staircase situated to the left spiralled down from the upper decks.

The room was unoccupied. Everything looked as it should except for one thing. Lule wondered why the floors, bed and sofa were covered in sheets of black plastic, taped at the edges and sealed at the joins.

She slipped in and closed the door behind her.

Keeping her back to the wall, Lule edged her way around until she was able to see to the top of the spiral staircase.

There was no one up there.

A muffled groan cut the silence. At the same time a loud cheer came from the upper deck and the music started pumping again.

The first door Lule tried led through to an en-suite bath and shower room. It too was empty. The second door on the other side of the bed opened into a dressing room large enough to accommodate a sofa and an armchair, with a huge mirror that spanned the width of the room and items of clothing – suits, jackets and shirts – hanging on a rail that ran the length of one wall. At one end of the sofa, his back pushed against the rear cushions, sat Ermir.

He was almost unrecognisable. His head had been shaved, accentuating his drawn, skeletal face. His legs were bound at the ankles and his hands tied behind his back. When he looked up and realised it was Lule standing in the doorway, tears started to stream down, over his thin, hollow cheeks. Thick tape across his mouth prevented him from speaking, but his eyes said everything.

He tried to shuffle forward, off the sofa, but Lule was already on her way, her hand held out in front of her, 'No, wait. You'll fall. Let me untie you first.'

Lule's eyes filled as she tugged and pulled at the bindings

around his wrists. The knots were tight, but she quickly managed to free his hands. While he tore at the tape covering his mouth, Lule worked on the rope around his ankles, talking through her tears as she picked the knots loose with her nails.

'I'm here, Ermir. I'm here, okay? Everything is going to be all right now. I am going to look after you: take you somewhere safe. No one will ever harm you again.' Lule's conscience was speaking for her, saying the things she should have said before. Talking to Ermir in a low whisper she continued, 'I'll be your mother, your sister and your best friend. Together we will be strong. Together we will take all the bad memories and roll them into a ball then throw them away, bury them in the dirt where they belong, and in their place we will put only good memories.'

When she'd finished and Ermir was finally free Lule scooped him up and held him in a tight embrace.

Eventually Lule whispered to Ermir, 'We have to get out of here,' then turned and headed out of the dressing room.

Two strides into the bedroom the butt of a pistol whipped across the back of her head and sent her sprawling to the floor. Lule stretched out her arms to break the fall and prevent herself from landing on top of Ermir. The Beretta she'd been holding slipped from her hand and bounced noiselessly across the plastic sheeting.

Down on all fours, she tried to scramble for the gun, but a kick to her abdomen forced the air from her lungs and knocked her onto her side. Then came another blow, followed by another. As she lay gasping for breath she felt the steel pressing roughly into her temple.

A guy in a suit was bending over her. 'You can keep

struggling and I blow your head through the floor or you can lie there for a minute and catch your breath, then have a chat with Mister Vedon and his friend. What's your call?'

Lule was breathing hard, trying to fill her lungs. She couldn't see Ermir, but could hear a commotion over by the spiral staircase. 'Please don't harm the boy,' replied Lule.

'Stand up,' said the guy, lifting the gun away from her head and pulling Lule to her feet.

Ermir was standing with his arms by his side, frozen, another one of Vedon's men pressing a gun into the back of the young boy's neck.

'Who the fuck are you?'

Lule turned to see a guy wearing a loose-fitting suit sitting on the bed with his back against the headboard and his legs stretched out in front. Where both trouser legs had ridden up, pale skin showed above the top of a pair of black socks. An older guy carrying too much weight was sitting on the sofa. He looked uneasy, but was still managing a smile. Lule recognised his face, but couldn't remember where from.

The guy on the bed was Verbër Vedon. Lule had seen him on the news plenty of times, but he looked different in real life.

'I was expecting the lawyer,' said Vedon before repeating, 'So who the fuck are you? You the boy's mother?'

'I'm his everything,' replied Lule.

'Whatever the hell that means . . . So where is the lawyer? I was told she was back in town and looking to party?'

'She's on her way with the Policia.'

'No, no, no, you must have missed the news. They've already been. A police officer friend of mine, and some of his guys were here already. Didn't find what they were looking for, but you've jogged my memory. I think my friend was going to meet up with the lawyer lady: wanted to "take her out". Vedon smiled to himself then added, 'If you know what I mean. What's the matter? You look like someone that's just done a shit then realised there's no toilet paper: can't figure out what to do next.'

'No, I was thinking, I don't think their date went too well. She called me a little while ago and said she was on her way back.'

'Well, let's see if she makes it.'

'I think she will make it, but I'm not so sure about your friend. What's with the fancy décor? I feel like I'm inside a bin bag.'

Vedon ignored Lule's question and asked, 'Did you kill Ibish and Kushtim?'

'Ibish called me a bitch and Kushtim looked as dumb as a chicken,' replied Lule.

'So you killed them . . . my friends?'

'I don't like being called a bitch by anyone other than people who know me and I think chickens are so dumb they deserve all they get.'

Vedon stared at Lule for a moment like he accepted her reasoning, then carried on, 'This is another friend of mine.' Vedon pointed to the fat guy on the sofa who was still grinning. 'Do you recognise him?'

'He looks familiar.'

'Where from?'

'Is he the guy stacks shelves in my local supermarket? Does it matter whether I recognise the big fat fuck or not?'

'I guess not,' replied Vedon. 'He's a professional man, a politician – married too, but he has a darkness in his soul –

don't they all.' Vedon gave a rueful smile and continued. 'His story is so common now it's almost a cliché. He craves power, but he is sick in the head. In the past they would have locked him in a cell and left him to rot, but these days you go into politics. It's funny, no? It's also good for business. We help him live out his fantasies and he helps us with our operations. He is very keen that your boy star in his next production. I will let you watch what he does to him and then I will let you see what happens to the children when they are finished with. The fancy décor in here is so we don't get it all messed up. All this is for killing my friends. If you can walk away from this in silence, without shedding a tear, I will let you live. You can then spend the rest of your life crying for what you have done. This is a new game. D'you like it?'

'I recognise you now,' said Lule to the fat guy in the chair. 'You're that slimeball, minister for health. You've always given me the fucking creeps – now I know why.'

Vedon ignored Lule and nodded to the guy holding Ermir, 'Bring the boy over and tie him to the bed. Make sure he's on his front with his ass in the air.'

Just as Vedon got up from the bed, the boat suddenly lurched to one side, the movement so violent that everyone was thrown to the floor. The fat guy tumbled over the sofa, and collapsed in a heap against the far wall. Screams could be heard from the upper deck as the boat rocked back in the opposite direction. The guy holding Lule was on his hands and knees, an arm stretched in front as he reached for the gun that had slipped from his grasp. Lule got there first, diving along the floor and snatching the handgun up. In the same movement she rolled, twisted and fired two shots at point-blank range.

Both bullets smashed through the top of his skull and exited near the base of his neck, killing him instantly.

Lule heard Ermir scream a warning and rolled off to one side as a bullet grazed her arm. A second bullet fizzed past her head as the boat lurched again and finally settled in the water. The movement was enough to throw the guy holding Ermir off balance and give Lule a brief opportunity to fire back. She didn't stop until she'd emptied the gun, the guy's body bucking and jolting as one bullet after another found its target.

Ermir cried out again, but too late this time for Lule to avoid the blunt toe of Vedon's leather shoe connecting with the side of her head. Lule raised her arms in time to deflect a second kick, but as she scrabbled along the carpet Vedon made contact again with the outside of his right foot against her nose, sending a shock of pain shooting to the back of Lule's skull.

Vedon was on top of her. He pulled the handgun from Lule's grasp, pointed at her head and squeezed the trigger.

There was a dull click as the hammer struck the empty chamber.

Vedon's cry of frustration was cut short by a loud crack of gunfire from the direction of the spiral staircase.

A ragged hole appeared in the ceiling above Vedon's head.

Ermir was standing with a gun clasped in both hands, his emaciated arms struggling under its weight. 'She is my sister and my mother and my friend . . . you will leave her alone.'

Thirty-three

It was just after midnight. There were still people sitting at tables on the terrace across from the pizzeria when the police car sped past doing over a hundred. It slowed as it approached the turn-off for the marina, but was still travelling too fast to take the turn and Keira had to fight to keep the Volkswagen from skidding off into the ditch.

The Cabrestrante was still serving. Everyone at the bar turned to watch the police car as it crashed through the gates and accelerated past, blue lights flashing, sirens wailing. The four henchmen standing guard on the shore side of the gang-plank looked towards the oncoming vehicle wondering when it would start to slow, but Keira had no intention of easing her foot off the accelerator.

She saw the men reach towards their holsters, but there was no time for them to draw their weapons. They just managed to dive clear as the dark-blue VW launched itself off of the end of the quayside and ploughed into the stern of the *Persephone*.

Momentum carried the car forward through the glass doors of the party deck, across the dance floor and on to punch a hole in the starboard side of the luxury yacht's hull. The force of the impact caused the boat to list violently to one side and ripped a hole in the stern where the yacht was tied off. A crack zig-zagged down the side of the hull, big enough to cause the lower decks to start taking in water.

The partygoers were pitched to the floor, tumbling one way then another as the yacht settled again. The front end of the police car was hanging out over the water, steam spewing from what was left of its engine bay. Keira put her shoulder to the driver's door and forced it open.

With an MP7 in each hand she stumbled from the wreckage onto the deck of the party lounge. Something her uncle had once told her crashed her thoughts, 'First thing to do in any situation is show people you're not fucking about.' Keira raised her left hand out to the side and squeezed off a burst of gunfire. A spray of bullets shattered the line of floor-to-ceiling windows opposite and initiated another round of screams and cries from the fallen partygoers. Some scrambled for the exits while others hid behind tables upended by the sudden listing of the yacht. Keira had no interest in the girls or the sorry collection of males wearing rip-off Armani suits and fake Rolexes: she was there to find Ermir and get him off the boat.

A movement from behind caught her attention. One of the henchman scrambling onto the stern, weapon raised. Keira felt the MP7s shudder as she opened fire on the turn and saw him jolt backwards a few steps before tumbling into the water.

Keira called out for Lule, but there was no response.

She tried again. 'Lule!'

A girl sitting with her back against the wall answered, 'Lule is downstairs.'

'Can you show me?' asked Keira.

'Please, I want no trouble.'

'Are you Verbër Vedon?'

The girl looked confused. 'No, my name is Odeta.'

'Then you won't have any trouble. Do you speak English?'

'Yes, a little.'

'Tell everyone to stay on the ground and I'll leave them alone. If everyone stays calm and keeps their guns in their pockets, everything will be fine – I'm here to have a word with Mister Vedon, take back what belongs to me, then I'll leave you all alone to enjoy the rest of your evening.'

Odeta translated.

'One more thing, Odeta, do you know what Mister Vedon looks like?'

'Yes.'

'Is he in this room right now?'

'No, he is also downstairs, I think.'

'Can you show me?' asked Keira.

Odeta led Keira down to the lower deck and pointed to the room where she'd last seen Lule. As she turned to leave, gunshots rang out from the room at the end of the hall.

'Get off the boat, Odeta,' whispered Keira as she squeezed past, heading in the direction the shots had come from.

The door at the end of the corridor was slightly ajar. Keira peered through the gap and saw Ermir on the far side of the room straining to level the gun he was holding. The way he stood, the tremor in his voice, the fear etched across his face, hit Keira hard. She looked down at her hands and saw they were trembling. She was no longer standing in the corridor of the *Persephone*, but walking up a set of darkened stairs to the sound of her father's groans as he lay wounded in the hallway below. She could feel the weight of the gun in her hands, the strain on her arms, the sensation that some invisible force was dragging the weapon down as she tried to lift it and aim at the man attacking her uncle on the landing above. She remembered the crack, the ringing in her ears as she squeezed the trigger and knowing – even as an eight-year-old – that her life would never be the same. Just as she knew now that this must not be Ermir's fate. He'd witnessed violence at a young age, just as Keira had, but she wouldn't let him become a killer . . . like she had.

A figure appeared and launched himself at Ermir. Keira quickly stepped into the room and opened fire, the bullets tearing through the fat guy's legs and shattering his kneecaps. As he buckled and fell, screaming in pain, the guy on top of Lule, Vedon, turned into Keira's wide arcing swing, which sent him tumbling. Blood poured from his face where the butt of the MP7 ripped his cheek open.

Lule was already on her feet and heading to Ermir.

'Get him off the boat,' barked Keira as she raised both guns and pointed them at Verbër Vedon, who was writhing around holding his face. 'I don't want to kill you in front of the boy, but I will, so stay on the floor and don't say a fucking word, understood?'

Lule grabbed the gun from Ermir and helped him climb the spiral staircase. 'Where to?' she called back to Keira.

'Along the beach back to the car. I'll be right behind you,' shouted Keira as they disappeared from view.

A second later Lule was back, calling over her shoulder to Ermir to stay put as she descended the staircase again and headed over to the fat guy lying on the other side of the bed groaning as he clutched his wounds.

'You are not going to fuck anything ever again Mister Health Minister,' said Lule as she forced the barrel of the handgun into his groin and pulled the trigger.

Verbër Vedon flipped round holding a small Sig P220 and

managed to get one round off before Keira fired a burst in return that knocked the gun from his hand and stopped him trying again.

'You okay?' asked Lule noticing Keira holding her arm.

'A graze,' replied Keira.

'Meet you at the pizzeria,' was thrown to Keira as Lule made her way back up the stairs.

*

'I'm surprised to see you, Miss Lynch,' said Vedon, pulling himself into a sitting position against the side of the bed.

'Not as surprised as I am to see you again, Mister Pasha. You and Fat-Joe Jesus played me good.'

'You're a smart lady, but you don't always get it right. Calling me a hustler at the foot-soldier end of the organisation. I'm the boss man, the *krye*. This is my fucking boat you're standing on. You think you get this shit spending your life "stuck in a traffic jam"? In this country you got to be smarter than every wise guy out there.'

'Yeah, you're so smart, I'm the one standing here holding the gun.'

'Fuck you. My friend Pavli told me he was going to kill you tonight, that's why I'm surprised to see you.'

'Yeah,' replied Keira.

'I can see from your face that he tried at least.'

'When they find his headless corpse you'll also see that he failed.'

'You sure you're a lawyer?'

'People ask me that a lot.'

'And what do you say?'

'I'm many things.'

'So, you've got the boy. If you make it out of Albania alive, you gonna get my friend Engjell E Zeze locked away for a very long time? Is that enough justice for you?'

'Your friend E Zeze won't survive till the end of his jail term. That's justice.'

Daud Pasha snorted, 'You going to have him killed in jail?'

'He's supernatural: he'll get over it.'

'You're just as bad as him.'

'Worse maybe. I have a conscience to deal with.'

'What now? Call the cops?'

'You're so naive, Mister Pasha,' replied Keira as she backed towards the spiral staircase. 'I have so many questions for you, but you answered every one of them the moment you took a six-year-old child hostage.'

Keira squeezed both triggers, emptied what bullets were left into Daud Pasha, and left the room.

She climbed the spiral staircase to the sound of a corrupt politician with no balls screaming for mercy as he lay on the floor bleeding to death.

There's no rejoicing in the death of others, thought Keira.

Thirty-four

The party room was empty: most had already left the yacht or were in the process of clambering off the wrecked boarding deck onto the quayside. Keira made her way past the police car embedded in the sidewall. Tables and chairs were scattered everywhere, food and drink littered the floor, lights flashed and the music continued to play.

A scream went up from those already on the quay as the *Persephone* listed a few degrees to starboard. Keira stumbled and had to hold on to a pillar to stop herself from falling over.

When she looked up Lule and Ermir were coming towards her, holding on to whatever they could to stay upright.

Lule called over the music, 'There's a boy downstairs.'

'What?'

'A boy! There's another boy down below.'

'Where?'

'In one of the bedrooms. You take Ermir; I'll go get him.'

'I'll go,' replied Keira.

'You don't know where he is.'

'I'll find him. Get Ermir off the boat.'

Lule hesitated.

'Get Ermir off the fucking boat,' shouted Keira as she turned and headed back towards the stairs.

As she disappeared into the darkness she heard Lule call after her, 'His name is Loran.'

The pitch of the boat meant that Keira had to brace herself against the wall as she made her way down the staircase. Just as she reached the bottom step the overhead lights started to flicker and the music suddenly stopped. The deck was already partly submerged. Keira stepped knee-deep into the icy water and felt the shock of cold running through her.

'Loran?'

Keira called along the corridor and listened.

She tried again, 'Loran?'

This time there was a response: a muffled cry.

The boat lurched again, more violently this time, causing Keira to lose her balance and fall headlong into the freezing seawater. In the same instant the lights flickered for the last time and extinguished, plunging the entire belowdecks into darkness. Keira stumbled to her feet, reached into the pitch black and – finding nothing to hold on to – fell again. Eventually, her hand grasped hold of the railing on the staircase and she was able to pull herself upright.

The boat was now taking on water fast. Even in the brief time she'd been belowdecks the level had already risen almost half a metre to just below her waist. The darkness was filled with sounds of rushing water gurgling its way through every crack and gap, and the eerie creaks and groans of the hull as it strained under the increasing pressure. Keira could feel a sense of rising panic. Even though the waters around the harbour were shallow they were still deep enough for the yacht to sink in. There was no question of her leaving the boy behind, but if she didn't free him soon they could both drown.

Keira waded further along the corridor, touching the walls

with her fingertips as she searched blindly for the bedroom door.

'Loran?'

This time she heard banging.

'Keep making a noise,' called Keira, following the sound until her fingers felt the door frame. As she fumbled underwater for the handle something brushed against her arm. There was something in the water floating alongside her. The unexpected contact sent a shock of adrenaline coursing through her. Keira lashed out, her clenched fists punching at whatever it was in an attempt to push it out of the way.

She felt the fingers of a hand try to grab hold of her.

'Fuck!'

Keira fell back, thrashing and striking out.

A bulkhead fitting at the end of the corridor started to glow dimly as the emergency lighting finally kicked in. Floating just inches away – his face hanging limp below the surface – was Vedon's corpse. Keira raised her leg out of the water and – using the flat of her shoe – kicked out, pushing against the dead weight.

'Get to fuck away from me.'

The body drifted slowly back along the corridor and disappeared into the gloom.

Loran was banging at the door.

The handle was now visible, just below the surface. Keira grabbed hold of it, twisted and tugged at the door, but it was stuck fast, the pressure of the water and the swollen wood making any movement impossible. With one foot braced against the wall and both hands gripping the handle, Keira tried again, but she was exhausted, the cold seawater sapping what little strength she had left.

Loran sobbed as he repeated the same phrase over and over again. *'Ju lutem mos më lër, ju lutem mos më lër, ju lutem mos më lër.'*

Aware that time was running out for both of them, but not ready to give up, Keira tried again. She pulled until her arms ached and her fingers were numb.

The door started to give way.

Keira forced her fingers into the small gap she'd created and after a few more tugs the opening was just wide enough for the young boy's head to squeeze through, followed by his shoulders and finally his hips.

Keira pulled the boy to her and waded back through the freezing water to the stairwell.

Neither of them spoke as Keira picked her way through the wreckage of the party deck, past the crumpled police car and out onto the boarding deck. The crowd gathered on the quayside was made up of crew – kitchen staff and cleaners, the girls bussed in for the party and patrons from the Cabrestrante looking on as the yacht sank deeper. The rest – Vedon's guests – had already fled.

Lule stood on the edge of the dock with her arms outstretched, offering to take the boy from her. Keira prised Loran's arms from around her neck and lifted him up for Lule to grab on to, then clambered off the yacht herself.

The four set off along the quayside, past the seafood restaurant and the Cabrestrante, walking around the marina and down onto the beach. They paused only once when a cry went up from the end of the quay and the *Persephone's* bow dipped below the surface leaving only its stern proud of the water.

'You fit to drive?' asked Keira.

'Where to?'

'Sarandë.'

'What's happening in Sarandë?'

'A ferry to Corfu, a flight to Belfast, then a quick skip to Stranraer. I'll call Kate and tell her we'll be needing another passport.'

Thirty-five

'Rennie at the *Record*'s come up with another belter,' said Kate, handing the newspaper to Keira.

The headline read, 'LAWYER'S ATTEMPT TO FLEE SETS SEVEN-TIME KILLER FREE.'

The Scottish criminal justice system was reeling today after it was revealed that drug-bust lawyer Keira Lynch's mysterious disappearance has prompted calls from Albanian killer Engjell E Zeze's defence team to abandon the case against him. Sources close to the multimillion-pound trial – one of the biggest in Scottish legal history – told the Record yesterday that Lynch's no-show could seriously undermine the integrity of the trial. In an exclusive interview with the Record, lead prosecutor, Advocate Depute Patrick Sellar told our reporter of his concern for the lawyer's safety and confirmed that her disappearance – despite the overwhelming evidence against E Zeze – was a major blow to the Crown's chances of securing a conviction. The paper can also reveal that there have been unconfirmed reports of Miss Lynch boarding a flight bound for New York, where she is rumoured to be in hiding. See pages five and six for this story in full.

Most of the front cover was taken up with a photograph of the

High Court building in Glasgow. In the bottom right a caption printed underneath a photograph of an unsmiling Sellar read: Prosecutor says killer could walk free in days.

Lule stretched her hand across the table and said, 'Can I have a look?'

'The cops raided our office,' continued Kate.

'What did they take?' asked Keira.

'Everything. Tidiest it's looked since you moved in. There's a pack of scabby journos camped outside the office too.'

The Holy Man walked into the kitchen carrying some beers from the back fridge and another bottle of wine. 'Anyone for another drink?'

'I'll have beer, please,' replied Keira as he placed the drinks on the table in front of her.

'It's the usual shite,' said the Holy Man. 'They've got me down as "shady crime boss" and Kate's a "wild child and former junkie". It's like reading something from the eighties. And I'll bet you a pinkie sling "sources close to the trial" is that greasy wee fucker Sellar.'

'Where are the boys?' asked Keira.

'Gillian's got them in the bath upstairs. Manky: the bathwater's like mud. Need some feeding up too. I'll take you, Lule and the boys down to yer ma's tomorrow, Keira. Youse can stay here tonight though, there's plenty space.'

'Thanks, Jim, I've got some things to do in the morning, but if you could take Lule and the boys that would be great.'

'Ye gonae hand yerself in?'

'After a fashion.'

'Might as well enjoy yer last night of freedom then, eh?'

'This won't be my last night.'

'They've got you down for contempt at the very least. Who knows what else they'll throw at ye.'

'I'll be fine.'

After the events of the last few days all Keira wanted was to drink until she couldn't stand up, draw the curtains then crawl into bed and sleep for a week. Apart from a few curious glances at the swelling and bruising on her face, the journey back from Sarandë had been uneventful. There were no awkward questions at border control and no one but the Holy Man waiting to pick them up when they arrived by ferry at Stranraer.

According to the Holy Man the port on Loch Ryan was the easiest entry point into the United Kingdom. It was chronically understaffed with none of the sophisticated surveillance available to larger hubs. 'Every ounce of coke I bring into Scotland comes via Stranraer. Only danger is the A77. It's a single-lane bastard to drive at night.'

Keira was aware that Lule was staring across the table at her, and asked, 'Are you okay?'

'Did you hear what I said?'

'Sorry, Lule, I wasn't paying attention.'

'I said, I know him.'

'Know who?'

'This man on the cover, the judge guy.'

'That isnae the judge, doll, that's the prosecutor,' said the Holy Man, looking over her shoulder at the photograph of Patrick Sellar.

'He was down to prosecute Fisnik Abazi,' said Keira. 'You might know him from that.'

'You knew Abazi?' asked the Holy Man, looking down at Lule. 'Small world right enough.'

'Sure. I am here before.'

'In Glasgow?'

'Keira has not told you my story?'

'It's not my story to tell,' replied Keira.

'Yes, and made to work for that son of bitch Abazi, but this is not why I know this man. I have seen him in the house with the other girls. He likes only the young ones, not me, but I have seen him for sure. In Albania the Clan run most of the prostitution, they have the judges and politicians, anyone who is anyone that visits the girls, the guy is only allowed to fuck with the condom on. We are to keep the sperm and freeze it, or one of the girls is made pregnant with it, then somewhere down the line the guy gets a call saying he better do what he's told. Abazi showed us this guy's photograph.'

Keira was staring at her. 'Patrick Sellar?'

'If any of us screwed him we were told to freeze the bag.'

'Are you one hundred per cent sure it's him?'

'Two hundred per cent,' replied Lule. 'He gives all the girls the creeps. None of them want chosen. He is nasty little fucker.'

'D'you have a phone I could use, Jim?' asked Keira.

'You can use the one in my office next door.'

'I'm calling Gary Hammond. Can the cops trace the call back to here?'

'Are ye kiddin'? My line's routed through Bangalore.'

*

Keira sat at the Holy Man's desk with the receiver jammed between her ear and her shoulder, leaving her hands free to roll a cigarette.

The voice on the end of the line said, 'DSI Hammond's away from his desk.'

'Is he sitting there having a coffee and can't be arsed, or he is actually away from his desk?'

The girl on the other end hesitated, 'Eh, can I get him to call you back?'

'It's important. Is it possible to slip a note in front of his nose saying that it's Keira Lynch holding for him?'

'I'll give it a try.'

The hold music hadn't played one bar before the voice at the other end said, 'Putting you through.'

'How's New York?'

'As far as I know it's grand. Why you asking me?'

'I've just been watching the CCTV images of you checking through customs at JFK.'

'You've just been watching the CCTV images of *someone* checking through customs.'

'Using your passport.'

'My passport was stolen in Albania. I flew back to the UK on Sunday night using a temporary visa, issued on behalf of and signed by the Albanian Policia.'

'I've always wanted one of those snow globes with the Empire State Building inside; will you bring me one back?'

'If you still don't believe me, check with customs at Glasgow airport.'

'So, where are you?'

'I've more chance of getting you a snow globe with the Duke of Wellington wearing a traffic cone on his head.'

'You saying you're in Glasgow?'

'You're the detective; work it out.'

'You're heating up again. I've got a screen full of alerts flashing red ... all of them relating to you and your activities. There's a few government agencies looking over my shoulder too.'

'A few?'

'Our lot and the Americans.'

'What's it got to do with them?'

'Who knows, but we've been asked to keep a soft eye on you. We raided your office. Took away a shitload of boxes. That's how hot you are right now.'

'I heard.'

'We were "encouraged" to seek a warrant. When we applied for it, one had already been written up. Seems to me that somebody's a bit over keen to do you some damage. Not allowed to mention any names, but that wee shite Sellar has been shouting his mouth off to anyone willing to listen. I wouldn't let him get behind you: you'll end up with his fangs in your neck.'

'I've got my back covered.'

'He's a sneaky wee fuck. Be careful.'

'Should you be telling me all this?'

'No.'

'Then you're the one better be careful.'

'Why did you go AWOL? I would've thought you, of all people, would be desperate to see that bastard E Zeze swinging from a rope.'

'I am and I will.'

'Where d'you want to meet?'

'I don't want to meet. I need you to do me a favour first.'

'In return for what?'

'I'll tell you where I'm going to be at nine o'clock tomorrow morning and you can make an arrest in front of the whole Scottish media.'

'What does the favour involve?'

'Were any DNA tests ever done on Kaltrina Dervishi's baby?'

'Fucksake, Keira, just a small favour, yeah?'

'Is it standard practice?'

'In a murder case, yes.'

'Where would the file be kept?'

'In a filing cabinet.'

'Can you find it and let me know?'

'That filing cabinet could be in the Procurator Fiscal's office, or the Advocate Depute's office. It could be anywhere.'

'No copies?'

Hammond was quiet for a moment, then, 'Is that it?'

'If I get a blood sample over to you, can you send it to a lab and get it tested?'

'You can't see me, but I'm sitting here shaking my head in disbelief at your bloody nerve.'

'How long will the results take?'

'If I fast track it, maybe twenty-four hours.'

'I'll stick it in a cab just now, but only if you promise not to arrest the driver and ask him where he picked it up from.'

'Only if *you* promise me this isn't going to land me in all kinds and colours of shit.'

'I promise.'

'Okay, then I won't arrest the driver. Where can I arrest you tomorrow morning?'

'At my office.'

'I don't like having my picture taken. Why don't you make

your way to Pitt Street and hand yourself in? I could do without the media scrum, to be honest.'

'I'll only hand myself in to you.'

'Don't worry, I'll be there.'

'Might be better: I'm not looking my best at the moment. See you at Pitt Street, nine a.m.'

'I can pick up the blood sample just now if you like. Where are you?'

'Bangalore,' replied Keira.

*

Keira sat with the fresh roll-up hanging limply between her lips staring the long stare.

There was a knock at the door and the Holy Man entered the room.

'Just checking yer okay, doll. You've been gone a while.'

'Enjoying the comforts of this chair: finding it hard to stand up.'

'Aye it's a Hermann Miller. Pure brilliant if you've got a dodgy back.'

'Do they make anything like this for a dodgy soul?'

'Glasgow's malt whisky.'

'I'll give that a try.'

'Ye want some? I've got a bottle of Auchentoshan over there in the drinks cabinet. None of yer high-street shite. This stuff's so good the angels wanted more than their fair share.'

'Sounds good.'

The Holy Man walked over to a retro drinks cabinet and flipped the mirrored lid down. The glass door panels showed a lake scene with Swans and willow trees silhouetted against a pale blue background.

'I like the cabinet.'

'Genuine article from the fifties: belonged to my ma. Only thing I kept after she died, everything else was shite. Da was an alkie: pawned anything decent my ma brought home so she stopped bringing stuff home and lived like a nun. First thing I did when I got some money was buy her a house, told her she could have anything she wanted, but by that point she wasn't interested. Just happy being on her own.'

McMaster had poured two glasses and handed one to Keira. 'It's been a tough couple of weeks.'

'Yeah.'

'Your face's some state, doll. I hope you gave as good as you got.'

'I might have to come to church with you on Sunday.'

'S'that right?'

Keira nodded.

'Confession?'

'Yes.'

'Mortal sin or venial?'

Keira shot McMaster a glance.

'Venial's a word.'

'I know.'

'Those are your two main types, but there's a whole range of options in each category. I'm a fuckin' expert in all of them. Venial is yer stuff like swearing and thinking bad thoughts, mortal is acting on those thoughts. It's a bit more serious: carries a heftier penalty.'

'I'll go for mortal, then.'

'How many times did you sin?'

'Three or four. I'd have to work it out.'

'No need to come to church, I'll give you absolution right now, Keira: knowing you, they must have deserved it. *Sláinte.*'

'*Sláinte*,' replied Keira, downing the whisky in one gulp. 'I feel like I owe you so much already, Jim, but d'you mind if I ask one more favour?'

'We've spoke about this already, doll. You don't owe me any-thing – I owe you everything. I'm your genie in the bottle. Whatever it is, ask: and if I can do, I will do.'

'Can you still pick a lock?'

Thirty-six

Patrick Sellar was sitting at his bespoke kitchen table – the one with the marble top and hand-turned legs designed to match the hand-painted cupboards. He was making noises about trying to catch up with some work when the doorbell rang. For a moment he considered hiding the half-empty bottle of white in the fridge, then thought *Who cares if I'm drinking at home on my own?* and left the bottle where it was. He'd stayed in the Clutha Bar longer than he'd intended, talking through the ramifications of Keira Lynch's disappearance with his friend Judge George Granville, the pair finally reaching a gentleman's agreement that Lynch was the perfect fall guy if the trial barrel-rolled on top of them. They would speak with one voice in their condemnation of Keira Lynch's behaviour, spend a little energy discrediting her, then move to have the bitch disbarred.

After three more for the road, Sellar had called a cab.

He staggered a little as he pushed back from the table and headed out into the hall to check the videophone. The security light had been triggered outside, but the small screen showed no one at the door. Sellar checked his watch. It was just after eleven: he wasn't expecting anyone and it was too late for a neighbour to call in.

He slipped into the front room without putting the light on and pulled the curtain aside, just enough to give a view of the front steps. The porch was empty, the driveway clear and there was no one on the street outside his house. There were no cars parked on the road either. Sellar made a growling noise and said in a loud voice, 'Fuck off, whoever you are, I have a dog here,' then added, 'that hasn't been fed,' as he made barking noises and growled his way back into the hall.

He stopped with a jolt, when he heard a voice from the kitchen reply, 'Miaow.'

Sellar stood framed in the doorway struggling to keep the twist of anger from his mouth. 'Are we adding breaking and entering to our list of crimes and misdemeanours, Miss Lynch?'

'If I'd come to the front door would you have let me in?'

'Certainly – after I'd phoned the police. If you keep racking up offences at this rate you'll be joining the lifers. I can't help but admire the theatricality behind your sudden appearance, but I still feel compelled to ask what the fuck you think you're doing in my kitchen? Shouldn't you be down at the nearest police station handing yourself in?'

'Got that appointment booked for tomorrow morning.'

'In that case I refer you to my previous question. What the fuck are you doing here?'

'I thought it was time we had that pre-trial meeting that we never got round to. Thought I'd run you through the prosecution's case: make sure we're singing Amen together.'

'We're a little beyond that, I'm afraid. You had your chance.'

'I'm not talking about E Zeze's trial . . . I'm talking about yours.'

Keira was spinning a kitchen knife on the marble surface of the table. Flicking the blade with her index finger, stopping it after one revolution then repeating. The noise was already starting to annoy Sellar. 'D'you mind? That one piece of marble alone cost nearly three grand: I'd be grateful if you didn't rout a fucking circle in the middle of it. Can you give me the knife.'

He held his hand out.

Keira ignored him and flicked again. 'Have you ever seen me throw a knife?'

'I can't say I have, but I've never seen you take a shit either, and right now each proposition seems as preposterous as the other. Have you broken into my house to show me your skills as a circus act?'

'Maybe. I haven't decided yet.'

'Have you been drinking?'

'I'll have a whisky.'

'I didn't ask if you wanted one, I asked if you'd already had some,' said Sellar retrieving the wine bottle from the table and pouring himself a large glass. 'It was a comment on your questionable mental state.'

Sellar leant back against the counter and took a slug, trying to look casual and making it clear that he wasn't about to offer Keira anything.

'You remember a few months ago you were attacked in here?'

'I remember it perfectly well. What is this, a re-enactment?'

'You told the police at the time you fought the attackers off . . . heroically. Nothing taken.'

Sellar was staring at Keira, his expression serious now. 'What the fuck does that have to do with anything?'

'You lied. Something was taken.'

Sellar took another drink of wine and said, 'If you don't stop spinning that knife I'll come over there and stick it in your throat.'

'You fold too easily under pressure, Patrick,' replied Keira. 'Maybe you should take up stripping.'

'Yes, well it's not every day someone breaks into your home and starts vandalising your property. It's an upsetting experience. More so, I'd say, the second time around. If I did happen to defend myself, it would be a perfectly reasonable response. Since the last break-in I've had security cameras installed; no doubt they'd show you, someone, the perpetrator sneaking in through the garage. "The lights were out; I had no idea what was going on. I was so frightened, especially in light of what happened a few months ago. They came at me with a knife, a struggle ensued, blah, blah, blah." Honestly, Miss Lynch, I thought you were smarter than this. I get the feeling you've not really thought this through. You're going to be charged with contempt, possibly even perjury, your actions so far may lead to a killer walking free, you've broken into my home and – at the very least – appear to be threatening me, with all your "Have you ever seen me throw a knife?" and "I'm talking about *your* trial" shit. Where is this all leading? From every angle you come at this story there's a big neon sign hanging above it saying "you're fucked" in capital letters.'

'A blood sample.'

'A what?'

'A blood sample.'

'Now you're just saying random words. Is it a game? Say the first thing that comes into your addled, alcohol-fuelled brain.'

'The people who broke in the last time didn't steal anything, but they took a blood sample.'

That got Sellar back up off of the counter, standing upright – his body language at odds with the front he was trying to put on.

'"A blood sample." What in the good gods' name are you talking about?'

'They told me.'

'Who told you?'

'The guys that broke in.'

'Friends of yours?'

'No.'

'Clients?'

'Possibly. They also told me your heroic efforts to fight them off consisted of you squealing like a stuck pig. It's been bugging me, why you've been so quick to let this case against E Zeze drop. I think even if I hadn't disappeared you would have found a way for it to take a tumble. You'd been given the nod by someone that E Zeze had to walk.'

'Your face looks like it has taken another beating since the last time I saw you, Miss Lynch – it's hard to believe that was only a few days ago – but it's obvious that the effects of the beating have damaged your mental capacity. Judging from your actions this evening I would surmise that the damage runs deeper than just bruising. Why don't I fix you a drink after all and – while you sit enjoying it – I'll call a doctor and we can get you attended to?'

'The blood sample that was taken from you is being analysed in a lab right now. When the results come back I'm fairly certain the DNA will match the sample taken from the child that Kaltrina Dervishi was carrying in her belly when she was murdered. Fisnik Abazi knew you would be prosecuting the case against him. He knew you were a frequent visitor to the girls he had working for him. The young, vulnerable females trafficked here for the personal gratification of guys that don't give a shit by guys that don't give a shit. You – in your position as upholder of the law – are charged to protect those people, these girls, you slimy fuck. Abazi took some of your sperm from a condom and used it to impregnate Kaltrina Dervishi with the intention to blackmail you when the time came for him to stand trial. I don't know if it's Engjell E Zeze's hand on the tiller, or Verbër Vedon's, but it doesn't matter, they're all members of the same crime organisation – the Clan. This is how they work. I have it on good authority from one of Kaltrina Dervishi's friends – a girl who used to work alongside her, a girl who's willing to testify in court that you were a frequent visitor to one of the houses Abazi ran as a brothel. Abazi was Johnnie Big Balls over here, Verbër Vedon was the man in Albania and Engjell E Zeze was the go-to guy if anyone stepped out of line. Two of them are dead and now, no matter what happens to the third . . . you are fucked because, unfortunately for all of you, I do give a shit.'

Patrick Sellar was visibly rattled, but he still tried to come back at Keira. It wasn't surprising – he was a first-rate prosecutor – and she was expecting it, but he'd blown it even before he'd started. 'You're smiling, Patrick,' continued Keira. 'My grandmother could predict which boxer was going to lose the fight. It was always the one smiling at the weigh-in.'

'Listen to yourself, Miss Lynch. Listen to the woman whose father was a terrorist, whose uncle was a hit man, who counts criminals as friends and employs their junkie daughters. It's too steep a climb out of the cesspit for you to get anywhere near the moral high ground. The traces of heroin found in your flat suggest a closer connection to the criminal underclass than is considered acceptable. Your office has been searched and evidence removed that will no doubt corroborate a lot of what I've been saying. Who knows what else we will uncover. Your assertions that I am culpable or guilty of any of the things your ludicrous rantings suggest will be dismissed as delusional: the product of a clearly unstable person's warped mind. I think, my dear, that it is you who are – as you so eloquently put it – fucked.'

Before his little speech had come to an end Sellar had managed to down the rest of his glass of wine and was heading back to the table for a refill. Keira spun the knife again, but before it had completed a full revolution Sellar made a grab for it. His fingers clutched the handle as he tried to snatch it up from the table but Keira – anticipating the move – slammed the palm of her right hand down on the flat of the blade, trapping Sellar's fingers.

'I've already asked you nicely. Now I'm telling you. Give me the fucking knife,' hissed Sellar. He tightened his grip and attempted to pull the knife free, but Keira pushed down harder. He moved his face close until she could smell the alcohol on his breath and said, 'Let it fucking go.'

Keira felt the razor-sharp edge of the blade catch and start to slice into the soft flesh below her knuckles. A small pool of blood started to form between her fingers, but Keira kept her hand where it was.

Noticing the blood, Sellar smiled and tried to draw the blade again.

Without flinching, Keira thumped the fist of her left hand down as hard as she could near the hilt and heard the crack of bones.

Sellar yelped and pulled away, clutching his hand to his chest, overplaying how painful it was. Keira snatched the knife from the table and watched him backing away, arms raised in surrender. That's when she caught him glancing up to the corner of the room, angling himself so that the pinhole security camera could get a better shot of the look of fear on his face.

Keira rose from the chair, knife in hand and started towards the advocate. When she was less than a metre away she sidestepped and slotted it back into the brushed-aluminium knife block sitting on the worktop behind, then turned and smiled up at the camera as she made for the door.

'You've picked a fight with the wrong man, Lynch,' called Patrick Sellar to Keira's back as she walked down the hallway to the front door, right hand hanging loosely by her side, letting the blood drip freely over his carpet.

'I didn't pick a fight with anyone, Sellar . . . you did.'

Keira didn't bother looking round as she delivered her exit line, she would see plenty of Patrick Sellar when he came to stand trial. 'You can't use any of the evidence collected from my office, by the way. Every single shred of it is protected by lawyer–client privilege. I'm sure it wouldn't bother a master criminal like yourself . . . but you'd be breaking the law.'

The smile was gone from Sellar's face as he grabbed a cleaver from the knife block and chased after Keira, screaming her name. '*Lynch!*'

As he blundered into the darkened hallway, he stopped dead.

The front door was wide open, but there was no sign of Keira Lynch.

Standing in her place framed in the doorway was the figure of a man silhouetted against the streetlight.

'Where the fuck d'ye think you're goin', pal?' asked the Holy Man.

Thirty-seven

Boats lay where they'd settled, keels stuck, bows pointing inland waiting for the turn of the tide to free them from the silt bed and pull them round to face back out to sea. A flock of gulls – their dark shapes silhouetted against the bright-blue afternoon sky – squawked and swooped their way across Urr Water to the far shore.

Kippford had one road that ran the length of the village. On the near side sat the Anchor, a pub in the middle of a row of low-rise houses, and on the opposite side a metre-high sea wall ran adjacent to a wide estuary that narrowed as it disappeared into the hills to the north.

Keira liked the Anchor; the interior was unpretentious and she knew the staff by name. In the winter a large open fire warmed the small bar area and in the summer patrons sat at the weathered wooden tables outside and watched the ebb and flow of tidal waters. There was something in the familiarity that made her feel safe.

It was warm enough to sit outside.

A wasp buzzed around the wooden table then flew into a spider's web strung between the bough of a potted bay tree and the rim of the pot. The harder it struggled the more the wasp became entangled. Keira watched the spider charge across the thin, silvery strands, numb its prey, then retreat into hiding while it waited for the wasp to die. When it was all over Keira shifted her attention back to the guy sitting thirty metres along to her right on the sea wall.

She felt uneasy: something about his presence was eating away at that feeling of safety.

The tide was out, giving Loran and Ermir the length of the beach to run their races. They'd been scrambling over the pebble shore for nearly an hour now, pulling at each other as they raced towards Lule, who was waiting to scoop the winner in her arms and throw him high in the air with a wild whoop.

In all that time the guy on the wall hadn't taken his eyes off them.

Keira had noticed the car when it first drove in from the top of the village. It made its way slowly past the pub and disappeared left at the end of the road, following Jubilee Path – a steep incline that snaked into the hillside past her mother's house. A few minutes later – possibly after discovering the road was a dead end – the car re-emerged. It parked in a bay at the end of the village set next to a concrete slipway that led down into the water.

Keira had made an exaggerated play of rolling a cigarette, but kept her focus on the guy as he'd walked past on the other side of the road. There was something about the way he was dressed, the way he was moving, that made Keira wary. The walking stick he was using made a hollow tap with every step and did nothing to help his slight limp. He wore a baseball cap pulled low and a pair of dark shades to hide his eyes. His beard, full and greying, concealed the rest of his face.

Twice – before he'd made it halfway along the road – the guy had checked over his shoulder as if expecting someone to come at him from behind.

After Patrick Sellar's 'dramatic resignation' another prosecutor was appointed and a new date set for Engjell E Zeze's trial. The story had attracted so much media attention that DSI Gary Hammond had warned Keira to be extra vigilant, but this guy didn't look like a journalist: he looked more dangerous than that.

The table was a mess of plates and glasses left over from lunch. Keira found herself instinctively scanning the debris for a suitable weapon. The waitress, Lindsey, appeared over her shoulder to deliver another beer and was starting to lift the plates when the guy climbed down from his perch on top of the wall and crossed the road, heading towards the pub. As he drew nearer Keira asked Lindsey for the bill – peering past her to get a good look at the guy's face, but he cut in along the alleyway and disappeared into the pub through a side door.

Keira was on her feet and over at the sea wall before Lindsey had finished clearing. She called down to Lule, who was standing twenty metres or so along the beach. Lule looked up and waved, then – seeing the expression on Keira's face, mouthed back, 'What's wrong?'

'Take the boys back to the house.'

Lule knew from the tone of Keira's voice not to ask any questions.

When Keira turned back, the guy was sitting at her table. He waited until Keira had taken her seat again before saying anything.

'You drinking the same beer as me?'

Keira looked at the pint sitting untouched on the table in front of her and replied, 'Looks like it.'

'What's this stuff called?'

'What did you ask for at the bar?'

'A beer.'

'It's called Criffel. Brewed locally.'

'D'you like it?'

'I only drink it when I'm here. Normally I'd go for a cold lager.'

'Me too. I think I like it. I'll tell you after I've had another three.'

'Don't bother. I'm not that interested,' replied Keira.

'You're Keira Lynch, right?'

'Says who?'

'The guy at the bar – the owner.'

'Well then, it must be true.'

'When you say you only drink it when you're here, does that mean you're not a local?'

'You've the makings of a detective there.'

Now the small talk was out of the way, Keira wondered how long it would be before the real questions started.

'The girl on the beach: she a friend of yours?'

This guy wasn't wasting any time.

'Not really.' As soon as the words were out Keira wished she'd said 'no'.

'Oh, sorry, I thought I saw you talking to her when I came out of the pub.'

'Yeah, well,' was all Keira could think to say in reply.

'Is she their mother?'

'Whose mother?'

'The boys.'

'No.'

'Are you?'

'No.'

'I was watching them running up and down the beach there,' said the guy.

'Yeah, I was watching you watching,' said Keira.

'Just wondering if they were brothers. Got the same colouring, but they look different.'

'Are you a journalist?'

'Fuck no. Is that why you're being so cagey?'

'Cagey?'

'Guarded, then.'

'Mister, I've no idea who you are and you've no idea what I've been through in the last wee while. None of it good. You could be a journalist, CIA, an Albanian hit man, all sorts of wild and whacky things. Section 1 of the Prevention of Crime Act 1953 prohibits the possession in any public place of an offensive weapon without lawful authority or excuse.'

'Is that word for word?'

'That's exactly what it says. If I called the cops they'd have you for that swordstick you're carrying. That's if the cops could find you. It's my guess if a squad car appeared at the top of the road you'd be gone before it had even reached the pub. Do you have the authority or excuse?'

'No I don't.'

'I don't know who the hell you are, and I don't want to know, so why don't you just sit there and enjoy your Criffel and I'll do the same, then we can both go our separate ways.'

'What are you, a psychic? A detective?'

'A lawyer.'

'Conveyancing? Corporate? What sort of lawyer?'

'Criminal. So I can smell a cell warrior fresh from the ding-wing at a hundred paces.'

'This cane sword is an antique, over a hundred years old. If the cops appeared at the top of the village I'd keep my arse parked right where it was. I'd be up on a bum beef. Antiques like this are exempt.'

The guy paused to sup some of his beer, before continuing, 'You probably knew that. I was only going to say that seeing the boys running up and down like that brought back some memories.'

Keira was giving him the stare now, but it wasn't working.

'Two boys running along a beach in Northern Ireland,' he continued. 'Racing each other just like those two today, only difference being, the boys on that beach *were* brothers. Racing each other to see who could reach their da first. The older boy letting the wee one win: that's how close they were, you know; they cared a lot about each other, those two. I'd go so far as to say they loved each other...'

'Do me a favour, mister,' interrupted Keira, her tone hardening. 'Go back to your news desk, or your crime boss, your sergeant or whoever it is sets your watch ticking in the morning and tell them you couldn't find me. Please. All I want is to be left alone.'

'Have you ever heard of Cushendun?'

Keira felt a punch of adrenaline in her stomach.

She'd been to Cushendun only once in her life, as an eight-year-old child with her mother and grandmother to stay at the Cushendun hotel.

The memory was seared into her brain.

It was the last time she'd seen her father alive.

'What the fuck does it have to do with you?' replied Keira, letting the danger creep into her voice.

'Well, I was just sitting on that wall over there thinking to myself I know you from somewhere, and now that I see you up close I'm almost certain. The boys from Northern Ireland were called Sean and Danny McGuire, and their ma watched on just like you were doing today . . . she would be your grandmother. Now, I have a confession to make. I wasn't just watching those boys on the beach, I was watching you too: and if you'd care to put that knife you stuck up your sleeve back on the table I'll tell you a few other things.'

'Like?'

The guy took his sunglasses off and folded them shut.

Sharp, black, familiar eyes stared back at her.

'Like . . . Your name is not Keira Lynch, it's Niamh McGuire. Like: you chose "Róisín Dubh" to play at your grandmother's funeral, which is exactly the music I would have chosen. Like: I know who taught you to throw a knife and I don't want you sticking me with a blade before I've had a chance to say everything I've come here to say.'

Keira let the knife slip into the palm of her hand, placed it back on top of the table and rose to her feet. 'How d'you know about "Róisín Dubh"?'

'I was there.'

Keira had tears streaming down her face as she asked, 'Who was it taught me to throw a knife?'

'Your uncle Danny . . .'

'And how would you know such a thing?'

The words choked in the man's throat as he answered, 'Because he was my wee brother.'

Keira stood motionless for a moment, then reached out, took hold of her father's hands and pulled him closer.

'You'll be all right, darlin', don't you worry now,' said Sean McGuire as he held his daughter tight and kissed her on the forehead for the first time.

Also by J. G. Sinclair

ff

Seventy Times Seven

*What happens when the man you have to kill is the only
man who has the answers you seek?*

A hit man trying to find answers to his brother's murder. An
informer trying to flee his past. A family under threat.

Rural Northern Ireland and small-town Alabama: Two places
connected by a deadly act – an act that draws two men, and
those closest to them, into a spiral of lies, violence and murder
as they try to lay their ghosts to rest.

But can you ever be forgiven for the sins of your past?

'One of the finest debuts of the decade.' Ken Bruen

'A brutal, extremely addictive and vivid portrayal of the sins of
men finally catching up with them. This is a very strong
debut tinged with sadness that will stay with you
long after the final page.' *Crimesquad.com*

'An impressive debut . . . Fast and bloody, though with
some moving touches, and Sinclair scores top marks
for the exceptionally vivid dialogue.' *The Times*

ff

Blood Whispers

How do you tell the truth in a world full of lies?

Keira Lynch is one of Glasgow's top defence lawyers with a reputation for keeping her clients out of prison. If Keira's in your corner then the opposition had better watch out.

But Keira has a past that she's spent years trying to put behind her – new country, new name, new start – until her latest case threatens to bring her back into the world she thought she'd left behind; a world of violence, where perhaps the most dangerous person isn't the one chasing you, but the one closest to you.